SYLVIA'S DILEMMA

A Novel By: Bertrand E. Brown

The siren screamed as the ambulance sped down the crowded city street. This was the third call this morning and the second suicide attempt.

"Damn, I know this recession is really bad but I'll be damned if I'm gonna kill myself 'cause I ain't got no money," the burly ambulance driver said to no one in general.

"I know that's right," the older EMS worker chided in.

"Hell, I ain't never had no money. Shit, I don't know what's happenin' to Black folks. We didn't used to do no shit like this. Suicide's always been a White thang up 'til Obama got in. Guess Black folks feel they equal now so they might as well jump on the band wagon," he laughed to no one in particular.

"They can keep the so-called equality if it means me killin' myself," the EMS driver laughed. "Give me 10cc's of adrenaline," the EMS worker shouted to his young assistant. Taking the enormous syringe from the cubicle he pulled back the plunger extracting the fluid from the bottle as his partner worked frantically to put the oxygen mask over Sylvia's nose and mouth.

"You got a pulse?" the older man asked.

"I thought I did but if there is it's almost too faint to tell. You'd better hurry with the injection if we're gonna save ol' girl. She looks like she's fading fast."

"Damn good lookin' woman too. Damn shame…Can't understand why a fine piece of ass like that would do something so goddamn stupid," the burly EMS driver stated. "Shit, I know a million women who would give their right arm just to have her looks and this stupid bitch I up here tryna kill her fool self. Just don't make no goddamn sense," he fumed now raising the huge needle and grasping it with both hands ready to plunge it down into her heart.

The adrenaline was a last resort but the CPR and defibrillator failed to bring her around and although it wasn't normal procedure the elderly EMS worker hated to see someone so young and so beautiful pass on without so much as giving life a second chance. Whatever had caused this beautiful, young woman to even consider taking her own life was her problem but in his mind she simply hadn't been thorough in her attempts and that was her problem. To his way of thinking he didn't have a thing to do with whatever was troubling her so deeply that she would contemplate suicide. His job had nothing to do with that. His job was to simply preserve life and he thought of little else as he brought his two hundred pound frame down thrusting the needle deeply into her chest cavity and into her heart. He was by no means squeamish but if there was a part of his job that he disliked more than any other it was this.

Pushing the plunger, releasing the adrenaline until the needle was empty he knew that if it were to have some affect the results were almost immediate. No sooner than the thought crossed his mind the woman released a screamed that made the driver swerve and had her sitting upright as if she'd been frightfully awakened from a sound sleep.

"What the…" she said before screaming again. Sylvia fell back on the gurney and seemed to be in shock as she stared at her torn blouse, her chest exposed and the huge needle protruding from her chest. Still, she made no attempt to move or remove it.

"Sit still little lady. You're goin' to be just fine. You had a close call but you're goin' to be just fine," the EMS said as he gently removed the six inch syringe and

3

taped a piece of gauze over the black and blue bruise forming quickly where the syringe had entered. "Had another young lady with a similar condition who wasn't quite so lucky. You've got quite a lot to be thankful for."

All in attendance breathed a collective sigh of relief. Well, all there but Sylvia, who turned her head to the side and let the tears fall leaving a dark, wet blotch on the clean white sheets of the gurney. Moments later she was wheeled into the emergency room of the hospital and admitted as an attempted suicide victim.

Adamant she made it plain to the nurse admitting her that she was fine had made a mistake with her meds and was quite capable of being released on her own recognizance. The nurse behind the desk who for some unknown reason reminded Sylvia of Judge Judy in a white uniform firmly stated that not only was she being admitted but she would most certainly undergo tests to see if the drug she'd ingested were legally prescribed followed by a psychiatric evaluation. Sylvia remembered the last time she'd been admitted into a hospital and shuddered at the thought. He hadn't been conscious then but when she did regain consciousness she could recall spending months in there for their so-called evaluation.

"Oh, hell no. I'll be damned if I stay here for some goddamned evaluation. I said I feel fine and who would know better how I feel than me. How you gonna tell me when and where I can go. Last time I looked this was a supposedly free society. I do have rights ya know."

The nurse peered over her glasses and spoke softly. It was obvious she'd dealt with overwrought, high strung people before. After all, she'd worked intake for the Emergency Room almost her entire career.

"Ma'm you may not be able to see the importance of our admitting you now. But if I were to let you walk out of here without having a thorough exam done and you were

4

to walk out those doors and fall out St. Luke's would be the one's liable and not only would I lose my job but the hospital would end up in a major lawsuit and believe you me this hospital ain't tryna pay nobody nothin'. You don't believe me just wait 'til Friday and I'll show you my paycheck," she said smiling. "Now lie back while I get an orderly to take you to your room. Best case scenario…You'll be out of here within a couple of hours."

Sylvia seeing no other alternative lay back and simply resigned herself to the fact that she was for all intensive purposes a ward of St. Lukes 'til further notice.

A week or so later, the hospital staff came to the conclusion that there had been no accidental overdose as Sylvia claimed but that she'd purposely tried to take her own life despite her protests. They'd found both the suicide note as well as an exorbitant amount of medication in her bloodstream. And despite her denials and attempts to present herself as a normal hard-working Black woman just like any other struggling Black woman out there the fact remained.

"I hear you Sylvia and believe me I sympathize with your plight. Let me tell you, I have three kids of my own, two twin girls that are about to enter college and one that's a junior and a husband that's unemployed and believes that he has sort of entitlement and refuses to even look for a job so I understand what hard times are. And the employment picture is looking bleaker by the day. There are days when I don't know if I'm going to make it. My mortgage is two months in arrears and I'm just wondering when the banks gonna foreclose on my house. And it doesn't do me any good to know that there are countless others out there in similar positions but the fact remains that we aren't trying to take our own lives."

"But doc…"

"Let me finish. That's what has me a little concerned. All of that's a part of life. And Lord knows this world can throw you some curves sometime but we have to some way in which we deal with and have the strength to combat the adversities that life throws our way."

Sylvia knew the woman in front of her was right and dropped her head. She was tired. Tired of life's adversities and had finally come to the end of her rope on that fateful day. All she wanted was out and had sought to get out the only way she knew possible. And she'd even fucked that up. But hell, if she had known she would end up here listening to this shit from some white lady half her age who called herself a shrink she surely wouldn't have tried it. Finally at her wits end with all this psychosocial melodrama bullshit Sylvia blurted out.

"So what the fuck do you have to offer me? Ya got a good man that'll love his woman unconditionally without lying and cheating and running the dick to get his dick licked. You got someone faithful and true that takes his marriage seriously instead of these pathetic motherfuckers who'll tell a good anything and everything so they can crawl up between my legs and fuck me 'til they grow tired of me and my pussy and then when they do they go off with those same bullshit lines 'til they find they find some other poor unsuspecting woman to bed down. C'mon doc tell me how you gonna help me with that?" Sylvia yelled.

Two orderlies hearing Sylvia's tirade stopped and waited outside the door just in case they had to aid the young doctor.

"Well, Sylvia that's a good question," the young doctor replied seemingly unnerved by Sylvia's ranting. "Perhaps those are some of the issues will have to come up with a plan to address. But let me ask you this? What do you think you could do to resolve this issue?"

6

"Cut their damn dicks off!" She screamed " They ain't nothing but penises anyway. They're mindless dicks."

The two orderlies laughed heartily before moving on.

"I'm serious. Women give their hearts and soul to these animals expecting them to have some heart and feeling and emotion. But these motherfuckers ain't got hearts or souls and no feelings whatsoever. They're animals. All they care about is themselves. They're selfless beasts and I'm tired of 'em."

"Okay, Sylvia. That's a good place to start. It really seems like the other sex is a sore spot for you."

"A sore spot? That's a good one. Hell, my husband beat my ass. I mean he whooped my ass. But being that he's head honcho in a big corporation he has license to do that and I can't do a damn thing about it."

"And where is he now?"

"Believe he just returned from his honeymoon. Married his secretary after I gave him the best years of my life," she said wearily the tears flowing in rivers now.

"Well, there are several ways you can look at that Sylvia."

"And how's that, doc?"

"Well ask yourself if you loved it when he beat on you?"

"Hell, no."

"Well then you can say and be grateful that he's out of your life. You see it's all a matter of how we look at things. We have to learn how to put things in perspective. We have to constantly ask ourselves if the glass is half empty or half full. And we certainly can't lug dead weight around with us. Life is too short and we have too far to go to be burdened with the weight of things past. Are you still carrying the burden of your being raped around?"

Sylvia looked up startled, surprised that this woman she'd only met days before knew anything about her being raped but kept her composure and answered coolly.

"It bothers me sometimes. It's not something that I'll ever forget. That's for damn sure."

"Tell me. How long has it been since this tragic event happened Sylvia?"

Sylvia laughed.

"Tragedy?" Sylvia repeated the words again as if she hadn't heard and saying it again would make it somehow okay. Taking a Newport from her pocketbook she lit it and inhaled deeply.

Ignoring the remarks the woman glanced down at her papers and commented.

"Well, from what your records indicate this *tragic event* happened in '94. Don't you think it's time you put this rather unfortunate occurrence behind you? My best advice to you is that you probably need to just let it go and move on Sylvia. That's what I'd suggest."

Sylvia looked at the doctor, her legs crossed, plaid dress and penny loafers swinging to and fro and fresh silk blouse, looking like a preppy little Catholic school girl and smiled. But there was no happiness and for the first time the doctor seemed unnerved by the woman sitting across from her.

Slyvia took a deep pull on her cigarette, leaned over and put face as close to the preppy young doctor's as was conceivably possible without touching her and smiled again. The doctor not wanting to appear intimidated refused to give an inch.

"Let me ask you somethin' doc. How old are you?"

"Twenty- six," the fear evident in her voice despite her unwavering posture.

"You're twenty-fuckin' six years old, a fuckin' baby and you're counseling a woman damn near fifteen years your senior and tellin' me how I should act and react to

8

different things you don't know shit about. You actually have the gall, the unmitigated gall, the arrogance to sit there looking like Polly Fuckin' Purebread and pass your little private school advice on to me."

The doctor who was in shock now quickly retreated to the little she had been taught when it came to deescalating an enraged patient.

"Sylvia, I really don't think there's a need for that kind of language or hostility towards me. We are simply talking about some of the issues that drove you to this point that you're sitting here in my office. But I will not be subject to your personal attacks and I don't see where my age has anything at all to do with your issues or the problems that confront you at this point in your life."

"And you wouldn't but let's flip the script doc. Let me ask you a few questions. Now you're twenty-six and although you don't think age doesn't have anything to do with my so-called issues let me just ask you a few questions and who knows maybe it will give me some insight into my problems and help me to come to some kind of resolution and who knows, maybe even allow me to, as you say, move on with my life as you so aptly put it. Fair enough?"

"Go ahead, Sylvia. Ask away," the doctor replied happy just to have a momentary reprieve and the woman out of her face.

"Okay the first thing I'd like to know is if you made love when you were in college."

"I can't say that I did," she replied her cheeks blushing a deep shade of crimson. "I went to an all-girls school in New Hampshire. There weren't a lot of prospects where I went and the town was full of redneck good ol' boys. Farmers and the like… You know the type…People I wasn't exactly drawn to. I didn't make love 'til I was married that I even thought about making love or having intercourse. I come from a long line of southern Baptists and pre-marital sex is not in the question," she replied smiling broadly.

"So I guess you've never been fucked either."

"No, I haven't Sylvia," she said again blushing deeply, "but let's stay on the subject and keep it focused. We have a lot of ground to cover and so little time."

"Oh, we're definitely focused and this definitely is one of my most prevalent issues, since we're centering this whole discussion of getting to the root of my issues and trying to come up with a means of solving them. Let me tell you something. I was brought up in a household very similar to yours. I was brought up an only child. My parents are very strict Methodists and pre-marital sex was a no-no. I too went to an all-girls college. So you see we're not as different as you may think. I never made love in college either. In fact, the only difference I can see is that I unlike you did get fucked. And maybe if it were one guy it would be different but there wasn't one guy. There were eleven. And they came back for seconds and thirds."

It was now quite obvious that despite that all the years of university training hadn't prepared her for this. And it was apparent that Sylvia's latest onslaught had shaken her.

"And I don't really believe that someone who hasn't experienced something as devastating as rape can advise me on shit. Maybe you can refer me to a group like Alcoholics Anonymous or Narcotics Anonymous with other poor souls who have been violated but you sittin' there lady not ever having such a dehumanizing experience as that can't tell me shit. Believe me I've been through hell and back trying to come to grips with it. I want that as bad as I've ever wanted anything in life. I've been through counseling, group meetings; you name it just so I can be as normal the next person. All to no avail. And believe me I've met some men out there…good men and all I ever wanted was to provide them with the love they've given me but the minute they touch me I have flashbacks. But I tried to trust men and act as if each is new and innocent until proven guilty. I try to act as if that one incident is an isolated affair and I have for all intensive purposes moved on but it doesn't matter if it's one individual or eleven, if they take my clothes off or leave me fully dressed I still feel like I'm getting fucked. And I 'm not sure if you're getting the big picture or not but these are not the run of the mill, low life, bottom feeding, hood rats I'm talking about. These are bright, highly educated professionals I'm talking about. Do you feel me?

The reason why I'm here today is that I came home after dating a brother, a good brother, for close to seven months and giving him my all only to find a note from him telling me basically that although he loved me it was time for him to take a new direction. And that hurt me. I mean that hurt me bad. But it was okay that he felt that his life was taking a turn or as he so aptly put it a new direction but why did he have to take everything including my good China and the furniture. I mean this brother had everything and a good job to boot. He's a school teacher. So, why was it so necessary to hurt me by not only taking my heart but my furniture too? That's what I can't understand?" Sylvia said the tears now flowing in waves.

There was a silence not reminiscent of the doctor's office but more like the uncomfortable silence when two people initially attracted to each other find they have nothing in common on a first date. But the young woman was speechless after hearing the graphic details of Sylvia's plight. Still somewhat aghast she sat speechless. She couldn't even imagine the thought of a man, let alone more having their way with her. She had only recently accepted her husband's forays when it came to sex. But eleven men having their way with her? No way!

"Do you still feel that age is just a number, doc? Or do you think you can still empathize with me and help me in my journey to recovery? I didn't even get to the part where they shook up theirs and inserted them into my vagina. Want me to share all the grimy details with you doc?"

"No Sylvia. I believe that's quite enough," said the young doctor still shaken and not sure of how to proceed at this juncture.

"So, what do you think doc? Still feel like you can help me?"

"To be honest with you Sylvia, I'm not really sure. I will admit though that I had no idea what you'd been through. I'm not really sure how I can be of assistance but if there's anything you feel I can do to help you through this or if you need someone to talk to I want you to feel free to come and talk to me anytime," the doctor said resignation apparent evident in her voice.

"What I could is for you to sign my discharge papers so I can get out of here and get on with my life."

The doctor smiled a patronizing smile before responding and chose her words carefully.

"I'd like to do that…"

"But?" Sylvia interjected.

Again the doctor chose her words carefully careful not to say anything to upset the woman who sat before her.

"As I was saying, I'd like to do that but I really want to believe that when you leave here they won't bring you back on a stretcher. I want to, no Sylvia I need to know that you'll be fine when you leave here."

"And how do you propose to do that?"

"Haven't quite figured that out yet but right now as close as I can figure the best I can do is monitor you as closely as I can for the next week or so and if everything proceeds as expected I'll have you out of here before you know it."

"And the pills?"

"Well, that's what got you in here in the first place so I won't write you a script for any but I'll leave instructions to give you one a day as needed. Will that suffice?"

"Guess it'll have to."

Both women smiled as the session ended. There was a mutual respect gained and though neither said it each knew they had grown in perspective in the others eye.

An orderly knocked breaking the easy silence.

"Yes Daniel?" the doctor answered. Whatever he had to say made neither doctor nor orderly happy but whatever it was that he'd whispered somehow affected Sylvia. She could just feel it.

"Everything okay doc?"

"Could you have a seat Sylvia?"

"Why what's wrong? Is there a problem?" Sylvia knew something was wrong now.

"Sylvia, it seems your father has passed away," the doctor whispered.

She had yet to sit and fell forward crumpling into the good doctor's arms.

The week that followed was a tumultuous time for Sylvia but she held it together well enough to elicit a discharge on the same morning as her father's funeral and caught the first flight out. Arriving in North Carolina she was greeted by her mother who seemed to be rather chipper despite her husband's death.

Seems he'd been sick for quite some time but had made it a point not to let Sylvia know.

"Baby girl, believe me your father is in a better place. He was in so much pain. And you know your father. He only wanted the best for his baby girl. He didn't want you to see him suffer," her mother confided as they waited her flight following the burial.

Sylvia had handled the ordeal as well as anyone could expect but as she boarded the flight she felt all the apprehension of a kindergartener approaching her first day of school and wondered why she'd chosen New York as her next destination. She'd been there on many occasions and hadn't particularly liked it. It was just as it was depicted by everyone who had the occasion to visit. It was dirty, grimy and the people were mean-spirited, crass and didn't welcome tourists or newcomers but Lord knows they were proud and loved their city. Thinking intently as the plane readied for its descent, Sylvia smiled. Maybe that's why she chose New York. After all she wasn't interested in a man, any man. What she wanted was to take back her life. And New York gave her the opportunity to find out who she was and do her with everything right there at her disposal. She liked the fact that people kept to themselves and valued their space. She could get lost in the people. And at this point that's all she wanted to do.

She knew one person there, a girl she had taught with early on in her career who had promised to put her up until she found a place of her own. Of course she'd already searched the internet and found a place but it was always good to have a contingent plan just in case. After landing at Kennedy and grabbing a bite to eat Sylvia took the advice of a cabbie and found a quaint little hotel down in the Village. After getting her gear stowed away securely Sylvia decided to see a little of the Village she had heard it was the culture capitol of New York and from what she had seen from the cab it was all true. People bustled along alone or in crowds and it just seemed so alive. Everyone was moving and although Atlanta was alive it couldn't hold a candle to this. Now she was a part of the hustle and bustle that was New York. And though she had only been there for an hour or two she suddenly and for the first in years felt at home.

Chapter 2

The next day crept through her window with all the freshness of an ocean breeze. And suddenly she realized it had been some time since she'd eaten and with all the gusto of a small child on Christmas morning she jumped from the hotel bed with the bad springs and made her to the window to take a deep breath and look out over the city skyline. Finding it exhilarating she felt the briskness of the spring air and slammed the window shut before climbing into the old dilapidated shower. Convinced she'd gotten all the dirt and filth of dirty cabs and flying coach she headed out searching for a restaurant that both appealed to her and appeared somewhat clean. When she couldn't find any to her liking she settled for a Starbucks with internet access. While here she called Mike the realtor and agreed to set up a meeting.

Seeing the seventeenth century Victorian building, she immediately fell in love and saw the endless possibilities. And the neighborhood was so quaint yet gorgeous and the fact that she had a doorman only added to her amazement. She moved in the next day and within two weeks had furnished her new abode. And she loved it. She loved the whole New York scene. She loved the people who despite the rumors who turned out to be extremely knowledgeable as a whole, cosmopolitan and despite the stereotypes rather warm. She loved the city despite its dirt and grime and truly believed that a person could be there all their lives and not take in half the things that it had to offer. She'd already met the local grocer, a very handsome young Puerto Rican gentleman around thirty who in two weeks had fallen in love with her and was now saving the choicest cuts of meat for mommy as he liked to call her. Then there was Sam the doorman, an elderly gentleman who also had eyes for her and couldn't do enough for her. They were men and so she took it for what it was worth smiled and kept it moving although she could have easily been swept away by the grocer five or six years ago. Still, the worst times of her life had always involved men and she adamantly vowed not to get caught up again. No, it was all about Sylvia now and New York was her new love providing with everything she wanted. The only thing that troubled her was how she would pay the rent which was well over two thousand dollars a month. Sure she had her 401K and the little money she'd saved while teaching but that would only last a few months with the cost of living being so high here. She dreaded the thought of returning to the classroom and knew that she still wouldn't be able to make ends meet on a teacher's salary even though they were some of the highest paid in the country. And then almost as if the good Lord knew her plight and grieved with her over her financial situation she received her father's will and though saddened by her father's passing was ecstatic when she found that he'd left her a six figure insurance settlement. If that weren't enough , William had voluntarily agreed to pay her thirty thousand a year in alimony. He must being doing quite well she thought as she thanked God for her most recent blessings.

The weeks following Sylvia spent at her leisure shopping at the small boutiques in the village buying all sorts of things from shoes and boots, to wool dresses and anything else that her little heart fancied and she thought she could afford. When she wasn't shopping she spent the majority of her time at the local bookstore or at the Schomburg library or at the museum. There were so many of them. She'd come home after days like this to a warm bubble bath and sit for hours relaxing before falling fast asleep dreaming of what tomorrow would afford her.

One morning like every morning, she awoke but for some reason she didn't feel like her usual self. Oh, she was up with her usual zest, vibrant and ready to go and explore and see what the city had to offer her today. But for some reason she felt a certain fatigue. Her usual appetite seemed to have gone south and she had to admit she felt somewhat lightheaded so after taking a vitamin and a cup of tablets of Vitamins B and C. She grabbed the latest novel from the kitchen table, checked the time on her cell phone and headed for the front door. Having broken from her normal she was running late today and wasn't sure she'd make the 8:05 bus that would take her down into Soho. Still, she had a chance when it hit her. Turning she ran towards the bathroom and made it just in time throwing up all over sink and toilet seat. 'Damn, must be that spicy Indian food I ate last night', Sylvia thought to herself. 'I love it but every time I eat it, it disagrees with me'. She smiled, cleaned herself up reapplied her lipstick and glanced her watch and figured she still had time to catch the 8:30. Rushing now she glanced at Sam the doorman shouted hello, though not waiting for him to grab the door and burst through. The strap on her handbag broke as she hit the door scattering the contents of her pocketbook everywhere.

"Aw shit" she said cursing the 8:30 bus as it slowly came to a full stop only feet from her. Before she half the contents picked up the bus pulled away. "Damn if this isn't the morning from hell," she muttered aloud.

"Need some help ma'm?"

"Thanks, but no thanks."

The man laughed irritating Sylvia even more than she already was and began helping her and Sam picking up the contents of her bag.

"Never could understand why women feel the need to carry so much junk when they're not going anywhere but to the grocery store," he laughed obviously trying to get her attention.

Sylvia had a good mind to curse him out but realized he would have liked nothing better to give him the chance to start a conversation so she bit her tongue and remained quiet and steadfast in gathering her belongings.

"Always rushing to go nowhere," he said picking up the latest book she 'd been reading, a rather thick volume of Langston's *I Wonder As I Wander.*

"I happen to have a very important interview this morning. Thank you," Sylvia replied growing agitated. She was having a bad morning already without having this joker making it worse.

Just then a long, black Lincoln limousine pulled up catching Sylvia's eye. She wondered who in her building had the means to pay that kind of rent and have a car and a driver to boot. Turning, half expecting Ashford and Simpson to exit the doors, (she'd heard they lived in a high rise just such as this), she was surprised when the driver made over to the handsome young man with her book in his hands and said, "Morning Mr. DuMont. I'm sorry I'm late. The West Side Highway is backed up bumper-to-bumper. If we hurry I can still get you o your meeting on time. It's at nine if I'm correct.

The impeccably dressed man in the charcoal gray suit, manicured nails and attaché case that easily cost as much as Sylvia's entire wardrobe ignoring his drivers comments about the meeting and seemed oblivious to everything but the book he now held in his hand. Staring at it he commented to everyone and no one.

"You know few people outside of his colleagues and a few scholars really understood Langston. He was far before his time. Always made me wonder if it's the times or the man that really marks one for greatness. In Langston's case it was the times that stopped him from achievement the heights of greatness he so richly deserved. Whereas people such as Martin came along at just the right time to aspire and reach greatness. I'm sorry to say that if Martin came along today he'd just be another Atlanta minister aspiring to be bishop. Langston grew up right here on a 145th and 8th. Right there in Harlem in the Dunbar but if you were to ask any of these kids out here who Langston Hughes was I'd bet you a dollar to a donut they wouldn't be able to tell you who he was."

Sylvia reached for the book now inspired by the man's knowledge.

"So you're a fan?"

"A fan?" he said a wide grin now etched on his face. "He's one of my favorites, if not my favorite. Your first time reading Langston's *I Wonder So I Wander?*" he asked the smile not dissipating an inch.

"Yes but not my first time reading Langston. I've read *The Ways of White Folks* and *The Big Sea.*"

Glancing at her watch she realized she was already late. She really did have an appointment. The way she had been shopping she knew her will and alimony checks couldn't last but so long with her current lifestyle so she'd answered an ad from some yuppie couple down in the East Village. Seems they were concerned about their son who attended The School of Arts and Sciences and was failing Language Arts miserably. They were located right by Village where she did most of her shopping and figured the hundred dollars and hour would at least offset some of now weekly shopping sprees.

"You should really try some of his books with Simple. Have you ready any?"

The man was a welcome relief from the cabbies and her friend the grocer and despite her initial reaction she found herself enamored by his wealth of knowledge concerning Langston but she really did have to run. She was already late.

Noticing her anxiety the man stopped.

"You said you were late for an appointment. Is there somewhere I can have Thomas drop you?" he asked matter-of-factly.

"No, there's a bus due in a few minutes. I'll be okay. Thanks anyway." She said leery of the impeccably dressed middle-aged brother.

"You sure now?"

"Positive," she answered.

"Well, in that case you have a good day, Ms...."

"Stanton..."

"Well have a good day, Ms. Stanton and I'll see you around. Maybe we can continue our conversation on Langston over a cup of espresso?"

"Maybe..." she replied hating herself the minute she heard the words. It was always like that with her. A few simple words and the next thing she knew she was cooking dinner for some man she hardly knew.

Thomas held the door as the gentleman got in. Sylvia watched as the driver pulled out of the parking space and sped out into the busy morning traffic. Sylvia walked the half-a-block up to Central Park East and stood on the corner waiting for the bus. Twenty minutes later she stood there still waiting and cursed herself for turning down the ride.

'Girl what the hell is wrong with you? The man lives in the same building as you and I'll bet he's not struggling to pay the rent. The rent...Hell, he's got a driver and a limousine the size of a Macy's Day Parade float, reads Langston Hughes and has shoes the price of my entire wardrobe. What the hell would he want with me outside of some comic relief? It's obvious that he's well read and well educated. He'd probably run circles around my country ass. But I sure could have the ride.' Sylvia glanced down the street but there was no bus to be seen. Damn, she said, how stupid can I be.

It was somewhere around six that evening when she arrived home tired, and exhausted. She was starved but had been too tired to stop and grab something though she knew her fridge and pantry were empty. Tomorrow was Saturday and she always did her grocery shopping on Saturday mornings but she was hungry now. With no recourse she decided to take a long hot shower and go to bed.

"Evening Sam."

"Evening Ms. Stanton. Hope you had a good day," he said smiling and holding the door for her.

Trudging to the elevator she heard her name.

"I almost completely forgot. I have a message for you from Mr. DuMont," Sam said reaching into his inside pocket.

"I don't believe I know a Mr. DuMont Sam," Sylvia said.

"Sure you do… He's the gentleman that helped pick up your stuff when you dropped your pocketbook this morning. He's the gentleman who has the penthouse on the top floor."

Sam handed her the note. Showing little interest other than in a shower and her warm bed Sylvia stuck the note deep into her pocketbook. A second later the elevator doors opened allowing her entry.

It was the first that someone had knocked at her door this late at night. In fact the only person that had ever knocked on her door was Sam to deliver a package from UPS. Other than that she had received no visitors so who the hell was this knocking at her door at seven o'clock at night.

Looking through the tiny peephole she saw a portly gentleman who could have easily passed as a bouncer in a butler's uniform. Sure he had the wrong apartment. Any place else she would have had second thoughts about opening the door, being a single female and all but security was so tight that even if they got by Sam they still were forced to check in at the front desk before being allowed up.

"Yes sir. May I help you?"

"Ms. Stanton I believe?"

"Yes."

"Mr. DuMont requests your company. I'm here to escort you up to his place."

"May I ask this is in regard to?"

"I haven't any idea. Overheard him say that he sent you a note and you must not have gotten it so he sent me to make sure his request had been at least received. That's all I know."

"Come in. You have me a little curious," Sylvia said. "By the way, I didn't get your name."

"Abdul ma'm. Abdul Rakman."

"Well, Mr. Rakman, sir I must tell you that I don't make it a habit of going to strange men's apartments just because they request it. A lady could get herself in trouble like that you know?" Sylvia said looking through her pocketbook in search of the note.

"I doubt that, ma'm. You'll find that Mr. DuMont is quite well respected. He's worked far too long and too hard to risk everything for any woman or a man for that matter, ma'm."

Still rummaging Sylvia made small talk in her vain attempts to buy time.

"And what is it that Mr. DuMont does anyway, if you don't mind me asking?"

"Don't tell me that you haven't heard of DuMont and DuMont Brokerage Firms?"

"Sorry to say I haven't but then I'm new to New York. I've only been here a month."

"Where are you from, if you don't mind me asking?"

"Well, I'm originally from North Carolina but I've been residing in Atlanta for the last ten or twelve years."

"I'm really surprised you haven't heard of it then. DuMont and DuMont has branches in both Charlotte and Atlanta. It's one of the largest and most prestigious firms in the country."

Sylvia suddenly found the tiny piece of paper she'd been searching for, opened it and read it. It was an invitation to dinner. Couldn't have come at a better time. She was starving and having already blown an opportunity for a job by declining a ride she considered refusing his invitation to dinner another blown opportunity and gladly accepted.

"Will you give me a few minutes to find something a little more suitable to wear?" she asked the very solemn and stoic Mr. Rakman.

Not a problem ma'm. I'll be waiting outside."

Chapter 3

Dressed in a gorgeous gold sequined evening gown with a pair of gold mules to match Sylvia looked like a star or better yet a runway model. Never one much for jewelry but tonight she donned a thin gold necklace with bracelet to match. As she exited her apartment, there stood Abdul waiting as he promised.

"Was I long? I'm sorry but you know how we women are?" Sylvia said cordially not half believing he'd actually waited until she changed, pampered herself and decided if she really wanted to go or not. She'd even taken the time to sit for a spell and reflect on her life, her dealings with men, and where a dinner with such a man as Mr. DuMont could lead to. She concluded that she'd come to New York to escape the trials and tribulations, and the utter chaos that men caused in her life and decided that dinner was totally out of the realm of possibility. It simply went against her very constitution. Still, another week had passed where once again she'd exceeded her budget buying clothes that nobody would ever get a chance to see and well, he'd been friendly enough and maybe, just maybe it wouldn't hurt just to have a friend. And besides all that and perhaps the biggest single factor in the whole equation was that she was starved.

"You never answered me Mr. Rakman? Was I long?" Sylvia asked as they got on the elevator.

"Does it matter ma'm? My job is in itself a waiting game but it doesn't matter to me I get paid by the hour."

"Guess that's a good philosophy to have."

"Doesn't hurt," he replied stoically.

Placing the key in the elevator, he then pushed twenty-six and the elevator moved from floor to floor with ease. Arriving at the floor, Abdul turned the key counter clockwise thus denying access to anyone accidentally hitting floor twenty-six. The door opened and all Sylvia could do was gasp. She'd been to some beautiful homes in Atlanta, palatial. There were homes that she would have killed to own but never in all her days had she seen anything to rival this suite. The floors were covered in expensive white carpet. A huge baby grand piano adorned the center of the room and though it was sparsely decorated what furniture that did exist was expensive and quite tasteful. On one wall hung a painting. Getting closer she noticed it was an original Basquiat. Impressed there were plenty of other pieces of the same ilk. Some of the pieces she recognized, others she did not.

"I'll tell Mr. DuMont you've arrived Ms. Stanton. He's probably in his study," Adul said before leaving.

The living room in itself was larger than her entire apartment Sylvia thought. Within moments Abdul was back.

"Mr. DuMont requests your presence in the study ma'm. Please follow me."

Sylvia followed directions and passed a galley styled kitchen with a long, free standing island with granite counters. It was the kitchen she'd always dreamed though long and narrow it had everything a woman could ask for. A rather attractive young white woman smiled cordially as she passed and soon entered Mr. DuMont's study which was even more impressive than the kitchen and living room yet equally as spacious. Around the walls were book cases and it occurred to Sylvia that this man's study had more books in it than the Elizabethtown library where she'd grown up. Her fascination apparent Mr. DuMont smiled extending a warm and gracious hand to the petite but shapely young woman before him.

"Welcome to my humble abode," he said.

"Wouldn't exactly call it humble, Mr. DuMont."

"It'll do but please don't call me Mr. DuMont. Call me Alex."

"Only if you call me…"

"Sylvia, I know…"

"Is there anything you don't know Alex," Sylvia smiled.

"Plenty which is one of the reasons I invited you here tonight. Figure you could help me feel in some of the blanks."

"I love your study or is it your library?" Sylvia inquired intent on stemming the flirtatious nature of the conversation.

"Call it what you like. I thought you'd enjoy it better than any other room being that you seem to love books. Can't blame you though. It's my favorite a s well. Not to sound too egotistical but I designed it personally and ordered every piece of writing in here. Literature is my passion you know which is why I was so intrigued by you. It's so seldom that I find a person who shares my interests so when I do, well I guess you know…" he said smiling.

"I suppose I do. First, an offer for a chauffeured limousine ride, and then a note left with Sam the doorman and finally Mr. Rakman, the butler comes down to my apartment to invite me to dinner. Are you sure our common interest in literature is what prompted all this?" Sylvia asked flirtatiously.

"Well, not entirely but in large part," he said caught off guard but her sudden forwardness. "Care for a glass of Merlot?"

"That would be wonderful. But you still haven't answered my question," Sylvia asked making it clear that she had no intention of letting the issue go. She needed to make it clear to Mr. DuMont that he shouldn't waste his time trying to woo her because those weren't her intentions. She could care less about how wealthy he was she would not be swayed again. Not in this lifetime. Not by him or any other man.

"Could you repeat your question, Sylvia?"

"I asked you what your intent was as far as I'm concerned?"

"I really don't understand, Sylvia. Why do I have to have intentions as far as you're concerned? I saw you were a reader and not just a reader but a reader of one of my favorite authors and I invited you to share a little bit of your perspectives on Hughes and some of the other authors you've read and may like. That's all."

"And that's all?" Sylvia asked still somewhat suspicious of why a man of Mr. DuMont's type would be interested for something other than a weekend tryst or simply because of their close proximity just being pillow pals for his convenience like a female Mini Market.

"Well, I must admit that you are a beautiful woman but the world's full of beautiful women. I see them all them the time. I even married a couple but when morning comes and you wake up I've found that it's so much more important to have someone you can share your thoughts and ideas with than simply a pretty face."

"I know that's right."

"But if it eases your mind any I am interested in you as a person and that's not to say that you don't appeal to me physically. You do. But all I really wanted was a nice quiet dinner and perhaps get to know you a little better. And you're here because you're curious about something as well. No?"

Sylvia smiled. Truth be told she was curious. She was curious about how the other half lived. She was curious about this Black man, what he did, how he could afford to live here, and have a chauffeured driven limousine. But most of all she was just plain hungry. Still, she played her cards close to the vest.

"Yes, I was curious as to how you knew about Langston and why you were so mesmerized when seeing his novel in my purse."

"And my interests were and are the same. So why are you so skeptical?"

"Just coming out of a bad relationship is all. I moved to New York to get lost in the shuffle and reacquaint myself with Sylvia Stanton. I asked you all of that because I am so skeptical of men at this juncture in my life, and so fragile that I make it a point to avoid the games, the drama and any type of involvement with the opposite sex. So, I had to ask what your intentions are because relationships and everything that goes along with them are out of the picture and I just wanted that to be clear from the outset."

"May I ask you something Sylvia?"

"What makes you so certain that I'm looking for anything or anybody? Listen. I've been married twice and in all honesty can't see doing that again. Secondly, I neither have the time nor the energy for a woman. My work won't permit me too. And now that's all said and done shall I have dinner served?

"By all means," Sylvia said glad to have cleared the air.

The pretty young brunette brought in course after course until Sylvia couldn't bring herself to lift her fork and had to push herself away from the small table brought in for just the occasion.

Dinner had been delightful. He'd given her a tour of his house before retiring back to the study where they finished off another bottle of wine and spoke in length about all the great Black writers of the twentieth century over coffee and pastry.

Alex DuMont excused himself at eight thirty saying he had to take a conference call and shaking Sylvia's hand, led her to Abdul who escorted her back to her apartment. Sylvia showered quickly and decided on starting one of the five books Alex had suggested she read but for some reason her thoughts continually drifted back to earlier that evening. It had certainly been a welcome change. Shit, she could get used

29

to some of the perks of being wealthy and although she could do without Abdul the

butler that white girl was certainly one helluva cook. She had to wonder much as she

hated to whether Alex was kickin' it with her in his spare time. She was cute as a

button. She hated when a brother picked up some scraggly white chick just so they

could they say they had a white girl but she was cute as she could be and had

obviously been to school to prepare the dishes she had. No, she was the real deal.

Wonder how much she was being paid. And the books… Oh, my God!! She would

never leave the study. All in all, it was another world. A world she would have had

no problem getting used to. And then there was Alex. A few months ago she knew

she would have had no problem taking him into the fold. He was her type alright

looking just as sexy as he wanted to in his charcoal grey trousers that fit just the way

she liked for them to fit and hugged just what she liked it to hug. Thinking about him

her thoughts drifted and she reached for the vibrator in her top drawer and the

Vaseline that made entry just that much easier. Lubricating it she slid into her now

wet vagina taking all twelve inches and gasping loudly. Damn, it felt good but it was

by no means what she needed. She needed a man. Still, it was the best she could do

and she relaxed easing back down onto the softness of the goose down pillows. Legs

now spread widely Sylvia eased the dark blue vibrator in and out in rapid succession

screaming loudly as she neared orgasm and thinking of what could have been if she

had let her guard down and let Alex DuMont take her. And she could very well

have. Truth of the matter was she'd never had any problem getting a man. The

problem was keeping one.

Chapter 4

The days and nights came and went quickly. Sylvia started tutoring and thought about opening her own tutorial service. There were so many kids in dire need of help and teaching was her passion. But real estate was so damn high in New York that it seemed inconceivable without financial backing and she knew of no one who had the kind of money that would be necessary.

There was always Alex DuMont but it had been weeks before she'd talked to him. And even then it hadn't really been more than a few words in passing. He'd been getting into his limo and heading off somewhere. He was always heading off somewhere and she had to ask herself once or twice what sense it made to even have such an extravagant home if you didn't get to enjoy it. Besides she hardly knew him. And certainly didn't know him well enough to borrow the type of money she needed.

A week later as she sat watching reruns of *Girlfriends* Sylvia resigned herself that she only had two options. She could either solicit Alex or let another of her dreams fall by the waste side. But his was a new beginning and the perfect time to seize the opportunity. All her life, she'd been supportive to men who continually sought to make their dreams a reality and she had helped always been very supportive letting her dreams sit dormant while helping them obtain theirs but no more. It was time for her to realize hers. She could recall daddy telling her when she was growing up that there was nothing in life worse than wasted potential. And he was right. She didn't have daddy here to tell her that anymore but the message was resounding nevertheless.

She awoke the next morning with a start, showered quickly and after throwing up two or three times went about the business of writing a proposal for The Literacy

Library a non-profit tutorial program for inner city kids struggling to finish high school. She'd been awake half the night working on the proposal in her mind so the words came easily that morning. In good spirits, she decided to run the idea by Alex, the go to the New York City Board of Education if he wasn't interested and then as a last resort, go the bank to seek funding in the name of a small businessman's loan. She hated to seek out the last but the dream was imbedded in her now. In all likeliness this is where she'd end up but there were always companies and major corporations which gave grants. She might even run it past her ex-husband's marketing firm and she couldn't see any reason why he'd turn her down. She was after all, one of the major reasons he was a partner in it now. Sylvia the years of teaching and incorporated it into the proposal before going to the library and completing her research.

A week later she was very proud of the thirty-three page proposal that sat before her on the coffee table in the living room. She had index cards and rehearsed her presentation through much of the following week until she was content and felt she was ready to present it to the world. She couldn't have been more proud of her efforts and was in such a wonderful state of mind that she had trouble understanding why she'd ever thought she needed a man. Well, those were thoughts until the sun was replaced by the moon and she lay in her bed tossing, turning and thinking. She'd started working and had even taken up running again across the street every night after dinner in Central Park. She's come home and takes a steaming, hot shower to relax her, before grabbing one of the books Alex had given her. Her intent was to read herself to sleep but she still found herself restless. And more than often the last thing that could be heard in the darkness at Apartment 2C was the steady drone of her blue dolphin as she rocked herself to sleep. It had almost become habitual but

32

still she didn't deem herself ready for a man. No, life was good, uncomplicated, she was happy and hadn't a care in the world. The only thing that bothered her was the constant throwing up in the morning. When it first started she thought nothing of it. But when it reoccurred she started examining all the possibilities. Pregnancy was impossible since doctors told her in college that after the rape she would not be able to bear children. What she feared most was that she may have cancer. Her mother had already had a mastectomy and her father had only recently passed from colon cancer. And as everyone knows cancer is hereditary so Sylvia avoided the doctor like the plague. Life was going far too well for any bad news. Besides that and despite her highly regimented exercise routine she was still a smoker. She told herself it was nothing more than the flu but after a week and it was still occurring she decided it best she see a doctor.

The next morning Sylvia left a note with Sam the doorman for Alex DuMont and headed to the library in search of information on starting a non-profit organization. She then had an appointment to see a lawyer so he could look over her proposal and then up town to Harlem to have a lunch with her friend Benny who had offered her a place to stay when she'd arrived and after two and a half months had yet to see although she did talk to her frequently using her as a sort of unofficial tour guide and information center.

By the time six o'clock had rolled around Sylvia still hadn't accomplished everything she'd started out to do but was so exhausted she headed home lamenting how there just weren't enough hours in the day. Stepping through the day revolving doors she glanced at Sam who was arguing with a delivery man who insisted on going up to a resident's apartment to get a signature for a package. Sam offered to take it up but the delivery a steadfast and persistent young Black boy insisted he do it.

"Yo, brotha I don't need nobody to do my job for me. I need this shit. My girl 'bout to have a baby," he said to Sam who was a stickler for the rules and the rules specifically said no unauthorized personal including deliverymen shall be permitted access to a resident's apartment.

"I hear you young brother but the rules clearly say…"

The young man noticeably in a hurry wasn't hearing or having it cut Sam off.

"Listen, nigga I already got two babies's to feed. Ya know what ahm saying? Plus I need ta eat myself. If this shit falls into the wrong hands, that's my ass. All I need to do is see the man's fuckin' I.D. and get a damn signature. Ain't nobody tryna commit no crime or nothin'"

Sam tired of trying to reason with the man simply said.

"Can't do it young brother. Tell your company the rules and let them call management and see if they can't work something out but for right now the answer is no. I cannot allow you to go upstairs."

"Man, fuck you," the young man said, "give a nigga a little authority and he swears he owns the shit. What you make nigga? Two fifty a week doin' the white man's biddin' and you think you own the fuckin' building. You ain't shit. You ain't no more than a field nigger workin' for the master. Shame on you," he said before turning and storming away.

Sylvia stood there awaiting the outcome, making sure Sam was okay and the young brother didn't become any more hostile than he already was. Sam wasn't the least bit shaken by the rudeness of the young man and turned to Sylvia who asked.

"Are you okay, Sam?"

"Just part of the job, Ms. Stanton… Just part of the job!"

"Alright, then Sam was just a little worried about you that's all Sylvia said genuine concern showing in her voice.

"Thanks for the concern. And how was your day, Ms. Stanton?"

"Busy , but fruitful overall."

"And how's your tutorial program coming?"

"Still just a work in progress but I have high hopes."

"Did you go and see the lawyer I told you about?"

"Had to reschedule with him… I've been running late all day. I have an appointment at nine a.m. tomorrow though."

"He's a good man. He should be able to help you out a lot. Oh, and by the way, I have a message from Mr. DuMont," Sam said handing her a piece of paper on the same monogrammed stationery he handed her the first time.

"Thank you, Sam and you have a good evening," Sylvia said before turning and heading to the elevators.

"Hey, Ms. Stanton," he yelled. "Would you like me to have a cab here for you at eight-thirty in the morning?"

"Sure Sam and thank you" she said stepping into the elevator.

Opening the envelope she read the note seeing where Mr. DuMont was requesting her company at seven p.m. It was six thirty now and she still had to take a shower and change. She had no idea of what to wear but she wanted to wear something conservative so he didn't get the wrong impression and would know how serious she was about the serious nature of her proposal.

Throwing on a black Jones of New York suit and some black heels, Sylvia smiled at her reflection in the mirror. Alex's a bad boy if he can refuse this proposal, Sylvia thought to herself. She then called the number on the paper and within minutes Abdul was buzzing the intercom. Grabbing the proposal from the coffee table she made her way upstairs. Nothing much had changed but she was as taken back by the overall appearance of the suite as she was the first time. Again she was led to the study where Alex DuMont sat behind his huge mahogany desk. Standing to greet he took her hand shook it graciously, his two large hands swallowing hers and seated her.

"It is a pleasure to be graced by your company once again Sylvia. My only question is… why so long? I gave it considerable thought and all I came up with was the fact that you didn't like the dinner or perhaps my company and that coupled with your aversion to men I was afraid to call on you again. But I am certainly glad you saw fit to call on me. Did you get a chance to read any of the books I gave you?"

"I certainly did. Read all of them and loved them. I especially loved Tip O'Neil's *Man Of The House* and Machiavelli's *The Prince.*"

"That's the equivalent of your Bible," he laughed. "Though not in a literal sense but when I change hats and head downtown it's his doctrine that I use for my business dealings," he laughed. "He's hardnosed and no-nonsense but if you look at politics…"

"I know. That coupled with Tip O'Neill's book and I got a whole different perspective on the inner workings of this country."

"I hear you. It was a wakeup call for me too. They changed my way of looking at things completely. You know, for a long time I saw things from a purely Black viewpoint but when I read Machiavelli and looked at the world instead of just from a racial outlook I understood things a whole lot better and a whole lot clearer."

"It was sort of like an epiphany for me. In all honesty, it was to say the least enlightening. That's why I believe reading for us is so important. And being a former English teacher is why I feel it so imperative that we as a people achieve literacy. That accomplished we can understand the world a bit better and deal with the things that ail us as a people and a nation."

"You are so right, Sylvia. I have a few more you might be interested in as well. Just finished one although it's not in the same vein as what you've just finished reading I think you may enjoy it. It's a bit more philosophical but a good read nonetheless. Hold on I'll get it for you."

Sylvia watched as Alex rose, slid from behind his desk and exited the room. Damn that man is fine. Elegant and intelligent to boot… Why couldn't have she have met him in another time and space…Damn

Alex DuMont returned moments later handing her a couple of books.

"Think you'll enjoy these," he commented. "You know you should really go with me one Saturday mornings. I hardly have any free time but I make time Saturday mornings to check out the book sales around the city. You know every now and then you can really find some keepers for little or nothing, he said smiling. "Do most of my clothing shopping that way too," he smiled as he watched her look of surprise on her face.

"You mean to tell me a man of your wealth and stature is out there yard sale shopping with the rest of us bottom feeders?"

"Wouldn't be where I am today if I hadn't cut some corners." He said ignoring her dig. "But seriously can I expect your company this Saturday?"

"Let me check my schedule and get back to you. I've been working on a little that's really kind of close to me and has me wrapped up at the moment. And to tell you the truth, since I started it I don't know whether I'm going or coming most of the time. I'm kind of caught in a world wind."

"If you don't mind me asking who or what is it that has your attention that you can't give up a Saturday morning for a friend that enjoys your company?"

"Actually, it's the reason I wanted to see you."

"And to think it was a purely platonic visit. I'm starting to think I should have asked your intentions. But anyway, tell me what's on your mind?"

"Well, I have this plan for a non-profit tutorial service for any city teens and…" Sylvia immediately went into her pre-rehearsed spiel. When she was finished Alex simply said, "It's a very interesting concept Sylvia and it's obvious you've done your homework. You present well. Ever considered financial marketing?"

There was no smile now. This was business and if it weren't profitable Alex was in general not interested. He'd almost shut down completely when she said non-profit but he'd been polite and listened anyway and by the time she'd finished come up with several ways in which her business would in some way facilitate his own. A non-profit would provide a nice tax shelter and now that the city was cracking down on absentee landlords it was extremely difficult to obtain real estate without maintaining a business or occupancy. Alex thought of the days when he could simply purchase a lot and sit and watch it appreciate in value. All in all, Sylvia ideas were not a bad one, giving him a valuable piece of property and also serve as a tax write off. Her proposal would also give him access to the very beautiful Sylvia Stanton who he'd thought about numerous times since their last encounter. Still, as he explained to her, he had to run it by his financial advisors before making a decision and so with much stoicism he let her know without any indication of what he was inevitably thinking but that he'd let her know Saturday morning when she joined him to go bargain hunting. Excusing himself for a conference call, he graciously shook her hand and said he would meet her Saturday morning at six a.m. in front of the building. A little bit disappointed she agreed acknowledging that the wine was once again exquisite and said farewell.

Disappointment evident she could do nothing but cross her fingers and wait.

Chapter 5

Saturday was on her before she knew it. Most people weren't up before nine or ten o'clock. And here she was way out on Long Island, some called Wyandanch rummaging through some old ladies rubbage looking for anything that caught his interest. She was herself having a splendid time but had slowed her shopping when Alex refused to let her pay for anything. That was half the fun of it, Sylvia thought. It was the thrill of getting a hundred dollar item and paying pennies for it. Half the time the stuff she bought at yard sales would go home and just become more clutter and she'd find herself asking herself what had possessed it in the first place. Still, the conversation was good and she got to see him a better light. He turned out to very witty and charming the total opposite of the very rigid, very serious Mr. DuMont she was so accustomed to seeing. He was almost like a little boy in a toy store, finding a doo dad here and there and screaming for her to come take a gander in spite of the crowds that each sought their own treasures.

He was dressed down. Adorned in a brown sweat suit and sneakers, the thirty-six year old Alex DuMont looked more like twenty-five and his close cut fade gave him the appearance of one of the fly brothers down at 14th Street Park not ready to ball but just there to impress the ladies. At five foot nine his dark brown frame had no steady gait. He seemed to float from item to item. On several occasions, Sylvia, dressed in a tight blue sweat suit of her own was caught looking but then she couldn't help it. He had nicest, ass she had seen on any man. And he wasn't least bit arrogánt or disconcerted when he caught her eyes on his ass. He seemed almost glad to finally have gotten her attention and smiled showing his dimples that made him even more attractive.

When Sylvia saw an item like that brass candelabra set that would fit so perfectly in her dining room she had to pull the elderly woman over to the side just to pay for it. Thomas the driver seemed to enjoy the game to, all the time keeping his eye on the comical antics of Ms. Stanton and rushing over every time he saw her purchasing an item on her own, grabbing it and racing back to the car and tossing it in the trunk.

Overall, the morning turned out to be a pleasant surprise. Both sipped wine in the back of the limo and by early afternoon were visibly tipsy. The only thing that seemed to irritate Syjvia was that there had been no mention of The Literacy Library, funding or anything else. It was as though Alex had just ignored her request. Perhaps she should ask she thought but on second thought didn't want to appear too forward or anxious. Still, wasn't that the agreement?

It was Alex who broke the easy silence.

"I think the wine's got me. Hope you don't mind if we stop and grab a bite to eat on the way home."

"Nothing extravagant, I hope. You've done far too much already."

"Don't think you'll have to worry about that. I've spent out. I was thinking the first Mickey D's or Burger King we see. That's all I can afford right now," he said smiling.

"That's fine."

"But listen, I'd be honored if you had dinner with me tonight. Would kind of make my day complete."

Sylvia was thinking now. Maybe he thinks he could let me down easier over dinner. But then again he could just be stringing me along. But being that she didn't know she accepted his offer.

Lunch had been somewhat jovial and before long they were home. Sylvia thanked him for her for the day and Thomas brought her newly acquired items up to the apartment for her. A few glasses of wine later and she found herself in a deep sleep. The phone ringing woke her with a start and she was pleasantly surprised to hear Benny's voice on the other end.

"Girl, I thought you were going to give me a call."

"Oh, Benny I'm so sorry. I do apologize but you know things are just hectic right through here. Half the time I don't know if I'm coming or I'm going," she said.

"Oh, shit girl what's his name? "

"Who's name?"

"The name of the brother that's got your nose wide open."

"Why would you say that Benny?"

"I told you I'm celibate. Men aren't even in the equation anymore. You know what they say about doing bad all by yourself, don't you?"

"I do but all that's talk and only talk right up until Mr. Right comes along and gets your panties in an uproar. And from what I'm hearing in your voice those bikini thigh high are all twisted up. So you gonna tell me about him or what?"

Sylvia laughed.

"I'm telling you the truth Benny there is no Mr. Right. I met a guy in my building who I think may be seriously considering financing the tutorial program I was telling you about that's all. He's a book collector and we went to some yard sales out on the Island but it's nothing serious."

"Nothing serious? That's husband and wifey shit. That's something that old married couples do. May not sound serious but I can read the shit and there's more."

"Benny there is definitely something wrong. Every time I talk to you I'm truly inclined to believe that someone blew the wick out on your candle," Sylvia laughed. "Okay, okay I'll leave you alone. Anyway, I Just called to see what you were doing tonight. Some of the girls and I were going down to the Latin Quarters and thought you might want to come."

"Can't Benny… I'm going out to dinner."

"Two months in New York and your ass is going out to dinner and you want me to believe that you haven't met anybody? What kind of fool do you think I am?" Sylvia laughed again.

"Ain't goin' nowhere but upstairs. Neighbor of mine invited me upstairs for dinner."

"Wouldn't be the same person that you went to the yard sales with would it?" Benny asked rather sarcastically.

Sylvia laughed.

"Yeah, he's one and the same," Sylvia said laughing.

"First yard sales in the morning and now dinner tonight and you mean to tell me there's nothing happening. C'mon Sill…I may not be the brightest star in the sky but Lord knows it doesn't take a rocket scientist to figure out there's interest there on someone's part. I don't know if it's you doing the pursuing or him. But one of you is certainly interested."

"Well, if you must know today is really the only day we've spent any time together and the only reason being is because he's considering funding my tutorial program."

"Oh, no he isn't. Okay, there's obviously something you're not telling me. You mean to tell me that you've been in New York City for only two months; in a city where it's hard to get directions on the subway you've already got a stranger to give you the money to open a business?

And then you expect me to believe that your financier has no interest in you other than being your friend? Oh, c'mon Sill, I may be naive but I'm not downright stupid. This is money-making Manhattan where people kill each other for a dollar and ain't nobody giving up shit. And you mean to tell me you have met someone who has known you for less than two months and he's agreed to… C'mon Sill level with me. At least tell me his name."

Sylvia chuckled lightly.

"If I told you would you his name you still wouldn't know him so what's the point."

"Humor me anyway. So, tell me his name."

"Listen, Benny. I told you what went down in Atlanta and what brought me here to begin with. I'm not interested in meeting *anybody*. My father just passed away and I'm really not ready for a relationship of any kind. And I make it clear to every man I meet that I'm not interested. Now if they are interested in being purely friends then that's the move. Anything other than that is out. You feel me?"

"I hear you. Don't know if I feel you but I definitely hear you. Still, if he means nothing to you…I mean if you're just friends then why are you being so secretive? Tell me the brother's name."

"Damn Benny! You're about a nosey heifer but if you must know his name is Alex. Alex DuMont, okay."

Benny screamed.

"Oh my God Sylvia you're not…Tell me you're not dating the Alex DuMont of DuMont and DuMont? Girl, do you know he's one of the richest Black men in New York? Oh, my God and he lives in your building. You don't have any idea of the power he wields do you? Did you know that he's considered one of the most eligible bachelors in New York? Oh, my God girl, you've really hit the jackpot this time."

Sylvia was unaware of most of the things Benny shared with her and now that she knew it still didn't matter all that much but she was elated that her girlfriend thought so much and held him in such high esteem.

"Told you we're just neighbors. That's it. But anyway let me get dressed I'm late for dinner already and I haven't even started getting ready. I'll call you when I get back."

"You'd better. I want to know all the juicy details girl."

"Don't know that there will be any juicy details but I'll call you when I get back home."

Sylvia arrived for dinner about an hour later, fashionably late as she referred to it only to find that Alex had to run out for a minute. Sylvia sat in the study leafing through some books which had drawn her attention. Deeply immersed in one she hardly noticed Alex's enter the room. Dressed in a pair of blue trousers and cream colored turtle neck he looked absolutely delicious. It was quite a contrast to the sweats he had on earlier and where he looked good before he looked absolutely ravishing now. Handing Sylvia a bottle of Dom Perignon and an envelope he smiled before bending down and giving her a light peck on the cheek. Sylvia was shocked by the gesture and though her mind told her that she wasn't there to be romanced she felt the warmth between her legs. Sylvia was still feeling the wine from earlier in the day and wanted to reach up and grab Alex and pull him to her and kiss him passionately but thought better of it and though difficult she refrained. She had to admit she was having a harder and harder time keeping Alex out of her thoughts these days. Perhaps he's different Sylvia thought to herself. Perhaps he's worthy of my time. She smiled but was glad she'd refrained from acting.

"Sylvia! Sylvia! You here with me?" Alex said staring, puzzled by her daydreaming.

"Sorry, I just have a lot on my mind."

Alex laughed.

"A very wise man once told me to never let anything live rent free in my mind for more than five minutes and I've tried to incorporate that into my very mantra. Makes dealing with the other houses on Wall Street just that much easier. "

"I hear you. Funny thing though, the thoughts weren't bad just came at a rather inopportune time is all. And I must admit I do have a lot on my mind right through here. I apologize."

"Well, I think if you open the envelope and then pour us a glass of champagne in that order it just may lessen your burden somewhat. Hold on, let me get Victoria to pop the cork and bring us a couple of glasses."

Alex picked up the cell on his desk and Victoria promptly appeared. After introducing the two women Alex insisted Sylvia open the envelope which she promptly did.

"Oh, my goodness Alex. Oh, my God! I thought you'd forgotten about my proposal altogether," she said rushing over and giving him the biggest hug and kiss she could muster.

"For that kind of reaction I'm tempted to write another check," he laughed.

"Thank you so much Alex. You've truly made my dreams a reality. Thank you.

"Not at all. I told my advisors about the way in which you presented and it was hard for them to turn down my request. I think they felt my enthusiasm…" he said smiling broadly, "and they were afraid not to buy into it." You know I'm a pretty good salesperson myself. I think they got the impression that they'd find themselves on the unemployment line if they would've refused. Probably right too. I gotta admit, I was probably as excited as you were just to be connected with such a valiant and much needed effort as yours," he said laughing loudly.

Sylvia sat there staring at the check in awe.

"Alex, you don't know what this means to me." She said, her eyes welling up with tears.

"It's the first of three over a year's time. Hope that'll be sufficient."

"Sufficient?!?! I think that's more than gracious.

Dinner was again both wonderful and delicious and the champagne had Sylvia swooning. But she was no novice, no amateur, no neophyte. When it came to the game she knew how men operated. And despite her wanting him to ease her wanting and her needs he wouldn't have her tonight simply because of a check and a bottle of champagne. Sylvia then waited for Alex to try his hand at seduction. The wine and the check made it almost impossible to refuse his overtures should he ask. And despite her convictions Sylvia knew that she wanted more than anything to relax them and make love to this man tonight but to her surprise there were no overtures and she lay in bed later that night she had to wonder if she'd lost something. She was after all, fast approaching middle age and the taut lithe body she used wear like a badge was started to gain a few pounds here and there and wilt where it used to be rigid and firm. Working out was now a necessity just to keep everything in its proper place. As to why Alex hadn't tried anything she was completely at a loss. Lying in bed thinking of all the beautiful women who made up the New York City landscape she was sure that Alex could have his choice of almost any of them if he wanted but it was she who he said appealed to him but he hadn't even attempted to make a move aside the friendly peck on the cheek. Well, if she didn't turn him on he certainly did turn her on and no matter how much she fought the idea in the daytime the reality of her passion became illuminated at night and tonight was like no other as she reached the bottle of Vaseline and let her hand other hand slide between her legs. Closing her eyes she rubbed her clitoris in tiny circles as she thought of his fine brown frame bending over to grab odd little statues at the yard sale earlier in the day. She recalled his perfectly formed ass and rubbed harder, moaning now, her clit on fire as beads of sweat formed on the bridge of her nose. Feeling the kiss on her cheek Sylvia's hip rose from the bed time and time again as the orgasm causing her to tremble and thrash wildly as she came time after time. Damn it was good she thought her eyes now closed and she now only half a heartbeat away from the much needed sleep she now craved could only think of thing she needed and wanted more than anything else after such a fruitful day. And that one thing was a man.

Sylvia awoke with a start. The night before was everything she could have asked for. There was champagne, a good meal with great company and most of all a fine, handsome, young, gentleman who showed interest. But this morning it was back to work and now it was time for her to make her plans and dreams come to fruition. Her first stop was to see the lawyer Sam referred her to make sure everything she was doing was within the legal parameters of a non-profit organization and to look over her proposal. She also needed to know if receiving monies from Alex DuMont was not only legitimate and fell under the umbrella of a non-profit, she needed to know what rights she had and what she needed to have in writing in case he changed his mind. She needed to know what she could do with the money, was it a gift or a loan, was it for materials, or a building. There were just so many things that were vague and unaccounted for and she needed some clarity, some clarification.

Riding downtown that morning in the cab Sam had arranged her mind was a jumbled mess. Why had Alex loaned her money without not so much as a question concerning her credit history. Or had he had her checked her out. And if he did how much of her past history did he know? Of course he'd had her checked out. He was a business man and from what she understood, one of the best in the city. And as everyone knows a business of Alex's caliber weighed every detail before he invested in anything. Money was his motivation and there was no way he was going to invest in a losing venture. But what was there to gain? There was no capitol to gain in investing a non-profit.

Sylvia was suddenly roused from her thoughts by the sudden lurch of the cab as he stopped in front of the lawyer's office. Entering the lobby she was pleased to find a rather pleasant atmosphere. A tall rather debonair dark-skinned gentleman approached her. He was dressed in a black suit of the highest quality and looking down to the huge hand that engulfed hers noticed his manicured fingernails and soft skin. A large rough hewn man though extremely handsome faced her with his chiseled chin he looked like Charlton Heston in black face.

"Names Chisolm. And the way Sam described you, you must be Sylvia. That man always did have good taste but his description hardly does you justice. You certainly are one beautiful woman."

There was no smile.

"Thank you Mr…."

"Chisum," he replied leading her by the hand past the receptionist desk.

"Hold all my calls, Trina," he said to the receptionist, a very shapely young stallion in her own right.

Leading Sylvia Stanton down the hall Chisum led Sylvia by his luxurious office giving her a brief tour and then took her into the conference room where he promptly pulled out her chair before seating himself adjacent to her.

"So, Ms. Stanton what is it that I can do for you today?" he said in a no-nonsense tone that let her know that time was money and that he was strictly business. "Well,…"

An hour later Sylvia stood and shook Robert Chisum's hand. Chisum walked her to the lobby and then the front door which he opted to open for her. He watched as she hailed a cab. The meeting had gone better than expected. She liked Robert Chisum despite his no-nonsense attitude and his penchant for getting to the heart of the matter. Hope he's not like that in bed else the whole sh-bang including the foreplay would last more two shakes of a dog's tail she chuckled to herself. Recounting the whole meeting she was nonetheless impressed. Knows his stuff she thought to herself. Now she had a plan and direction she though as she read over the page and a half of notes she'd taken. All she had now was implement it.

Still, one thing bothered her and though he didn't elaborate when he saw the signature of the check he seemed visibly shaken telling her that she might consider other avenues for revenues other than a single entity. It unnerved her and she wondered why and who was he considering. Or was he insinuating that there was something wrong her particular financier. Whatever his displeasure he deftly avoided her follow up questions on what was wrong with her receiving monies from one Alex DuMont. The only response he gave was to, 'be careful' thus skirting the issue and moving on to the next line of questioning. Knowing time was of the essence, Sylvia, promptly moved on with her questioning but Chisum's reaction left her perplexed. A bird in the hand is always worth more than two in the bush Sylvia concluded before asking herself who in their right mind would possibly turn down that much money. It'd be like turning down one of God's blessings. Still, the thought worried her.

Sylvia thanked Sam and over the next couple of weeks saw Alex more and more. They were an item much to Sylvia's chagrin. Benny had been right about Alex's celebrity status. It seemed like every posh steakhouse Alex took her to a bevy of reporters crowded around to snap the couples pictures. At first Sylvia was thrilled when Benny called to say she'd seen Sill's picture in the daily tabloid but after awhile the ducking of photographers and other media hounds became burdensome and Alex noticing the strain on Sylvia opted to just have a quiet dinner at home and watch the latest bootleg movie Thomas would pick up on the street.

By this time, Sylvia had grown accustomed to Alex's ways and found that he was both thoughtful and insightful. The two were spending more and more time together. Sylvia enjoyed his company and for the first time in her life she had to admit that she'd met a brother that was both intelligent and wasn't preoccupied with jumping her bones and bedding her down. She on the other hand, had definite plans for him. Yet, whenever the occasion arose something always seemed to come between them whether it was that damn Mr. Rakman or Ashley the chef. It was always something. She'd finally resigned herself to the fact that even if she wanted to seduce him there were just too many…

Tonight was different though. Both Abdul and Ashley were off and Sylvia couldn't remember a time when they'd actually been alone together but here they were cuddled up in his sitting room watching *Brooklyn's Finest* starring Wesley Snipes and Don Cheadle. The movie wasn't anything spectacular and both acknowledged their disappointment.

"With Snipes and Cheadle I thought it would be better," Sylvia commented.

"We're in a recession you know. I guess the brothas are just trying to get paid. Can't really blame them… Sometimes you just have to take what's available."

Alex turned toward her drew her face toward her and kissed her lightly. Immediately feeling the heat rising she withdrew. Seeing the obvious look of disgust and rejection on his face she made herself more comfortable and leaned over returning the kiss. Her nipples immediately grew erect and she only hoped that he hadn't noticed the passion rising in her.

Sylvia leaned forward returning his kiss. The months of being without were immediately recognized and Alex smiled without letting her know that he sensed her frustration and longing. Taking both his hands in hers, he pressed his lips to hers before moving to her ear where he sucked lightly. "You taste so sweet. "She emitted a sigh as he nibbled her neck and began unbuttoning her blouse. Sylvia reached for his member and felt it suddenly grow hard to her touch. Without a word, Alex grabbed her hand and led her down the hall to his bedroom and to his bed. Removing her blouse, Alex pressed his body to hers and kissed her deeply. She could feel his hand slowly moving to find the clasp of her bra. She moved closer to him allowing easier access. Sylvia pulled him closer to her bosom letting him fill his mouth with her breast. His breath was warm and hot as he suckled her breast causing her knees to buckle slightly as she moaned in sheer pleasure. Sylvia closed her eyes thinking she would orgasm at any second. "Lay down on the bed baby and let me love you." he whispered.

Sylvia eased her body down on his king size bed gazing into his eyes waiting for direction afraid to lose the moment and waiting patiently for direction. Alex's tongue trailed from her bosom to her stomach licking around her belly button and unbuttoning her skirt. Sylvia raised her buttocks off the bed allowing him to pull her skirt from around her hips. "You are a beautiful woman Sylvia. I dreamt about this moment since the first day I laid eyes on you." Alex reached between her legs and felt the moisture seeping through her thong indicating her eagerness to have him.

Sylvia moaned at his touch, "Take me Alex. I want to feel your touch and warmth."

She unleashed his hands from between her legs and removed her thong. Sylvia felt

she would lose it at any moment but held on reaching for his pants to unleash his

throbbing penis. "Take me baby. Make love to me." Sylvia straddled her body across

the bed giving Alex a full view her curvaceous figure. Alex entered her sweetness

gently thrusting meeting the rhythm of her strokes. Each was in tune with the other

as they held on to one another until reaching their peak of ecstasy. "I'm cumming

Alex! Oh! Oh!.... Pumping faster he felt her tunnel tighten and jerk in intense

delight. Overcome with excitement, Alex released and fell to her side breathing

heavily and satisfied. "You were beautiful Sylvia". Sylvia kissed his lips and turned

away allowing him to spoon against her warm body. Stroking her hair and holding

her tightly he whispered in her ear, "I love you Sylvia" before falling asleep.

Stunned, Sylvia stared at the wall in front of her. A tear dripping from her eye she

didn't know if it was the joy of waiting so long to be physically pleased, the

happiness of knowing Alex loved her or simply having the strength or was it the

weakness of getting back to trusting again.

As he slept Sylvia showered before slipping on her clothes and finding her way back

to her own apartment.

Early the next morning she awoke to the ringing of her doorbell and wondered who

could possibly be ringing this early. It was a little after eight o'clock. Peeping

through the peephole she recognized Sam the doorman. Opening the front doorway,

Sylvia could only gasp. There were roses all the way down the hall to the elevator

and two deliveryman were still bringing them. There were red roses, yellow roses,

pink and white roses.

"My God Sam!" Sylvia said smiling knowing at once where they were from.

"Who are you telling?" Sam said the sweat pouring from his brow. He had done nothing more than escort the deliveryman up to her floor but the utter volume of the undertaking had him drenched in sweat.

"Sam, where pray tell am I supposed to put all these?"

"I don't know Ms. Stanton but the lobby's full as well and I've got to get them out of there," he said the seriousness obvious in his voice.

Sylvia opened the door even wider letting the two delivery man enter with bouquet after bouquet when one of the deliverymen commented.

"Must be a lot of love here," to which the other responded, after glancing Sylvia, "and I can understand why, too."

Sylvia ran to the bathroom and vomited.

"Was it something I said?" the delivery boy said looking to his friend. "Nah, probably just had a lil' too much to drink last night."

"Or a 'lil too much of something she did and believe me worked somebody to get this much love." Both men laughed.

Sylvia overheard them and had to smile herself before dropping a twenty-dollar bill into Sam's hands and asking him to handle the flower problem. She had to call Alex to thank him for the beautiful night and the flowers but before any of that she needed to find a doctor. The persistent throwing up was now beginning to scare her. She had not only changed her diet and her strenuous exercising regiment she had even gone so far as to stop smoking something she thought she would never be able to do but she continued to throw up every morning. She considered the thought that perhaps she was pregnant but it was hard to get pregnant when one wasn't indulging in sex. And she hadn't had sex for four or five months. The last person she'd had the occasion to sleep with was Terrance almost four months ago when she was in Atlanta. But there was no way she could be pregnant. Her insides had been so battered and torn up following the rape that doctors told her there was little or no chance of her becoming pregnant so that was out. All that remained was the thought of cancer. Both mom and dad had had bouts with it. Her mother had had a mastectomy and it was colon cancer that had only recently taken her fathers' life. Sylvia believed in her heart and soul that she was destined to contract it but had a hard time believing that it attacked one so young as she. Still, it was a well-known fact that if it were diagnosed early enough it could be treated. And she could live a healthy, productive life.

When Sylvia was done arranging the flowers in her apartment she made it a point to call Benny. If anyone could help her locate a reputable gynecologist or a general practitioner it would be Benny.

"Hey girl, it's me Sill."

"Hey Sill, how are you?" She asked expectantly. "I was waiting to hear from you last night when you got in. Wanted to hear all the intimate details but I guess I fell asleep before you called."

"I don't know what intimate details you're expecting to hear," Sill replied. "Ain't nothing but two friends getting together over a glass of wine, some popcorn and a movie. Saw that new joint with Wesley Snipes and Don Cheadle."

"No you didn't! I've been dying to see that. But I've been too lazy to go. And I hate going to the movies by myself. So, he took you to see that? That's nice. Then what did you do?"

"Actually we stayed home and watched it."

"You couldn't have. The movie just came out last week, so it can't be out on DVD yet. How the hell did you get a copy?"

"I didn't. Alex did. I'm pretty sure it was bootleg. Probably picked it up off the street. I really don't know. All I know is that I watched it."

"Uh huh. Well, I guess that's to be expected. You don't get to be where he is by doing things straight and by the book," Benny remarked.

"And what's that supposed to mean?"

"Nothing Sill. I was just saying…"

"No I want you to tell me what you know."

"Don't get your panties all in an uproar Sill. I was just talking."

"No I was just saying that regular folks like you and I who play strictly by the books never get anywhere but some people take risks and well… if they don't get caught while they're dabbling in illegal activities come out with millions and smelling like roses. That's all."

"You sure that's all?"

"That's all. Believe me Sill, I don't know a bit more about Alex DuMont than what you've told me and what I've read in the newspaper. That's it. Why you asking anyway?"

"I'm just curious is all. I was at this lawyer's office yesterday and he made me think. I showed him the check Alex had given me and he gave me a strange look and asked me if I had thought about seeking other means of funding. Here I am with a signed check in my hand that's going to cover the expensive of the building and every other thing I'll need to get my program up and running and he asks me if I've considered other sources of funding. It just didn't sit right with me that's all. And even though he answered any and all questions I asked him about the program when

I asked why I should seek alternative methods of funding when I already had the money in hand he avoided me like the plague and never did answer my question."

"Should tell you something… Don'tcha think?"

"So what are you saying, Benny? If you know something then tell me."

"Well, being that you're just friends I don't think you'll have anything to really worry about. I mean it's not like you're in love and his future or his dealings affect you in any way. You know what I'm saying? I'm sure you care about his overall welfare but live or die it really doesn't have any affect on you."

"Okay Benny save the games. I think I'm falling in love with Alex and I'm really interested in knowing the low down. I've been in one bad relationship after another. That's the main reason I'm in New York so if you consider me a friend then please tell me what you know.."

"Oh, so Mr. DuMont *does* have your attention despite all the denials?"

"I guess he does. We made love last night for the very first time and oh, Benny it was beautiful. The brother had me speaking in tongues. I cursed my momma and daddy for not telling me how good it could be. We started off with a little small talk watching a movie but he made some big talk when he got in bed girl. Benny, this man had me screaming, calling his name. The boy made a friend for life. He had me crying , toes curlin', and my head whirlin'. I'm telling you I went there with straight hair and came home with Shirley Temple curls. Girl, he was all that."

"I hear you Sill. I'm truly happy for you."

"Thanks. But as good as he was, I still don't want nobody caught up in no sheisty ass business dealings. So if you know anything tell me now."

"Sill, I'm serious, if there was something to tell you I would. I really don't know anything other than what I read in the papers. I know he's been brought up on charges or allegations of insider trading. That's all they were, were allegations and as far as I know nothing's ever come of it or you wouldn't have gotten the chance to meet him. Isn't that right? I've seen him here at the park during the Rucker Tournament hanging out with the high rollas and the playas but you know how that is. I don't think he's involved in that circle."

"Sorry, for asking. I'm just a little leery of men ya know. Been through hell at their expense."

"I hear you… And I don't blame you a bit. You can't be too careful nowadays."

"Anyway, the reason I called you is because I was kinda hoping you could refer me to a good gynecologist."

"You okay?"

Careful not to say too much, Sylvia downplayed it.

"Yeah, it's just time for my annual check-up and I haven't had a chance to look for a gynecologist and wouldn't know where to look if you paid me."

The information had, Sylvia hung up the phone and wondered if Benny had been straight with her. There was something wrong, a feeling she had that she wasn't exactly sure of but a feeling just the same. She wasn't sure what was wrong but she had bad vibes. Maybe too many bad experiences in the past were clouding her judgment.

Chapter 6

Sylvia and Alex spent virtually every waking moment together looking for a place for Sylvia to open her leaning center. It was difficult to tell who was happier she or Alex. When they had agreed on a place Sylvia spent her days working on it and only stopped when Alex came to pick her up in the evening. She couldn't have been more ecstatic. And although she didn't like all the attention he garnered by his mere presence there, Sylvia was still in awe of all the people he knew and could call on when there was something that needed to be done. He had a special way of handling people and had the electricians, and the contractors all eating out of his hand by the time he was finished with them.

What was even more surprising was the fact that he knew all the homeboys on the block that surrounded the property. She knew that a lot of them were up to no good but for some reason the bad language and all other illegal dealings would come to an end when she was in the vicinity. She wasn't exactly sure why but she knew Alex's influence had something to do with it. Alex DuMont not only wielded power downtown but also had something to do with the happenings uptown although she couldn't exactly figure out why or how.

Then one late July evening she noticed something she'd never noticed before. It was the first time she'd ever seen Alex shook and although she didn't know the particulars she could tell something had disturbed him greatly. Standing outside of the property she glanced through the window admiring her work and had to admit that it was coming along nicely and she was sure that even though the contractors had given her an August 15th date for all work to be completed that they were far ahead of schedule. As Sylvia glanced in the window she noticed the black limo across the street on the far corner. A dozen or so people crowded around and she could the cursing and yelling from where she stood and immediately recognized Thomas the chauffeur standing apart from the crowd. Straining to see better she could fairly make out Alex standing in the center. There were several people standing, yelling and pointing fingers. Confused and fearing for her man she started over to see what all the commotion was about when Thomas caught her eye and headed in her direction.

"Thomas! Thomas! What's wrong? Is everything alright?"

"It's no problem Ms. Stanton. I wouldn't have left Alex alone in this neighborhood if there were a problem. Just a neighborhood problem with the neighborhood watch group. You know Alex's on the board for Safety In Our Community and there's been a rash of break ins and purse snatching as of late so the community watch and a couple of neighborhood groups gathered out here to speak to Alex and to address their concerns. But believe me he's not in harms way by any means. I don't know if you know it or not but Alex grew up on these streets and is as loved if not more than any politician in office today. I told him to run for office but he says he's already overwhelmed with trying to run the brokerage house and his real estate business to take on any new ventures."

"Well, I'm certainly glad to know it's nothing serious. I was beginning to worry when I heard all that screaming and cursing."

Thomas laughed heartily.

"You know how our people are. We have a tendency to be loud and obnoxious at times."

Sylvia smiled not at all comforted by the older man's words despite his attempts at trying to soothe her.

"Anyway, he told me to inform you to give him a couple of minutes and he'll be ready to go."

"That's fine Thomas. I'm just going to go back inside and tie up a few loose ends 'til he's ready. Ask him to call me on my cell when he's ready," Sylvia said a little more at ease now.

"I'll do that Ms. Stanton," Thomas said sure that he'd carried out his boss' wishes with utmost care and tact.

Sylvia waited at her desk in the inner office thoughts rushing through her head. She wanted to rush over there and see what was really going on but he'd ask her to stay put and so she'd chosen by her man's wishes and trust his better judgment when she heard a cadence of loud pops.

Running almost falling she reached the front door to see the long black limousine come screeching to a halt. Only this time did not get out walk around and open the door. The door swung open and Thomas screamed, "Get in Ms. Stanton! Hurry!" No sooner had Sylvia gotten in than she noticed the blood.

"Oh, my God Alex. You've been shot. Hurry Thomas. Get Mr. DuMont to the hospital. What's the closest hospital?"

"Harlem Hospital's the closest but Mr. DuMont refuses to go there. Says he would rather go to St. Luke's right up the hill by Columbia."

"I'm okay baby," Alex moaned. "It's just a flesh wound. Nothing serious…" he said trying his best to elicit a smile through the pain. "Just an irate resident angry that the neighborhood isn't being cleaned up as quickly as City Hall promised is all. Nothing to be alarmed at. I can't blame them. I grew up a block or so from there and it's always been rough there. Some people are just fed up is all. Nothing personal…"

"Nothing personal? They tried to kill you."

His weak attempt at a smile did nothing little to soothe Sylvia's anxiety or his own pain.

"Does it hurt much, baby?" Sylvia asked more than a little concerned. "Thomas how much further is the damn hospital?"

"Only a couple of blocks, MS. Stanton. Only a couple of more blocks. You hang in there Mr. DuMont. You hear…"

"I'm alright Thomas. It's just a flesh wound. Burns like hell but it's nothing serious."

By the time they arrived at St. Luke's Alex DuMont was drenched in sweat and seemed to be in and out of consciousness. Sylvia rushed into the hospital and within moments two orderlies appeared with a gurney, place the injured man on it and raced him inside.

Sylvia paced the halls with Thomas but as the doctor said, 'it was a waiting game now'.

"What happened Thomas?"

Thomas seemed a bit distant and at a loss for words, the concern showing on his face.

"To be honest, I'm not exactly sure Ms. Stanton. It all happened so quickly I don't have a handle on it myself. The crowd was jockeying for position screaming and yelling at Mr. DuMont. Most were just airing their grievances. It all seemed harmless enough when these two young thugs walked up and pushed through the crowd. One of them had a gun and started shooting. He fired a couple of shots and then took off running. I real don't think it had anything to do with the rally. It's the most bizarre thing I've ever seen. I don't even think they knew Mr. DuMont. It was like more of a gang initiation or something. But to be honest I still don't know what happened. I can't figure it out. I just hope Mr. DuMont's alright." Glancing down with sorrow and pity in his eyes, he spoke again this time in almost a whisper.

"I would have never stopped to let him speak if I had known something like this was going to happen."

"Don't blame yourself Thomas," Sylvia said placing a soothing arm around the older man's shoulder. "It's going to be alright," she heard herself say if not in attempt to pacify him but also herself.

Moments later Abdul Rakman appeared but hardly looked like the butler Sylvia had come to know and dislike so much. Instead of his usual navy blue butler's uniform he now donned a black and gray camouflage outfit with a black beret. She wondered how he'd gotten word of Alex's misfortune but then nothing surprised her anymore when it came to Alex's wheelings and dealings. Speaking briefly to Thomas in a tone not much above a whisper an inaudible to Sylvia who was now seated not more than five feet from her Rakman turned and left just as quickly as he'd come.

"What was that all about?" she heard herself ask Thomas.

"Not much, I'm afraid. Rakman is a man of few words. He simply wanted to know how Mr. DuMont was and where the shooting took place.

'That man scares me."

"I think that's his job," Thomas snickered. "Rakman scares a lot of people. But he's one of the few people Mr. DuMont knows and trusts. I think they were childhood friends. And I do know this. If Rakman had been there tonight I doubt this would have happened."

The doctor was before them now with a cordial smile adorning his face.

"Good news people, Mr. DuMont is going to be fine. It's just a flesh wound. The bullet ripped a small hole on the right side of his chest. I'll tell you though, a few more inches to the left and it would have been over. He's a lucky man," the doctor said staring a Sylvia and smiling broadly. "Are you his wife?"

"No, just a close friend," Sylvia answered ignoring the doctor's flirtatious nature.

"Will he be here for some time."

"No, actually the nurse is just finishing up his paperwork and he should be discharged shortly. I'm prescribing a couple of antibiotics to prevent infection from setting in and some Darvocet for the pain. See that he takes these regularly and he should be fine. Now if you go down to the far hallway you can meet Mr. DuMont. We're opening the back doors at his wishes to avoid the reporters. You may want to pull the car around back," the doctor said nodding at Thomas.

'It was two a.m. when Sylvia decided to leave Alex. He'd been asleep since nine. The Darvocet alleviating most of the pain and allowing him to sleep peacefully still Sylvia remained just in case he needed something.

The following day Sylvia let go all of her regular affairs to look after Alex, making sure he took his medicines at the prescribed times and was mesmerized by both his demeanor and his attitude the day after he'd been shot. Still, she figured it was all a cover up to put her mind at ease. After all, who could bounce back after something traumatic as being shot for no apparent reason. But this man she loved was no average man and that was one of the reasons she was so attracted to him. She had so many questions she wanted to ask him about the shooting, the motive, and so forth but could never really garner the courage or felt it was the right time to do so. And then almost as if déjà vu she heard the lawyer, what was his name—oh yeah—

Chisum asking her if she couldn't find someone else to provide her with start up money for her program when she was sitting there with Alex's check in plain view. Dismissing the thought, she knew she was searching for reasons for withdrawing, for running away again. Her mother had long ago told her that she had a fear of success. And perhaps that was true but she'd attributed it more to her always having had a suspicious mind. Trust had always been hard to come by and following the rape it was next to impossible no matter how many therapeutic counseling sessions she attended or how hard she tried to convince herself. Now this. In all her life she'd never known anyone personally to have gotten shot but then again how many millionaires had she known for that matter. There were so many questions she needed the answers to and before she got in any deeper she had to know.

Bringing Alex his midday medications she sat opposite the bed while Ashley brought him his lunch. It consisted of asparagus spears, a baked potato and baked chicken. Looking absolutely scrumptious Sylvia decided to join him for lunch much to Alex's delight.

"Alex can I ask you something personal?"

"Anything, Sill. Anything at all," he replied placing a large doolop of sour cream on his potato.

"Alex, it seems awfully strange and a little unnerving to me that the man I choose to fall in love with is shot on a Tuesday and acting as if it never occurred on Wednesday the day after. You make it almost seem like it's a work related accident that you were expecting to occur and now that it has you can go ahead with your career and it will never happen again. When in reality, someone wanted you dead and just sent the wrong person to complete the job," she said reluctantly.

"Interesting observation," Alex said smiling before pushing the tray away from him. He had picked over his breakfast too and Sill was worried that perhaps she was the cause of his losing his appetite now. "The simple truth is that I fight the same battles everyday in the boardrooms. Only difference is the weapon of choice. Both are deadly and over the years I've become resilient. I've had too."

"Yes, baby. I hear you but in the board room they're not trying to killing you."

Alex laughed so heartily he grabbed his side in pain. "Now I see how little you know about playin' hardball with the big boys. They'll cut your throat in a heartbeat. You've always got to be on your guard."

"I know that but it's not like someone taking a shot at you in the street," Sill responded.

"I grew up two blocks from there Sill. It's not nice. It never has been but I feel safer and more secure there than I downtown with those sharks. Every now and then things pop off and I'll admit that's never good but its all a part of life in Harlem. It's not what one would wish for anyone but it is what it is. I'm doing my best to make it a better place for little Black boys and girls but it takes time. Harlem has been like that for a long time. Since the Harlem Renaissance it's been on a downward spiral. But we're gonna bring it back. That's why I found a place for you there."

"You make me feel a little suspicious, a little reluctant," Sylvia replied.

"Don't be. Ninety-nine percent of the people there are good hard-working people. There's always that one per cent that make it bad for the lot but we have to keep our eyes on the prize and focus on the good people."

"You're right."

"So, you see I can't think about the shooting. There's too much to do tomorrow to worry about yesterday. Ya feel me Sill?"

"I understand what you're saying Alex but isn't there even the least bit of interest in knowing who did this and what their motive was? Don't you feel the least bit vengeful? It happened to you, the man I love and I wanted blood but you on the other hand haven't even mentioned it," Sylvia said still not quite getting it.

"Have you ever heard the old saying 'vengeance is mine said the Lord' or the Law of Karma which says 'what goes around comes around'? Well, I believe in both of those but neither one of those merits my time or my consideration. I can't concentrate on negativity. Again, I just don't have the time."

"That's something Alex. You know everyday you grow a little larger in my eyes," Sill said beaming with confidence. She pulled him to her ever so gently and hugged him tightly.

"I love you so much Alex" In a matter of minutes, Alex DuMont had once again restored her confidence and made her feel good about loving him.

Rakman was always but always interrupting something. This time she was intent on loving him down but here he was again. Only this time, he walked in without so much as giving her a nod or acknowledging her presence walked across the room and bent over and whispered in Alex's ear.

"It's done," he said whispering but loud enough for Sill to hear. She had to wonder what all the secrets were about when it came to Rakman but figuring she'd asked enough questions for one day and refrained.

Alex appeared fairly busy the next two days. And Sylvia although hesitant at first headed back uptown to continue to work on her building and her program. Sitting in her office supervising the construction workers she picked up the Daily News and began to flip through the pages. She liked the paper although she'd become tired of seeing her face donning the gossip pages every time she stepped out. Flipping through the pages she caught sight of two African American males ages eighteen and nineteen that had been brutally murdered on the next corner. The paper reported they'd both been murdered gangland style. Both had been shot in the back of the head by a small caliber gun possibly a .22 by a single gunman. There were few leads but witnesses said they saw a thirty to thirty-five year old gentleman wearing camouflage utilities and ski mask fleeing the scene of the crime. It just so happened that the murders had been on the exact same corner where Alex had been shot. Sylvia put on her reading glasses and glanced closer at the paper. Recognizing the younger of the two victims as a hard young thug who was always out there. And then it dawned on her that the description of the assailant fit Rakman's description to a tee. And hadn't he been wearing black and gray camouflage utilities on the day Alex was shot when he made his brief visit to the hospital. Sylvia stopped momentarily. The murder had happened on the same corner that Alex had been shot. And witnesses, including Thomas had reported seeing two young assailants fleeing that shooting as well although only one had been the triggerman. Oh my God! No! Could Alex have been behind the murder of these two young men? Wasn't he after all the one who had talked about The Law of Karma? Saying that what goes around comes around. Oh my God, Sylvia thought to herself. The pieces fit together all too well. She hated to think that her man, the man she'd chosen, the man she'd finally given in to this time, the man she felt so sure of could be a killer. Benny had told her that there were few if any who played in that high stakes game could go unscathed. But murder?

Still, wasn't it Alex himself who had downplayed his own shooting and handled it with utter cool who made the remark that it was nothing in comparison with swimming with the sharks downtown. He'd known all the time how'd he'd enact revenge when the time came. And he'd certainly made short work of it.

She knew and she knew she was in danger. But how would she play it? She could always play it off and go along with their daily ritual. Did she have a choice? It was dinner at seven and maybe a movie afterwards before she'd retire to leaf through the mountains of mail and materials she received each day as she gathered the newest, innovative ways of teaching those who needed remedial help in the worst way. Yes, she'd use that as a way out and cut dinner short. She had a doctor's appointment in the morning. But that was downtown and being that it was her initial visit; she nor he knew where it was so she knew she'd be safe there. But then what? She could always go home to North Carolina. He'd once asked where she was but the only information she'd given was that she was from a small town in North Carolina with one stop light on Main Street. She'd likened it to Andy Griffith's Mayberry but then how many towns in North Carolina fit that description. He'd never be able to locate her there. But then there was the matter of The Literacy Library and how many months had she devoted to making it a reality. She couldn't just let it fall by the wayside. She'd by her own account spent too much time and energy. And maybe, just maybe those two boys wouldn't have met with such a tragic end if it had been there years before. How many kids could she prevent from following the tragic end those two had met if she were just allowed to get her program up and running.

And then there was the building; she invested all of the check he'd given to her as well twenty thousand of her own money. She couldn't just let it all go to waste but how could she continue her tryst with a killer, a murderer. Could she stay and play along or were the police an alternative. She thought about the police but men like Alex DuMont controlled the police. And besides with his pull and lawyers he'd

69

certainly wriggle free with some legal loophole. Then where would she be but stretched out in some Jersey Swamp? The alternatives seemed few and doomed and Sylvia who only a week ago seemed so energized and so ready to begin a new life faced the unenviable position of being hopeless once more.

Dinner was nice but Sill was distant and once or twice Alex noticed and asked Sill what was wrong. She was tempted to ask him about his involvement in the two killings up on 116th St. but thought better of it. Her need to keep everything hush-hush despite the constant coverage in the daily tabloids now turned out to be harmful whereas in the beginning it had been a ploy to keep everything on the down low and quiet. In the beginning she hadn't wanted anybody to know her business including Benny, her one and only friend in the Apple but here she was stuck in this killers apartment. Should she say anything or just slip up and say the wrong thing she might end up just another statistic in the city's homicide directory, which had only recently increased by two. And then it dawned on Sylvia that the lawyer that Sam had introduced hadn't seemed particularly fond of Alex and had questioned her receiving money from him. Perhaps she could confide in him. But first she'd talk to Benny. Excusing herself from dinner she passing Rakman, nodded, and headed for the elevator telling him there was no need for him to escort her this evening. As soon as the words left her lips she was sorry she'd said anything. She was trying to keep everything as normal as possible. He escorted her every night. Telling him might arouse suspicion. But it was too late now. Once in the apartment Sylvia took a long, hot shower changed into her nightie, laid down and staring at the ceiling and ran the events of the past few days over in her mind.

She could be wrong. It could be all a matter of coincidence. After all, how many brothas in New York had she seen wearing camouflages and hadn't Alex told her

70

that vengeance was the Lord's? If she loved him as she did then why was it so hard to trust. Too many bad relationships she guessed… Still, how good he'd been to her, advancing her the start up money for her project and how many times had he expressed his interest in Harlem's youth. No, she simply had a problem with Rakman and even if Rakman was responsible he had certainly done so without his bosses consent. Thomas said he had an uncommon dying sense of loyalty and he had looked crazy when he came to the hospital but then Rakman always looked like he hadn't his medicine. Yeah, he'd probably gone out and exacted revenge without Alex's knowledge.

Sylvia felt better about things now and decided that she'd let Alex know in time. Turning over on her side Sylvia closed her eyes, her mind now at peace and rested easily.

She was running late again. Her doctor's appointment was at nine a.m. and although she'd gotten up in ample times she was still running late. It was already eight thirty and she hadn't even left the house yet. She had asked Benny to meet her and make a day of it. They'd do lunch and a little light shopping and then come back and crash at her place, maybe even take her up to meet Alex. The real reason that she'd asked Benny to accompany her was that she was scared. Nothing the doctor could say could be good. She'd been throwin' up for close to three months and had hoped it would end on its own but it hadn't and though the doctor was a final alternative she prayed that she hadn't waited too long. Approaching the front door, there stood Thomas waiting. The two spoke.

"We're you rushing off to on this fine morning Ms. Stanton?"

"Have a doctor's appointment Thomas."

The two had grown rather close over the last several months and Sylvia genuinely liked the elderly driver and it was obvious Thomas liked her as well bringing her fruits and vegetables from his wife's garden now and on occasion.

"Everything okay?" he asked the concern showing on his face.

"I certainly hope so." Sylvia replied.

"Where's your appointment?"

"Oh, it's not far. I believe it's on 110th and Lexington Avenue."

"C'mon, I don't think Mr. DuMont will mind. I'm not due to pick him up 'til ten. I just stopped to see what new lies my buddy Sam had in store for me today," Thomas said holding the door open for Sylvia.

"Why thank you Thomas. You're a lifesaver. I was running late as usual and am supposed to meet my girlfriend up there."

"The young lady you introduced me to a couple of weeks ago?"

"The very same."

"Oh yeah Bernie isn't it?"

"Bennie…" Sylvia corrected.

Yeah yeah Bennie. Attractive girl. If I was twenty years younger she'd be in trouble," Thomas said smiling glancing in the rearview mirror as he weaved in and out of rush hour traffic. They were there in a matter of minutes.

"You have my number. Call me if you need a ride home, ya hear."

"Thanks a lot Thomas but it's girls day out and I don't think you'll want to hang a pair of old gossipy women all day," Sylvia said smiling as she exited the limo. Bennie was already there. The two women hugged each other and Sylvia filled out the standard forms before being led through the huge doors that separated the waiting room from the the examining rooms. A half hour later Sylvia exited the

72

same two doors she'd entered. Only now she appeared puzzled, bewildered even. Seeing Sylvia in this state was unnerving and Bennie rose from her chair and rushed towards her girlfriend.

"You okay, Sill?"

When Sylvia did not respond Bennie grabbed Sylvia's arm and led her to a seat to gather her senses. Sylvia appeared disoriented, her eyes distant and glassy.

"Are you okay baby," Bennie asked again concern and panic setting in in earnest now. When Sylvia refused to answer again and it appeared that something really was amiss Bennie rushed to the desk and demanded to see the doctor who appeared minutes later. The doctor a rather stout and jovial manner entered the waiting room and headed towards Sylvia but Bennie intercepted him.

Doctor I don't know what's wrong with her. I've never seen her like this before. She seems to be almost incoherent. I ask her a question and there's no sign of anything. Almost like she's in shock."

"She may be," the doctor said smiling.

"And you let her out? What kind of doctor are you?"

Not at all disturbed by the woman's attack the doctor continued grinning.

"There are different types of shock, ma'm. What Ms. Stanton is suffering is just a mild form. She was given some rather disturbing news. Good news but nonetheless disturbing to her."

"Is she very sick?"

"I believe she'd probably like to tell you herself. Just give her a few minutes. She'll come around. You have a good day ma'm."

"You too doc."

Bennie was besides herself but after several minutes of prodding that ended with her slapping cold water on her face and making faces like she was a kindergartener out for recess. Still, there was nothing. Sylvia sat there just as she'd done some fifteen years earlier following her rape. All that she was was on the inside and there was no outsider who could pierce this deeply sensitive woman. But the doctor had commented on her news being good so what was the dilemma that had her sitting there looking like she was autistic?

After several minutes, Bennie took the doctor's advice and sat back with the latest issue of Ebony. Sade was on the cover and being one of Bennie's favorite artists who hardly ever interviewed it made for interesting reading. Midway through the article she felt Sill tap her arm.

"Girl, I thought you were dead. I'm sittin' here talkin' to you and you're lookin' like you used to when you were in Mr. Dean's physics class. You alright?"

Still, there was no reply from Sill.

"C'mon let's go," Bennie said grabbing Sylvia's purse.

Sylvia followed still somewhat in a daze.

"Cab or subway? Oh never mind we'll be here 'til they put the tree up in Rockefeller Center waiting on an answer from you at this rate and here it is mid July. I don't know what that doctor gave you but I sure as hell want some," Bennie laughed.

Bennie summoned one of New York's many cabs, held the door open for Sill before sliding in herself. Sak's Fifth Avenue she told the driver.

"I'm pregnant."

"What?!?" Bennie yelled.

"I'm pregnant," Sylvia, repeated almost as if she didn't believe it herself.

74

"Oh, my God! You're not serious! Oh my God! That's beautiful Sill!

Sylvia still dazed and a bit confused begged Benny's forgiveness choosing to cancel their luncheon and shopping spree opting to go home instead. No wonder she had been feeling so fatigued. Her head and heart were in limbo. On the one hand, she welcomed the blessing the Almighty had bestowed on her. Doctors had told her that she chances of her ever becoming pregnant were at the very least remote and now this. Her pregnancy was truly a miracle. She knew that she'd been truly blessed. Still, there was the much deeper underlying question of whom the baby belonged to. And that's what gnawed at her very soul. She couldn't recall when she'd had her last period. It bothered her and she thought of the choices she'd made. Chances were more than likely that Terrance had fathered her child but truth be told it could very well be Alex's. Terrance had been bad news and Alex worse. Despite all her attempts to rationalize the events of the past week something still bothered and much as she hated to think about it deep in the recesses of her mind she truly believed that Alex's shooting was in some way connected with those boy's deaths. There was no way of proving it but there were far too many coincidences.

No way would she ever consider bringing a baby into such a quagmire of such unfathomable happenings. No, a new life should be exactly that—a new life—not mired in the remnants of a life gone astray or covered in other people's blood. Her baby would be born in innocence, a fresh slate of his own and begin his journey as she had. Her parents had afforded her everything a child could want and so she would with her baby. Sylvia lay in her bed eyes fixated on the ceiling and daydreamed, her emotions mixed. But one thing was for sure she would never let her child grow up knowing either of those two men. Because she had made bad choices didn't mean her child would be subject to her mistakes. And it was here that she decided that she would have to escape all his wealth and all the tragedy and mystery that came along with it. There would be no sideways glances or whispering in dark corners. There would be no innuendos or rumors directed towards her child. But how, by the grace of God could she just up and leave with his knowing. And Lord knows if he ever found out there would surely be hell to pay. There was no telling what a man with his power and influence could do to make her life miserable but her child would never be exposed to his wrath of this she was sure. And then it came to her that if she tried to leave with his child there was no telling what he might do. After all, hadn't he been responsible for the deaths of two teens on a whim.

Sylvia was at once afraid as she'd never been in her life and it was at that very moment that her thoughts cleared and she knew exactly what she had to do.

Chapter 7

Benny was in total disagreement.

"Sylvia., I'm feelin' your pain girl. I understand. Believe me I do but don't you think you're being a bit hasty. I mean you've laid the groundwork for a beautiful existence here in only a few short months and now you're just going to throw it all away. And why? Because your suspicions tell you that this man has committed murder. C'mon Sill let's be reasonable and think this through."

"I have thought it through Benny. And I wouldn't bring a child into this world with a cloud of his father being incarcerated or worse yet a murderer."

"But those are only accusations, Sill."

"True, but I have enough suspicion and evidence to make them a formal accusation if I chose to do so. I'm not trying to do that. And forget those boys that were killed. I don't want any part of it. I just want out. I'm not trying to 'cause anyone any pain or hardship. I'm not trying to tear down empires. I'm not trying to do anything but get out before I get in any deeper. Is that a crime?"

"But baby don't you think you're jumping the gun just a bit. I mean I'm sure your baby won't suffer or want for anything but look what he could have with Alex as his father. And Lord knows you wouldn't want for anything ever."

"My baby will have love and what more can you give a child, Benny?"

"I hear you but a million here and there doesn't hurt either," Benny said elbowing Sill gently and grinning broadly.

"Sho' you right," Sylvia agreed a slight grin forming. "But I don't need all the added extras, all the benefits for simply being pillow pals."

"Oh, Sill don't downplay your relationship with Alex. Let's fess up and be honest. We're friends aren't we and have been since damn near high school. Am I lying?"

"No, that's true."

"And if there's anyone that knows you it's me. I was there when you finally laid Barney down for the last time and told Lucretia Thompson that you didn't have time for Barney or her anymore because you had a new best friend and her name was Benny Monroe. Do you remember that? I think we were six or seven at the time. Do you remember that?"

Sill smiled as she remembered back.

"Am I lying?" Benny asked again.

"No, you're not lying."

"And who knows you better than I do?"

"So then why do you think you can lie to me now, Sill?"

"I'm not lying to you Benny."

Well at first you claimed there was nothing going on between you and Alex. You wouldn't even divulge his name when I asked. And here I am supposed to be your best friend. But you spent your ever-waking hour in that man's presence. Who are you trying to fool? Then you suspect him of some hideous crime and decide to just up and leave everything that you worked so hard to build. I just don't understand. The only thing I can gather is that you're letting all your past experiences cloud your vision. All the Chad's and Terrance's are all coming into play because you allow them to. I really believe you mom was right when she told you had a fear of success. You're bright with drop-dead looks that most women including me wish they had and you fall in love with someone equally as bright and when he shows some interest what does your ass do? You turn tail and high tail it out of town. What kind of shit is that?"

"Benny, have you heard one word I said? Two teenaged boys were killed at this man's instruction!"

"And how do you know that?"

"I'd have to be a fool not to be able to put the pieces together. I don't need a truck to hit me, Benny."

"You're crazier than a rabid dog Sill. I'm convinced. Listen, if you're so certain of this then why don't you do what any logical person would do?"

"And what that be?"

"To sit down with the man and ask me if what you believe is true. If he loves you I doubt that true or not he wouldn't let you come to any harm. After all, his love for you automatically puts you in his inner circle. C'mon Sill know matter what you know or think you know he's gonna continue to love you and even if he falls out of love he's going to continue to love and provide for his son. From what I know Alex's a decent "No, Benny. Besides it'll be nice to get away for awhile. It'll give me a chance to think and put things in perspective. It's not everyday that I get pregnant or meet a welthy businessman and fall in love. It's just a lot even for me the master of catastrophe," Sill laughed. "Don't worry. I'll be back. I just need to get my life in order and figure out what my next step is. You have the keys to my apartment and the building uptown so I know everything will be taken care of and I'll be back before you know it," Sill said reassuringly.

"The last time you said that I didn't see you for what was it…twelve years?" Benny said pessimistically.

"A month at best Benny. Remember I've got a program to get started," Sill said exiting the cab and then turning to Benny and giving her a hug that let Benny know that it would certainly be some time before the two friends would meet again.

Benny watched as her best friend exit the cab and make her way into the main lobby at LaGuardia Airport. She hadn't told her destination to Benny or anyone else for that matter where her final destination was just in case of reprisals. And she most definitely hadn't informed Alex. He was away on a three day business trip and Sylvia figured she'd put some time in between his leaving and hers hoping that the time apart would afford her a clean getaway. She was sure he'd come looking for her but in three days she'd really have a chance to get ghost and after the news of her pregnancy she really didn't want him to see her. No, wonder she was gaining weight she was three to four months pregnant and really beginning to show. That's all she needed now was for him to see her in that condition and swear it was his. If she was open and honest about the whole situation what was he liable to think? Especially when he found out she had been intimate just months before with Terrance or any man for that matter. The minute she told him she knew it could not only be the end of her, their relationship and after what she'd just witnessed perhaps her child too. No, the best thing to do was to get out of town leaving no forwarding address, find a safe haven, and just give everything a chance to blow over. She had never told him where she was from although he'd inquired on more than one occasion. And she prayed that despite his money, power and connections he wouldn't be able to locate her now.

No sooner than Sylvia checked her bags she heard the boarding call for Raleigh, North Carolina and turned she had been followed. She hadn't talked to Alex today and their daily phone calls had become almost ritual. She was pretty sure hat he'd sent Rakman to her apartment earlier that day but she refused to open the door after peeping through the peephole and saw him standing there. She'd become deathly afraid of him since the shooting and made sure that Alex was present whenever

Rakman was present. But today she was so intent on packing and getting out of there that she hadn't given him a second thought. Assured that she hadn't been followed Sylvia made her way to the gate and was soon boarding Flight 106. A gentle peace came over her and Sylvia woke to the subtle sounds of the captain's voice as he announced their arrival. Since she hadn't told anyone other than Benny of her plans she was forced to rent a car and find her way to her tiny hometown of Elizabethtown. She hadn't really spoken to her mother more than a couple of times since her father's death and when she found her mother in fairly good spirits after her father's death and so she hadn't called since. She would be overjoyed to see her only daughter and her spending time and with her news she knew her mother would simply be overjoyed to see her only daughter. Smiling as she eased into the Charger and pulling onto I-95 she smiled at the thought of seeing her mother again. There was nothing like the quiet serenity of going home again. No matter what had transpired her mother would be there with open arms compassionate and loving. And hour or so later as she eased into the driveway she was greeted with exactly what she expected. Her mother always glad to see her only child embraced her only daughter long and hard and with such force that Sylvia could hardly breathe. Her mother was not the only one happy to have her daughter home. Sylvia was ecstatic to be back as well and let her mother know. It was home and in the ensuing days as Sylvia sat on the front porch waving at the occasional car that passed by she no longer wondered what her haste was to leave Elizathbethtown. And for once she understood her parents love for the small town with no other claim to fame than Main Street which ran through it and led to here or there or anywhere. Once upon a time, here or there or anywhere was all she'd yearned for but after being savagely raped, one failed marriage, countless failed relationships and now with a baby on the

81

way without a father she could rightfully confirm here, there or anywhere seemed like nowhere and she was quite content to leave all those transgressions and afflictions right where they were and was just as content as she could recall in recent memory to wave at the passing parade of cars.

Every blue moon while sitting there watching the passing vehicles and her mother crochet this and that for the baby she'd let her mind drift, her thoughts would inevitably drift to Alex and she wondered if she truly loved him and if she was doing the right thing. She'd let the contract on her phone expire and was completely without contact with anyone just as she'd done when she'd left Atlanta. And had only called Benny once to make sure the rent on her apartment and building were paid. When Benny assured her that all was well she'd ceased to call Benny. Instead she called the landlord to make sure everything was in order. When he assured her that all was well she had stopped calling altogether and was content to just sit back and wait. The two women enjoyed each other's company as they always had and where Sylvia entertained her mother with stories of the big city her mother kept her up the on all latest happenings in Elizathbethtown. Within a month she was well abreast of all her classmates, how many children each had, and who had married, died, who was having an affair and who'd divorced who. Sylvia found it quite entertaining and wondered if there wasn't more happening in this little one horse town with it's Main Street than in all of Atlanta and New York combined. It was funny too that her mother who seldom left the house could acquire all the latest gossip without ever seeming to go anywhere. Sylvia chuckled at the very thought. Several months passed and Sylvia was never more satisfied or happier. The idea that perhaps she'd wrongfully blamed Alex who'd she'd somehow convinced herself had no parts in the killing of those boys had now dissipated. Thoroughly convinced that

82

he no longer was a threat to her or her child's safety all thoughts had become no more than a distant memory. All drama gone from her thoughts, her memories, she had one thing on her mind these days and that was nurturing the miracle growing within.

The first few months she'd hardly shown but with the passing months combined with her mother's constant cooking Sylvia's petite figure had ballooned into someone she hardly recognized. But she was happy and her happiness made her mother happy in turn. In her spare time and aside from keeping up with the soaps and all the small town gossip there was little to occupy her time, (although Sylvia soon found that just trying to stay abreast of all the latest gossip was a full time job in itself), Sylvia began to wary of doing nothing and abandoning her dream of starting a foundation to help children. All she had ever really wanted to do was teach and help children so with her mother's prodding she began to pick up the remnants of her dream and began working on The Literacy Library again although he was somehow disposed of returning to New York City under any circumstances. But as her mother had told her it's not important where you start it, our kids need help everywhere. And so with that rather solid piece of advice in mind Sylvia grabbed the bull by the horns and spent her every waking minute working on her dream and enjoying the old woman's company while her mom occupied herself redecorating the house. She was eight and a half months now and in her words looked like a pregnant cow but it hardly ceased her male suitors who flocked to the house now since word had gotten word that she was back in town and still single. Most were men who had been high school classmates but there were quite a few she'd met at her mother's insistence while attending church.

"Picture that. How desperate are men that they'll approach a woman eight months pregnant," but her mother only smiled seemingly grateful for the attention her daughter was getting.

"Well, you know what they've always said…"

"No, I'm afraid I don't. Please clue me in momma? What's up?"

"Well, the word around and the way it was passed down to me is that you ain't had a real woman until you've had a Stanton woman," she said chuckling lightly.

"Oh mommy behave yourself and stop being ornery."

"I just know you're not telling me to behave yourself sitting up there lookin' like a beached whale and a male visitor every other day."

"Oh. no you didn't. It wouldn't be anyone here if you didn't go to church making announcements about your pregnant daughter being home and trying to introduce me to every man out there like I'm desperate and looking for a man to raise my child."

"Well, now that you bring it up ain't nothing wrong with a child having two loving, caring parents. Good as I am, and I'm *damn* good I don't think I could have raised you without your father's help. All that stuff they talkin' about when it comes to single parenting is all a bunch a hog wash coming from ol' ugly women who can't get no man. We is Stanton women and you know as well as I do that getting a man is the least of our problems. I gots men that prayed for me when I had to go into the hospital to get my mastectomy ringing the doorbell now trying to date me and here I is a seventy-four year old widow with one tit and the other one that hangs below my right knee and here they is knockin' down my door. I goes to church and ol'ass Clara Jenkins…You know Miss Clara"

"Yes mama I know Miss Clara."

"Here Clara telling me that she sure could use a man and here she is with two good breastes and one a dem thirty-five dollar Wonderbra that got her titties damn near in her mouth and she can't get no man. So, don't blame it on me if you just born young and lucky as a Stanton woman. T'aint my fault," she said grinning from ear-to-ear.

"I hear you mama."

Sylvia didn't give much thought to Alex anymore but neither did she her new suitors either. For the first time in her life, she was not only comfortable but at peace with herself. No longer did she try to avoid men or have to think when it came to the pain they'd caused her in her life. They could stop by anytime they chose to, with all their smooth lines, proposals and promises but she simply wasn't interested. It wasn't that she didn't like them. She just wasn't interested. In fact, she had to admit that their small town dreams and Southern charm were a welcome relief from the slick, sophisticated ways of the New York men in their fancy clothes. But the bottom line was she just wasn't interested.

Soon, it came to be known that the Stanton woman was neither looking for a good time nor a man to take care of her baby. In fact, the word was hat neither mother nor daughter needed much of anything. It seemed they were rather comfortable financially, and didn't seem to be looking for either income or the excitement that a man with a job in the mill could bring. And so the suitors lessened with each day and life went back to normal, well, except the older gentlemen that still sought her mother's company.

Not long after that—maybe a week or so later—Sylvia drove herself to Fayetteville and admitted herself into Cape Fear Valley Hospital. A day later she was the proud mother of a baby boy, whom she named, Josh Hunter after her father and whom she immediately fell in love with. She now had a man in her life—a man to replace the only in her life—her father. A week or so later Sylvia was back home in Elizabethtown with her mother putting the finishing touches on 'lil Josh's room. And from all the visitors who came to see MariBelle's newest and only grand the resounding echo was that this baby would never want for anything as long as Sylvia and MariBelle were in the picture. There was a lone pathway to the crib. The newly hardwood floors were strewn with stuffed animals and all types of toys he was yet unable to play with. Stopping her mother from shopping for 'lil Josh was quite the task and when she'd finally convinced her mother that it was simply too much and that he baby was being spoiled rotten before he could even imagine the toys and clothes that now filled his closets Sylvia went on a shopping spree all her own. When she'd finished her mother continued as if her very livelihood depended on buying in excess. This went on for several weeks until obviously tired both women stopped. Sylvia became totally absorbed in her young son's life and went from caring for her young son to working on The Literacy Library in her spare time and then when he awoke she returned to his needs. This went on for several weeks until one-day there arrived a bouquet of roses. Flowers had arrived continuously for weeks on end wishing congratulations but this one was somehow different. There was no card or attachment and the driver had driven too quickly for Sylvia to inquire about the whereabouts of the sender. Sylvia didn't sleep well that night and for several nights after that had a recurring dream which did little to alleviate her fear. And then as if by no coincidence she received a package. There was no return address and Sylvia was more than a little hesitant about opening it. Her mother inquired about the contents and Sylvia's face wrought with fear since she was sure no one knew of her whereabouts refused to discuss the strange package only arousing her mother's curiosity that much more.

After two days of sitting unopened the package remained sitting in the middle of the kitchen table.

"You don't open it I will," her mother said one morning as Sylvia came down for breakfast. When Sylvia did not respond her mother grabbed the small box, tore off the brown wrapping paper and proceeded to open it disclosing the contents. In it was a cell phone—a Blackberry to be precise. When turned on it disclosed several text messages. The message was the same one repeated numerous times stating, "I've searched the world over for you. I've spent a lifetime seeking the woman that would somehow complete me and give this meager existence meaning. When I finally think I've found her she disappears right before my eyes. I feel abandoned, lost without you, my love. Whatever it takes to have you back in my life. That I promise I will do. The phone number hasn't changed. Impatiently, lovesick, and soulless I await your call if only to hear your voice."

Sylvia dropped her head.

"What's wrong baby?" her mother asked.

"He's found me mommy," Sylvia responded not quite sure how she felt about this recent turn of events.

"And?"

"I don't know. I just don't know mommy."

"Well, the best solution to any problem is to confront it head on and let the chips fall where they may."

"It's not that easy mommy. Alex is a very, very, powerful man. He lifts his hand in New York and three or for people die in Miami. That's the kind of power he wields."

"I don't know about what he does in New York but if he comes down here waving his hand he may just pull back a nub. If you want to get your school started then go ahead and do it. I can raise 'lil Josh til you get situated and everything up and running. If you need me to I can go up to New York and look after things at home while you go to work."

"Oh, thank you mommy but I just need time to think."

"I'll tell you what I think young lady." Sylvia looked up. Her mother always referred to her as young lady when her patience was wearing thin and Sylvia was in trouble. It had been quite some time since she'd heard it used and was surprised to hear her use it now but gave her the same undivided attention she'd given her when she was a child about to be reprimanded.

"If that's that boys father then he has just as right to know him and try to raise him as you do. If you don't think he's adequate or sufficient then your 'lil hot ass shouldn't have laid down with him."

"How did I or was supposed to know he was a killer or would be in any way connected with a murder?"

"The same way I knew your father was a good decent man before I married him. You take your time before you jump into bed with anybody. If you had taken your time to get know him you would have discovered this long before you had a child by him. That's what I hate about you younguns nowadays. Y'all so ready to blame somebody 'bout he ain't no decent man 'stead a taken responsibility for your actions. If your 'lil hot ass had taken the time to get to know the man this baby probably wouldn't be here now. Do you know it was three years after me and your father had been married when we even thought about bringin' a youngun' in the world. By this time I knew him as well as you can know a man and he knew me well enough to know that he knew I was the woman he wanted to conceive his child. And here you is still makin' stupid, mistakes at your age. Thirty-somethin'and still makin' ol' dumb, childish choices concerning your life and that of this here baby. And don't look like neither of you know enough to raise no child. What do you know 'bout raisin' a child. That's why there so many dumbass niggas runnin' round here now robbin' and shootin' and killin' innocent people. 'Cause they don't know nothin' and the reason they don't know nothin' is because there simple ass parents just wanted to lay down and screw around long enough for them to feel good. Ain't neither of them thinkin' a'bout a child and when they get up they confronted with the idea of a child but they find out they don't hardly like each other let alone know each other. And who gets stuck holdin' the bag. The baby does, that's who. He gotta grow up with one parent or be shuffled back-and-forth all confused and tryna make heads-or-tails out of a situation he ain't even create. And do you know why Sylvia. It's because simple ass women like you don't think past what makes 'em feel good right then and there. You ought to be shamed of yo'self. I'm almost ashamed to say you're my daughter. Layin' down wit' just any ol' somebody and then afraid or not likin' the man you laid down with and wantin' him as a father for your son. Only thing it tells me is your sense of self-esteem and your self worth ain't shit. How you gonna lay down long enough and enough tomes to let a nigga off the streets impregnate you and you get up and you don't want him as a father fo' yo' child. Only thing that tells me is you don't give a good goddamn about yourself or the way your parents raised you. I raised my daughter to think but I can tell you this, you're just lucky this man loves you 'cause you done slept with enough that you've just been lucky is all I can say. This child could have been a number of men's. Now tell me I'm lying."

"Mama…"

"Don't say shit to me girl. Every word I spoke is true. Get yo'self together and confront the man you layed down and spread your legs for. You ain't even sho' it's his chile is you?"

"But mama…"

"Don't but mama me. If yo' daddy was alive this would surely kill him dead. I'm just lucky he ain't have a chance to witness this is all. He probably rollin' over in his grave as we speak."

"But mama you don't understand. This man has enough money and power that he can say Josh is his and can gain full custody if he takes me to court. He goes for custody and both you and I can kiss 'lil Josh goodbye."

"They say you lay down with dogs you're almost certain to get up with fleas, young lady. Why I always told you to be careful with whom you lay down with. Guess you're at his whim if you plan on keeping your son. Sometimes we make mistakes and the best we can do is right the ship the only way we know how. Which may be too simply marry him with the agreement that he keep the business and home life completely separate. Seems to me that's all you can do and try as best you can to insulate your son."

"But mama he scares me."

"Didn't scare you enough to keep your legs from spreading, now did it?"

Sylvia hung her head in shame.

"Go get that boy. Don't you hear him crying?" her mother said.

Sylvia hadn't seen her mother this angry in years. She was seventy-four years of age and whereas when she was younger she used to bite her tongue to save her daughters feelings she was old enough and felt she had earned the right to express herself in anyway she deemed necessary. Nowadays you had better come with your shit correct or simply don't come.

"Give me that baby," she said and deal with that man, she said handing her the phone before grabbing the bottle and a pamper and heading out to the front porch. Sylvia took the phone though hesitantly.

Scrolling through the messages until she came to the final message, which for some reason mesmerized her. It read. I sent this phone last Friday. It was to arrive Monday. I received confirmation that it did indeed arrive and you signed for it. I have the confirmation slip in my hand as we speak with your signature on it. It is now Friday and I'm somewhat concerned, if not a little worried as to why you have not answered either my calls or texts. I am therefore leaving this evening and will arrive rather late tonight. And as you are staying with your elderly mother I will not attempt to contact you tonight but will wait and see you bright and early tomorrow morning.

All of this was a bit more than Sylvia had bargained for and she wondered how he'd managed to find her. But find her he had and now there would surely be hell to pay. Sylvia's thoughts were in total disarray. The time for fear had long since passed. But her mind was still a jumbled mess of conflicting thoughts, not the least being her weight. In the two months prior to Josh being born she'd gained close to fifty pounds. She'd lost a good deal of it but all were efforts to lose were in vain as her mother continued to cook all of her favorite meals. Now here he was on his way expecting the Sill he'd last seen. She caught herself. What did she care about how she looked for him or any other man at this point in her life? What did it matter? When she had that resolved in her mind it went to another thought equally as trauma filled. How would she answer when he asked why she'd left so quickly and without

91

so much as a notice or at least some forewarning? What is it that he'd done? Had he offended her in some way? Is this the way she'd sought to repay his kindness and generosity? And then there was the question of her past. If he'd gone through the trouble of locating her he must have definitely found out that she'd had two stints in the psychiatric ward in the last fifteen years. One even as recent as a month before she'd met him. And why hadn't she revealed her rather checkered past during their many long hours and discussions together. But the thing that bothered Sylvia most were the questions concerning 'lil Josh. Was he his? Why didn't she tell him she was pregnant? And if it were his why would she take his son and run away with him? What was it that she was so terribly afraid of?

Sylvia laid down. It was close to seven in the morning before her mind stopped marching to the band of questions that plagued her and refused to let her sleep. When she finally did doze off she heard that old familiar sound that awoke her countless mornings as a schoolgirl. It was the all too familiar sound of the school bus pulling to the curb and coming to a halting stop on the red that adorned the curb in front of the house. Only his was no school bus and she was no more that used to rush out of the house book bag in one hand lunch box in the other. Sylvia peeked through the blinds only to see the long black limousine she was all too familiar with backing into the driveway. The car took up the major portion of the driveway the front end sticking its nose out partially into the street. Before the driver had turned off the engine she saw her mother move down the porch steps her car keys in one hand, baby in the other addressing the driver who after some discussion took the keys from her mother and eased the old Plymouth into the garage before pulling the nose of the limo out of traffic.

Sill sat down as she watched her mother shake hands with the driver and the handsome gentlemen now exiting the car. After shaking hands the man embraced the elderly woman and took the baby from her arms and held it a distance staring at 'lil Josh a smile illuminating his entire face.

The two chatted for several minutes. And whatever the two were talking about Sill could tell from her mother's expression that she was totally taken by the man who stood in front of her. 'He's won her over just like he did me' Sill thought. 'Oh how I despise that man,' she heard herself say aloud but damn he looked better than even she remembered.

It was obvious he'd taken special care assembling his clothes for their reunion. Dressed in a burgundy turtleneck, gray trousers and a charcoal blazer with a pair of burgundy Cole Haan penny loafers with tassels he looked quite the gentleman. If nothing else Sill had to appreciate her taste in men. She smiled briefly as she watched her mother dissect Alex DuMont with her eyes and nod approvingly.

Sill, dressed in a house robe now far too small for her and some turned over slipper featuring Fred Flintstone Sylvia made no attempts to clean herself up to make herself more presentable. Alex DuMont was no more and no less than any other suitor that had tried to win her over during her last months of pregnancy. She'd been cordial in dismissing them and she intended to be just that with Alex. Sure, he'd driven a ton farther than the locals that pounded on her door in their hopeless attempts at wooing her but the outcome was inevitably the same. Sure she owed him a good deal. There was the matter of the real estate partnership but it was she who was paying the mortgage and though she hated to she would simply give him the money back and seek other investors if that were the case. All in all she owed him nothing more than being cordial. But she knew it wouldn't be that simple and so she did as she'd always done. She closed her eyes and looked to her heavenly father as she did every morning and asked for his help. Hearing the screen door slam Sylvia made her way to the bathroom where she brushed her teeth before taking a long look in the mirror. She had certainly changed since she'd left New York and after looking at her reflection for several minutes she had to admit that she liked herself even if she didn't resemble the woman she'd previously been or that Alex knew.

Wrapping the robe around her she exited the bathroom and made her way into the kitchen where Alex was feeding the baby and engrossed in conversation about Sylvia's childhood.

"Oh, mommy stop. You have no shame when it comes to putting my personal business out there in the street," she said smiling but never once bothering to look at or acknowledge Alex.

"I know you're not talking about anyone having shame. And speaking of being ashamed I know I didn't raise a child that comes into a room at my house and doesn't see fit to acknowledge a stranger in the house."

Alex dropped his head to conceal the emerging smile. Sylvia obviously embarrassed turned to Alex and nodded.

"I know you're going to do better than nodding at someone who you had no problem laying down with and consummated a child with."

"Mommy!" Sylvia screamed more than a little embarrassed now by her mother's remarks.

"You have to excuse my daughter Mr. DuMont."

Alex smiled openly now.

"It's okay Mrs. Stanton but please call me Alex."

"No, it's not okay I raised her better than that. Now stand up and give Mr. DuMont—uh Alex a hug. The man said he's been searching for you for months and then he had the goodness in his heart to drive what—nine hours to see you. The least you can do is give him a hug."

Sylvia stood up and Alex gave the child to Mrs. Stanton before turning and embracing Sylvia intensely. She felt her legs turn to rubber in his embrace. She knew then at that moment and as much as she hated to admit that this man still had a significant piece of her heart.

"I've missed you so much Sylvia," he whispered softly in her ear. "Is there somewhere we can go and talk in private," he asked.

"Not at no seven-thirty in the morning. This ain't no New York. This city sleeps. These are hard working people that sleep late on Saturday mornings but I'm going to the Giant Eagle. Ain't nothin' in the house to eat and now that we has Mr. Alex staying with us a few days I'm a need to buy some groceries so yous two can have the house to yo'self 'til I get back."

"Who's staying a few days?"

"Mr. DuMont here."

"Alex's fine, Ms. Stanton."

"Sorry, Alex but anyway Alex's staying for a few days. I do believe that's what I said the first time."

"I'm sure Alex has much more pressing issues than to be hanging around Elizabethtown," Sylvia commented.

"Actually, I cleared my schedule when I finally located you and Elizabethtown is just the break I need to get away from the hustle and bustle of New York," he said smiling and stealing a sly wink at the older Mrs. Stanton who smiled back.

"Well, that's settled then. Any special foods or dietary concerns I should know about?"

"Anything you prepare will be fine, Mrs. Stanton and by the way people around here all refer to me as mama and they don't have half the right to do that as you do so please call me mama Alex."

"I'd like that mama."

"Good then that's settled. Now let me leave you young folks be. You've got some pretty serious issues to work out so I'll let you be. Don't worry about me it's gonna take me a minute and then I'm gonna probably stop by Sista Clara's house. She's been calling me for a couple of days and I ain't returned none a her calls. She don't want to do nothing but cry over dead husband then ask me why she can't get no man."

"You didn't tell me Mr. Jenkins died mama," Sill said, genuine shock on her face.

"Yeah, he passed a week or two before yo' daddy did. You know they was tight. I think that played a large part in yo' daddy's death too. You know he seein' his closest friends dying around him I guess he just figured it was just his time to go and join them. But anyway, I'm goin' to stop by Clara's and listen to her bitch and moan for awhile then I'll probably stop by the flea market and see what I can see."

Alex heard the words flea market and his eyes suddenly blazed but he had to take care of one small matter before he could indulge his passions. And after eight months he knew that the task at hand was no easy one but he was determined.

"I'm leaving Josh so he and his father can get acquainted and make sure that there's no hanky panky going on while I'm gone. Don't want to come back to find out there's a little girl on the way," she chuckled.

"Mommy!"

Sylvia's head dropped again. She had never understood why mommy always said the first thing on her mind but that was mommy and at seventy-four there was little chance of changing her.

The old woman let the screen door as she exited.

Alex whose eyes had been fixated on the old woman suddenly turned to Sylvia.

"I like her. She's beautiful," he said laughing.

"She's a mess," Sylvia replied.

"So, what's new, sweetheart?"

"Nothing Alex. I'm here in Elizabethtown. What the hell could possibly be new?"

"Well, I'm a father, although I would have never known if I hadn't found you."

Sill knowing what he'd said had more than a 'lil truth in it had no reply.

"So, how have you been?"

"I can't complain. I'm blessed," she replied curtly.

"You look good. You look better anyway. You look like life agrees with you here. I see you've gained a little weight. It's really becoming."

"I'm fat. Between the baby and mommy constantly shoving this and that in my mouth I can't lose a pound. You know I promised myself that as soon as the baby was born I was going to drop the weight but like I said mommy would rather see me like this than…" Alex cut her off.

"Sylvia, the truth…what happened to us?"

"Nothing happened to us Alex. I guess we just ran the course."

"What course? Baby I was just starting. Everything felt real good. I mean it just felt right. Right as rain baby…and then you were gone. There was no word, no hint, no nothing. You just walked out of my life and it would have been alright if you had forewarned me and allowed me to prepare myself but you didn't say a word. I mean

97

there was nothing but me and my broken heart. It took me months to get a lead on you and you still haven't given me a clue as to what I did. All I know is that after that little incident uptown you weren't the same. I know it must've been pretty traumatic for you but the least you could have done was to sit down and talk to me about it baby."

"I did try to talk to you Alex. But you evaded my questions. The Alex that I knew was a different Alex after the shooting. You were cold and distant. You started telling me about karma and shit like that. Here, I am witnessing the man I love getting shot on a corner in Harlem as he comes to pick me up and the only thing he tells me to reassure me is that The Law of Karma is in effect. Not the most reassuring thing for a woman to here. And then two weeks later I'm sitting in my office and come across an article in the Daily News that read about two teens that were murdered on the same corner you were shot only a matter of a couple of days later. Coincidence? The description of the assailant fit Rakman to a tee and he came to the hospital spoke to Thomas to see what happened when they took you into ER and left quickly. Didn't even speak."

"There's no doubt Rakman's a hard case but what you're saying is that you think happened is a bit far fetched Sill. Don't you think?"

"That's what I'm saying, Alex. I didn't know and you didn't help with you sweeping it under the rug like you did. And if there's a chance that you were involved in any way then I had to divorce myself of the situation. You know it's often hard for us to see ourselves but you give off an aura as if you're untouchable and can control the events that are out of our control. You see as cool as you were after the shooting I just knew that you had it all under control and would have it all taken care of. A day or so later it seemed like retribution had been had by you. A

98

day or so later I went to the doctor and he informed me that I was pregnant and I certainly didn't want my child growing up with a question mark over his head concerning his daddy and his business dealings. There were just too many unanswered questions. So, I thought my best option was to leave, clear my head, and enable my baby to have a fresh start. Can you blame me?"

Alex smiled.

"Why didn't you simply ask me Sill?"

"Was none of my business and if you did have anything to do with those murders then what's to say my knowing wouldn't or couldn't have met with the same fate. It's better that I just leave cutting all ties and start fresh."

"So, what are you saying? Are you telling me that it's that easy to just up and walk away from all that we had."

"It's never easy Alex. But it wasn't just my life I had to think about now."

"I understand. And if you are that adamant about Rakman I'll look into it. He's very loyal and very protective. Always has been. You know we grew up together. We used to gang bang together as teenagers on those same streets. From 110th up to 135th Street and from Seventh Avenue to St Nick. I was warlord and save his ass many a day. He's been loyal ever since. The Spades were something back in the day. But you know for most of us that was a particular time in our lives. Some of us moved on. Rakman unfortunately didn't. He did a few bids at Rikers and Attica before I took him under my wing just as I did when we were kids. He's bitter now after two or three bids upstate but we're talking something rather serious when we're talking murder. I don't think Rakman wants to have anything to do with being incarcerated again. I know for a fact that he's two-time offender and isn't even considering a third strike. I pay him a rather handsome salary just to make sure that he doesn't have to worry about hustling on the side to make ends meet. Still, your allegations may prove correct. I can't speak about anyone's motivations other than my own and I can assure you that I'm not in the least bit motivated to seek retribution on anyone. But I will look into it if it'll ease your mind. To tell you the truth I haven't thought about the events of that day or those boys since it happened. I left the streets alone a long time ago. If you haven't realized it yet I'm a successful businessman and I've just about had my fill of that. Don't know if you realize it or not but it's a totally different playing field. There are no guns and knives involved in the boardroom but it can be just as rough and tough and as ruthless as any of the mean streets in Harlem. And to tell you the truth, with the right partner I wouldn't mind buying me an old beat up Ford 150 and getting a few hens and a cow or two grab a couple of acres of land and sit back and just breathe easy."

"You'd die down here Alex," Sill laughed.

"I'm dying there," Alex, said the humor gone from his voice.

Sylvia looked at him again noticing how much he'd aged during their conversation.

"The best thing about the last year was knowing that I had you to come home to. It made going to work each day almost bearable. But I'm tired Sill. I've got enough saved for our children to be comfortable and when I get tired there's of here there's no reason why we couldn't fly to wherever to break up the monotony."

Sill didn't know how to read him. She had never seen him like this. She wondered what had transpired since she'd been gone. Whatever it was it had certainly changed him and Sill had to wonder just how serious Alex really was. And then as if that wasn't enough to turn a girl's head and make her wet.

"Sylvia, you still haven't acknowledged that Josh is my son. And I really don't want to get into all the details but I do want you and Josh and I to be a family."

Sylvia was shocked by this latest revelation but not as shocked when Alex with Josh in his arms knelt down on one knee and pulled the largest diamond ring out of his pocket, looked her in the eyes and said, "Sylvia I have never loved any woman as much as I love you. Will you take me as your husband?"

Shocked at the audaciousness of the proposal. Sylvia stood there speechless but soon gathered both her thoughts and her voice. More than modestly pleased by his proposal she nevertheless refused to smile and give the impression that she somehow would even think she'd consider his proposal. Sylvia stared down at Alex who was still on one knee staring up at her, his eyes pleading.

"Baby, I know you can't be serious. I haven't seen you in close to ten months, have questions concerning your criminal involvement in a murder during the time we were together and you show up here like it was yesterday and nothing ever happened."

"Sill, as far as I'm concerned nothing has happened when it comes to the way I feel about you. And it would have been yesterday if I could have found you. You don't know what you mean to me. From the very first time I met you I raised my hands and thanked God for allowing me to experience such a swirl of beauty and culture in my life. I thanked Him for allowing you to enter into my life. I never stopped thanking Him and I was sincere. I had money, a name, the prestige that went along that with it and thought that I was living. That was until I met you Sill. When you up and left me I admit that at first I was angry. I kept thinking, how could she? I never thought about chasing you down. I thought that I could go ahead with my life and just chalk you to the fact that good things come and good things go. I tried to rationalize our time together and your sudden departure. I reasoned that you were no more than a temporary blessing. But as the days and weeks went on I found that I couldn't get you out of mind. No matter how angry I got, I just couldn't let you go.

I continued to pay the mortgage on the building subconsciously hoping and praying

that you'd return if for no more than to fulfill one of your dreams. But when all was

said and done the fact remained that you were the sunshine in my dark and gloomy

existence and I needed you like I have never needed anyone in my life. I know now

what it is that completes me and makes me whole. I, who never needed anyone need

you Sill."

Alex dropped his head, a lonely teardrop falling from the corner of his eye.

Never a compassionate person, Sill felt a sense of remorse. The months had

somehow softened her. Still, there were just too many unanswered questions and

that thirst that had at first had her seeking the big city, the hot lights and being

amongst the beautiful people was now gone diffused. She no longer needed to be

amongst the beautiful people needed to feel important or needed to know she was

amongst the rich and famous therefore she had no need for Alex DuMont, his crowd

or anyone and any of the shenanigans that went along with it. She'd finally found

the peace and quiet that she had once so hated. And with her newborn, the place to

raise her child. The chaos that she'd once found so exciting, so exhilarating, was

now old hat.

Just then a car pulled up in the driveway. Sylvia smiled a sigh of relief.

Recognizing the familiar sound of daddy's old Plymouth Sylvia turned to Alex.

"Can we continue this conversation at another time? Mommy's home and tends be a

bit nosy."

"That's how mother's are," Alex said matter-of-factly. "Let me go give her a hand

with the groceries. But don't worry, I'll be here for a week or more. Or at least as long as it takes me to convince you that you need me in your life as much as I need you."

"Don't wanna say that better men than you have tried, but what I can say is that others have tried and as you can see I'm still quite single."

Alex laughed.

"That's a temporary situation."

"We'll see. Now, would you please help mommy with the groceries?"

"I'm right here, Mrs. Stanton," Alex shouted at the elderly woman struggling with bagfuls of groceries.

That night Alex stayed at the Stanton household. Sylvia's mother so grateful for the company went against her daughter's every request in making Alex DuMont as comfortable. And he had to admit that with his cook, butler and chauffeur he had never been made to feel more comfortable. She cooked dishes she hadn't made since Sylvia was a small child, cleaned and pressed his clothes and every other thing she could imagine to make Alex's stay just that much nicer. And no matter what Sylvia did to proclaim he was no more than a friend who she had no intentions on making a family member, her mother had thoughts of her own and was mesmerized by his mere presence. What made matters worse was when Alex sent Thomas back to New York, bought a small pick-up truck to get him around town and commenced to scour the town for things he figured the elder Stanton would like. He had exquisite taste and of course money was no object when it came time to purchase anything he thought would put a smile on the older woman's face. He bought her dresses, suits, and assorted household accessories they'd seen on the Home Shopping Network and mentioned she liked. He'd already depleted the charge card he carried for petty cash and the older woman even went so far as to say one day as they all sat around after another fabulous dinner that, she hadn't had that many visits from the men in brown in the twenty something years she'd been living there and that had been more than twenty years. He smiled. He had to admit that he'd grown quite fond of her. She was everything he'd always wanted in a mother and welcomed the fact that she'd so easily accepted him into the family and even proclaimed that he was the son that she'd always wished for. It was during one of these tribute paying trite sessions that Sylvia swore she felt herself throw up in her mouth. Nevertheless, they seemed to genuinely like each other, they got along well, and certainly enjoyed each other's company. Sylvia no longer had to stress over Alex's presence. She rarely saw him and when she did, nine times out of ten he'd be out on the front porch shucking corn or popping beans while engrossed in some world saving discussion or sitting their like two lovebirds gazing at the stars. A couple of times she'd even found that ol' familiar lil' green monster rearing it's ugly head. And she had to remind herself on more than one occasion that Alex was only there because he was trying to woo her. And after all her mother was twice his age and as far as she'd only been seen one man her in her entire life and that was daddy and Alex as smooth as he was certainly not her father although he did have his good qualities. Deep down inside though she was smiling. She was in a strange kind of way glad momma liked Alex. She'd always applauded her mother's good judgment and if mommy thought Alex to be reputable then chances are her accusations were probably unfounded. Sylvia was still curious as to what the two had so much to talk about.

One particular warm summer evening, after Sylvia had come in from her daily run she found the two in their usual position on the front porch, mommy rocking in that old rocker daddy had given her on her seventieth birthday while Alex sat on the porch swing he'd adopted as his own. Approaching she heard the baby crying and ran straight past the two to find him crying his heart out. Sweaty, she picked him up and rocked him only the way a mother can do 'til he was once again quiet. She then grabbed his bottle which she'd already warmed and headed through the kitchen to give the baby to Alex or mommy 'til she'd showered and dressed. It was one of the nights Alex had asked her out and she'd been excited all week when he informed her that he had tickets and not only tickets but VIP tickets to see Sade in Fayetteville. Yet, when she headed out of the porch door to hand the baby to her mother she was bushed off. No matter she thought turning to hand the small child to Alex she was greeted with the same admonishment.

"Talking business baby," was all he said.

Too stunned to protest Sylvia simply went in the house and to her room where she continued to rock her son until he was fast asleep. Putting him into his crib she returned to her room pulled back the blinds and once again glanced at the two people lost in what seemed deep conversation. What business dealings could those two possibly be involved in, she wondered watching as her mother continually broke up in laughter while continually pointing to the vast expanse of land across the road. The land belonged to her parents for as long as she could remember and consisted of sixteen or seventeen acres of prime farmland smattered with a grove of trees here and there and a couple of small ponds. Daddy had been approached several times around it's sale and no matter what the price offered had always declined telling her after each prospective sale that one day that land would be hers and she should never sell it. And she had always adhered to his wishes at least in principal so why was mommy continuing pointing to it in her talks with Alex. Whatever it was, she knew mommy wasn't in the league to deal with the likes of one Alex DuMont and especially without her lawyer being present. She wanted to charge back out there and put an end to whatever they were discussing. Any business dealings with Alex and mommy would end up broke and destitute in a nursing home crocheting with some other old ladies ten years her senior.

Sylvia not wanting to interrupt, and not wanting to chance being shooed away again decided to wait until she and Alex were alone and she could get to the bottom of mommy's so-called business dealings. There were some other things she needed to discuss as well. It was going on two weeks since Thomas had pulled the long black limo into the narrow driveway and to her way of thinking and what she'd seen he didn't seem hardly as pressed as he was in New York and really didn't seem like he was in any rush to leave to get back to the business which seemed to obsess and possessed him during her brief tenure there. In the last two weeks she'd gotten a chance to see him in a different vein, a different light, a different venue. He was relaxed and unassuming. No longer did he dictate and delegate. He simply sat back and enjoyed the simpler things in life including his newly adopted son who he was content to hold and care for hours on end.

He seldom moved from the swing on the front porch and seemed equally content talking to the old woman or reading a book of poetry by Langston Hughes. If he moved it was to find something the old woman had mentioned or referred to in her idle chatter. The only other time she saw him move with any fervor was to accompany the elder Mrs. Stanton to the local flea market on Saturday mornings. Dressing quickly, Sylvia met Alex in the kitchen. Already dressed Sylvia felt a hot flash run down her inner thigh as she glanced Alex in an outfit she had never seen before. He was dressed in a suit somewhere between tan and brown that hugged him just the way she used to like hug him and a crème colored t-shirt made of the finest

Egyptian cotton with a matching fedora identical to the one Denzel paraded in Mo Better Blues. Sylvia glanced then did a double take. Jazzmen were always some of the smoothest dressed brothers she'd come across and she had to admit that all he was missing was a horn tonight. It was always a pleasant surprise when it was time to go out and she had to admit that he had impeccable taste but then most of the brothers she'd run across from New York could dress. They were so unlike the Bama's she'd met in Atlanta who'd as easily don some white shoes along with a white three-piece suit to go to a black tie affair. No, Alex had class. And with his class came two characteristics she embodied and sought in a mate. He was both subtle in his approach whether it be his dress or his approach to the most critical of issues. But the quality she most admired was his humility. Despite the obvious achievements in the financial world he never flaunted his business acumen and if one were meeting him f, Sill thought and smiled at her revelations. He'd made it. There was no question for the first time one would be hard pressed to gather whether he was a high school English teacher or a case manager for some division of social services. Aside from the fact that the New York tabloids announced his every movement on the regular to know and be around this man one wouldn't have guessed he possessed anymore than the next nine to five Joe Blow out there trying to gain a foothold into the American Dream. Now, here he was trying to woo her and her mother into letting him become part of a family that held no more prestige than any average American family. Sylvia wondered never having any great sense of self what it was that so attracted this man who seemingly had everything to her. She'd never felt that there was anything-particular special about her. She really was no more special than anyone else. Oh yeah, she had an education. But she possessed no more knowledge than anyone who'd graduated the same year and probably far

107

less than many who'd graduated at the same time. She was attractive or so she'd been told. But again she was no more attractive than many who traversed the streets of the city. So what was it that attracted this man who had elevated himself to the next plateau to be interested in her, a common, everyday soul who had also done her very best to elevate herself and far too often fallen short. Sylvia wondered but whatever it was she would find the answers too many of her queries tonight.

"Oh, don't both of my children look so nice tonight. Y'all headed up to Fayetteville to see that Sade, huh? Now her I like. She ain't like all the rest of those so-called singers out there. She reminds me of my Sill for the world," Mrs. Stanton said staring directly at Alex. "What I like is that she's a song stylist. Meaning that she's no great singer but she has the ability to put a song across and her lyrics have some meaning. You know she dresses them up nicely leaving some intrigue."

"I didn't know you were a music connoisseur," Alex said smiling broadly. Sade was perhaps his favorite contemporary artist and hearing the old woman speak so fondly of her only endeared her to him more.

"Oh, yeah I like my music although there's not a lot out there for me to choose from nowadays."

"You got that right. I wish I had known. I would have gotten you a ticket as well."

"No, you two run along. Someone has to stay with the baby. But yeah I do like Sade. She reminds me so of my Sill. She's got an elegant but quiet sophistication that you don't see too often nowadays. When you see her, you get one thing. And that's the music. You don't see her taking off all her clothes and gyrating like she's crazy. She doesn't have to do all that. She's good and she's confident that she has a quality product that will sell itself and that's her music and that's what I like about her."

"All right mommy. I left everything you should need on the bassinet. C'mon Alex. We've got an hours drive and we don't wanna be late," Sylvia said in an attempt to cut mommy short. If it was one thing mommy could do it was talk.

"You right. Y'all run along for you be late. Have a good time and behave yourselves. I don't want you coming home with another bun in the other. This boy's a handful enough as it is."

"Oh, mommy!" Sill said slightly exasperated but still smiling as Alex held the door for her.

"I didn't know your mommy liked Sade."

"I'm surprised there's something you don't know about mommy as much time as you two spend together."

"Do I detect a note of jealousy?"

"Of mommy?" Sylvia laughed.

"Just sounded like it," Alex teased. "But now that you mention it. They say the fruit doesn't fall far from the tree and it just seems to me that a piece of fruit is fine but the best would be the bearer of the fruit. What would you say?"

"Are you saying that you're interested in my mother?" Sylvia asked. The brow of her nose was beading up quickly.

"Well, being that she's the only one that's paying me attention and catering to my needs I do find myself somewhat attracted to her."

Sylvia was caught somewhere between dumbfounded and livid but before she jumped down his throat she thought about her mother's words comparing her to Sade. A quiet and reserved elegance and she bit her tongue. Alex was trying to bait her, goad her into a conversation, trying to make her lose it. He was a master of manipulating her mind, and her thoughts. He'd soon have her angry, spitting out words she'd soon regret and her pressure up. So. Remained calm and steadfast.

"Well, I am pleased that you and mommy have bonded so well. You have a way with bringing people into the fold."

"I really don't think it's as cold and calculating as you think, Sill. Truth of the matter is that your mother and I simply share a lot of the same things in common but there was no way for me to know this when I first met her and that's one of the reasons I had Thomas stick around for the first few days after I arrived. Like I said we just kind of hit it off. She's a beautiful person and it's not hard to love her. She doesn't have any hidden agenda. She tells you exactly what's on her mind and how she feels about something. And after being in the company of those sheisty characters down on Wall Street day in and day out she certainly is a welcome relief. That's all."

"I think she's fond of you as well."

"Just wish her daughter would show me the same love her mother does."

Sylvia did not comment instead choosing to breathe deeply. She had chosen the ride there to resolve some of their issues which up until now had remained in limbo but she had to admit she liked Sade as much if not more than he did and wanted nothing more than to enjoy an *Evening with Sade*, as it was being billed but she needed to talk to Alex. This was the end of the third week and he seemed no closer to leaving than he had. Still, in her eyes it was time for him to go. She had a man in her life, a man that gave her everything she could ask for and more. He gave her unconditional love filling the void that had been with her since her inception. And in all reality, she didn't know how she could juggle him and not just a husband but anything else

110

in her life with him. He was a full time job and if it weren't for mommy she was quite sure she wouldn't have made it.

"On a serious note and I think this has been a long time in coming but I have to ask you what your intentions are?"

"My intentions? I think I made that plain when I first arrived. My intentions are to marry you…"

"Lofty goals…" Sylvia remarked.

"In your case, I'd agree. I see the way men look at you and you act as if they don't exist but I'm not just your average Joe."

"No. You're not but what I don't think you understand is that average Joe or not I'm just not interested at present. Don't get me wrong, I do find you attractive and if I were interested you'd probably be my first choice but the fact remains that I'm not interested at present. I don't know what you want me to say."

"I don't want you to say anything other than how you feel and although I don't understand I respect your feelings."

"I'm glad and hope you know it's nothing personal. So tell me this now that we've gotten that out of the way. When will you be leaving?"

"That I can't say."

"But I thought we'd come to an agreement. What's the point of you hanging around when I made it plain that the reason for you being here is all but moot now? You said initially that you came here to marry me and now that you know that that's out of the question why stick around other than to aggravate me?"

Alex laughed deeply.

"It's funny, Sill, but you can't imagine how many times I've put forth a proposal in my work and it's been rejected. But I've always been a firm believer that persistence overcomes resistance. Besides that you're absolutely right. When I first arrived it was strictly of a personal nature. I was coming to ask the woman I love to marry me. That was personal. But I met another wonderful woman who just so happens to be your mother and she enticed me into a venture, which no longer makes it solely for personal reasons. Now it's business. So to answer your question, when we finish conducting our business I suppose I'll be leaving. Don't when that'll be so I guess you're stuck with me until then."

"And if you don't mind me asking what kind of transaction have you involved mommy in?"

"I'm really not at liberty to say at this juncture. All things in time…"

"Alex please don't have this woman get caught up in something. She doesn't know anything about investing or anything like that. The only thing she has is the house and some money daddy left her. If she loses that she's basically destitute."

"Did I look out for you when you first arrived in New York?"

"Yes, but…"

"Then what makes you think that I wouldn't do the same for your mother. Besides don't play your mother cheap. She's got savvy and a better business acumen than half the brokers down on Wall Street. Trust me she can take care of herself."

"I just hope so. Mind telling me what you two are involved in?"

"I would but she asked me not too, it'll be obvious to you though in a couple of weeks when the project gets started. Trust me."

Sylvia was really curious now but knew better than to ask.

Moments later they were only feet from Sade as she crooned her latest hit single, *Soldier of Love.*

The ride home was quiet. Sylvia was tired and Alex appeared so as well. When they arrived home they found the old woman sleeping the baby nestled gently in the crook of her arm. Alex took the baby and placed him in his crib while Sylvia escorted her mother to her room. Tomorrow was Monday and Sylvia was intent on heading to the local library to work on her program. She was pretty adamant about not starting it in New York although Lord knows they were in dire need of it. But whether it was in Elizabethtown or in Harlem the need remained.

The following morning at the crack of dawn Sylvia was awakened to the sound of a loud thunderous thud. Seldom was there any noise besides the chirping of a lone robin who had commenced to making the big oak in the front yard his home. Sylvia peeked through the half closed blinds of her bedroom only to see two large bulldozers clearing the heavy underbrush and thicket that had grown long and tall since her father's death. Seeing the construction crew on her father's property across the road grabbed her robe and burst into the kitchen screaming.

"Mommy, do you see those men on daddy's land?"

"Whoa baby. I think a good morning would be more appropriate."

"Morning mommy. Now do you see those men tearing up daddy's land? I know you and Alex done schemed up something. I don't know what you two are up to but mommy you should know better. Daddy bought that land and never wanted it touched."

"Your daddy's not here now baby. And I believe he left the land to his wife to do with as she sees fit."

"Oh my God! Mommy you done lost your mind. You let that silver-tongued scheister come down here and in less than a month let him talk you into giving up the land your husband worked his whole life to purchase. How you gonna just let him do that? Don't you see that's what he does? That's his claim to fame. He ain't nothin' but a common street hustler. And you let him swindle you. Mommy I thought you were smarter than that."

"Girl, who are you talking to? I don't where you've been or what you've been doing but I'll be damn if you talk to me like that. But let's say what you're saying is true. Why the hell would you bring some common street hustler to your mother's home? Better yet why would you spread your legs with that kind of trash?"

Sylvia dropped her head in embarrassment her silence admitting her mistake.

"If I had thoughts of telling you or including you in what was going on, I sure as hell don't now. Picture that, you walkin' round here with a newborn and you don't even know who his father is and you're gonna admonish me for something\'. Lord, chile you done brought the devil out in me. What I suggest you do is go in there and clean yourself up and come in here like you got some sense and try that again. You might just wanna start by dropping to your knees and thanking the good Lord for allowing you another day on his green earth and then ask him to forgive your transgressions. How 'bout that?"

But Sylvia wasn't finished and she knew if there was anyone to blame it was Alex. There hadn't been an ill word between the two women in the entire time she'd been there. This was the first time and of course Alex was at the center of it all. Why he couldn't have just stayed in New York, stayed in his element with all the rest of crooks she didn't know. Hell, things had been the same here since she had been a little girl and there was no need for change now. No, everything was as it had always been…well that was up until Alex had shown up. Sylvia showered and then exiting the shower she yelled.

"Alex, Alex! I need to talk to you this instant. Now dammit!"

"Sylvia what's wrong with you?" her mother yelled back. Alex's been long gone. Caught an eight o'clock flight out of Raleigh. He's long gone. Left about five this morning."

"And he didn't even say goodbye. Now I know he's up to no good. Didn't I tell you he can't be trusted?"

"Why in the world would he say goodbye? You act like he doesn't exist when he is here. Young man comes to me every night asking me why you're so darn cold towards him. Told him you're either eccentric or half-crazy. Couldn't tell him which 'cause to tell you the truth I'm not sure which one it is myself but he just smiles telling me some mess about how persistence overcomes resistance. Tellin' me how he's in it for the long haul. I tol' him he waits on your crazy behind he's liable to end up ol' and gray before your stubborn ass comes around but he's willing to wait. Never seen two more stubborn young people in all my life. Nice young fella too. He's got you up on some kind of pedestal. Calls you a diva. And no matter how many times I tell him that there's a thin line between deranged and diva he still believes you to be the latter. Nice as he is when the topic comes to you I swear he ain't the sharpest crayon in the box. He got the world at his feet, can have any woman in New York and he picks your half baked behind. Lord! Lord! Lord!"

"Well," Sylvia said looking somewhat pitiful and a tad dejected after hearing of his leaving. "I'm glad he's gone."

Chapter 8

Sylvia found herself recollecting on the past three weeks and had to admit that she did feel a little remorse at Alex's departure. She hated feeling this way and kicked herself letting him get the best of her again. She promised herself she wouldn't dwell on him anymore. If he's gone he's gone. But despite her denial the fact remained that she missed his presence. She was not the only one. Mommy did too retiring early. The house had grown solemn and the usual chatter and laughter that had now become a part of the household was now gone from the front porch. And when she asked mommy if she wanted to spend some time she dejectedly declined. Seemed everyone was feeling the brunt of Alex's departure. Curious she crossed the road and approached the driver of a flatbed delivery truck delivering two by fours.

"Excuse me sir. I'm the owner of this land and I don't believe I ordered anything."

The driver took out the billing statement and viewed it closely.

"RFD Box 335 Rte 5?"

"Yes," Sylvia answered.

"Then this load of two by fours is yours ma'am."

"Do you know what it's for?"

"I'm a truck driver. I deliver lumber to wherever they tell me. I'm not a contractor ma'am. 'Scuse me ma'am, I gotta go."

Sylvia received the same rather calloused responses from the bulldozer drivers clearing the land who seemed so incensed by the interruption that Sylvia decided to simply wait on Alex and mommy's response or slip up since it was obvious she wasn't making any headway with the construction workers. Crossing the highway a F-350 narrowly missed her as she made her way back to the house.

"Sylvia Stanton! Sylvia Stanton!"

Sylvia turned and stared as the man got out of the truck's cab and made his way over to Sylvia with all the haste of a newborn getting back to the shelter of his mother's arms.

With outstretched arms he reached out and hugged the tiny woman tightly.

"It's me Sill. Tristan! Damn it's been a long time! And you ain't changed a bit."

Sylvia was still trying to place the face when it dawned on her who Tristan was. And then it came to her. Tristan had been every little high school girl's dream when she was a freshman and sophomore. He was the cutest little point guard on Elizabethtown's basketball team and was headed to Notre Dame or UNC and was destined for the pros or everyone thought. She had dated him briefly as a freshman and was devastated when the short-lived relationship came to an end. She then spent the next two years coyly plotting and scheming how to get him back only to dump him a week after she had him firmly entrapped. She had after all, never been dumped and wasn't going to allow him to do that without making him pay. She had seen him or paid any attention to him after that. And this had to be the first time in more than twenty years that she'd laid eyes on him.

They'd had some good times and she broke into a broad grin as she recognized him. I was all coming back now but the Lord knows he was no longer the skinny point guard anymore. He'd certainly grown into his six foot two inch frame and had to be standing at least six foot seven or better and had picked up a good bit of weight besides. There was nothing skinny or cute about him now. No, the man that stood before her now looked like a cross between Hercules and Adonis. His good looks were not only ravishing but also strikingly good-looking. Sylvia had to admit that he had certainly grown and come into his own.

"Oh my goodness, Tristan. How long has it been? Well, you certainly have changed. But it's all for the better. You really look good. What are you doing for yourself?"

"Not a lot. Workin'. Bought a small lumberyard and just tryin' to make a go of it is all. How 'bout yourself?"

"Well, I graduated from "T" as you probably know and got a teaching job in Atlanta, got married and divorced, stayed there for umpteen years before heading north to New York where I've been for the last six or seven months 'til I returned home about a year ago. I have a newborn and that's about it. Nothing earth shaking."

"Sounds earthshaking to a small town boy like me," Tristan chuckled. "I've never left E-Town," he said chuckling again.

"Last thing I heard was that you were undecided but had options to go to either Notre Dame or UNC. Everyone had NBA written all over you. From what I heard pro scouts were on you like white on rice before you even got out of high school and Coach Dunleavy had to cordon off a piece of his office just for all the mail you were receiving from colleges."

"I think you received some misinformation Miss Stanton. Is it still Miss Stanton?"

"I'm afraid so. But what happened to college and the big time basketball star?" Sylvia asked sorry she'd said anything. Was she still smarting over his reaction some twenty years earlier? Or was it just that he was a man and Lord knows she had no use for that species of being.

"Well. The big time basketball star never listened to his mother's advice or anyone else's for that matter and decided to attend the University of North Carolina on a basketball scholarship instead of an academic one and I tore up my knee in a scrimmage before I even had the opportunity to suit up for a game. UNC rescinded

118

my scholarship and here I am. It hasn't been that bad though. It took me about a year to rehab my knee. After I had it where it was better than new I signed on to play over in Italy for a couple of years and I got a chance to see Europe and save a couple of bucks before the NBA came around and signed me but after a year or two I lost my passion for the game and ended up right back here where it all started."

"So, let me get this right, you gave up a lifelong dream to come back to Elizabethtown?"

"You did it. Why can't I?"

"Touche…"

"In all reality though I think this may have been my best move yet. You see I was smart enough to save up a couple of bucks and when I returned I took a few online classes in Business Management and ol' man DeKlirk who owned the lumberyard remembered me from high school when I used to work part time for him at the very same lumberyard. He was a big basketball fan then. Well, he used to ask my parents how I was doing on the regular and he followed my career over in Europe and when I got back to the states. I used to send him clippings and keep in touch. Anyway, he never had any kids so I guess I was like an adopted son or something to him. So, he gave me a job as a foreman when I got back. At about the same time my mother got breast cancer so I was supporting her and working for him at the same time. He thought this was so commendable. Anyway, he had a hard attack a few months later and you should have seen the white folks in E-Town when they read his last will and statement saying he left the lumberyard to yours truly."

"No, he didn't," Sill shouted, probably sounding as stunned as those at the actual reading.

"Oh, but he did," laughed Tristan. "I said the same thing when I saw that the net worth of the lumberyard was in the neighborhood of six point something million."

"No, he didn't" Sill repeated.

"Sorry you dumped me now aren't you?" Tristan replied still smiling. "Still, I might forget all that if you'd consider having dinner with me this Friday night."

"I might if you'd tell me one thing."

"And that is?"

"What are they constructing on my daddy's land?"

"That's all you wanna know and I can have dinner with the woman I've waited damn near forever on."

"That's it. I don't come at too high a price do I?" Sylvia said laughing.

"A lot cheaper than used to be."

"I don't know if I should take that as a compliment or not."

"I've always been complimentary when it came to you, Sill. Remember you were the one who kicked me to the curb."

"Only in response to your initial dismissal."

"A moment of temporary insanity I must admit but God knows you made me pay. I still lay awake at night wondering what the hell was on my mind."

"Oh, you need to stop, Tristan. You ain't no more thinking about me..."

"That's where you're wrong Sylvia. I've had many a wet dream with you playing the starring role," he laughed. "But in all seriousness all I do is check on the load and make sure it was delivered, especially when it's an order of this size. Just good business to make sure everything's in order but as far as what's to be constructed... I haven't a clue. Tell you what though, I'll see what I can find out and let you know when I pick you up. Say about eight?"

120

Tristan jumped into the huge Ford pickup before she could answer.

Sylvia felt a warm glow within. She'd always liked Tristan more than a lil bit. After all he'd been her first and now that the competition was between zero and none and the adoring crowds had thinned to just her she might finally have a chance to get to come to know her high school heartthrob without interference.

Sylvia entered the house to the smell of baked apples and homemade biscuits. She was smiling. Grabbing the baby and the bottle from her mother's arms she spun around and kicked her heels up the way she had seen the Rockettes do it at Radio City Music Hall.

"Well, somebody's mood has certainly changed from earlier," her mother, said noticing the sudden mood change. "Who done got you all in an uproar now?"

"Do you remember Tristan from high school?"

"Oh, you talking about Tristan from the lumberyard?"

Sylvia was slightly surprised that mommy remembered.

"How could I forget? You used to be crazy 'bout that boy. Your father stayed up many a night hoping you didn't get married to that boy before you finished your schooling. Yeah, I know Tristan."

"I just saw him. He really looks good, mommy."

"Lord girl, I don't know what I'm going to do with you. How many men does it take?"

"Mommy it's nothing serious. We're just old friends going out for dinner to talk over old times."

"And what about Alex?"

"What about Alex. I'm neither married to Alex nor thinking about his sheisty ass."

"Sylvia! I'm telling you for the last time. Leave the streets in the streets. This is a Christian home and I'll have none of that foul language here. Your father would roll over in his grave if he heard his daughter talking like that."

"Sorry mommy, but you act like I owe Alex something…"

"Sylvia can't you see that Alex loves you. He's a good man baby. He's wealthy and he loves you."

"And because he has money I guess I'm supposed to do back flips. And since when has money changed you mommy."

"It hasn't and I'm sorry I said that but I won't be around much longer baby and I just want to see you settled down with a good man that can take care of you and treat you and the baby the way your father and I think our baby girl should be treated. You have that in Alex. And from I've seen and I've always been a pretty good judge of character he can provide for you and love you the way it should be done."

"All that's probably true mommy but their remains one small thing you're missing in the whole equation."

"And what's that Sill?"

"The fact that I don't love him."

"Well, something you did gave him that impression."

"I may have. But you know what they say mommy."

"No, what's that?"

"Two tears in a bucket and say fuck it."

"That's the last time Sill. I swear 'fo God. You say another foul under this roof and you can start packin' your baby's bags as well as yours and catch the next thing to fly your foul mouthed behind up outta here. Do you hear me young lady?"

122

"Yes mommy. I just want you to understand that what ever Alex and I had is over. That's all. I don't want him or his money. I came down here because the only thing I do want is to be left alone."

"Then why are you going out with Tristan then if you just wanna be left alone?"

"I don't want Tristan either mommy. We are at least old friends. And since when did dinner between old friends become a crime?"

"You forget I know you Sylvia and you drop men like old people drop dead."

"Oh mommy," Sylvia said the exhaustion dripping in beads like the sweat from a tobacco farmer at noon in the Carolina sun. "You'll see."

"You're right. I'll see just as soon as Alex gets back from his business trip. But I'm gonna tell you this. I don't want no drama in my house 'cause of none a your foolishness."

"He don't bring no drama, won't be no drama."

"Im telling you he ain't gonna like the idea of you seein' Tristan one bit," the elder woman said as she pulled the golden, brown biscuits from the rack in the oven and placed them on top of the stove.

"Don't know what to say mommy. He better get used to it or he better get over it. That's all I know. Ain't a man alive gonna tell me what to do with my life 'cept daddy and he's dead and gone."

"Okay. Okay. Do whatcha gonna do, Sill. You always have, least long as I can remember. All I'm sayin' is he ain't gonna like it one bit."

Chapter 9

The days passed quickly. The nights lingered on for what seemed an eternity.

During the days Sylvia hardly had time to breathe between the baby, getting her

proposal in order and preparing for her date when Alex happened upon the scene.

She'd gone to Lumberton to shop for a dress and was pleasantly surprised to find

something elegant yet sophisticated and after a day of shopping she'd come across

something not only elegant but something sexy and revealing. Truth is she needed

to know that she still had it, that she still had what it took to turn a man on and turn

him out. She'd come across a little black dress that was thigh high and low cut. The

sides were sheer and the rest form fitting accentuating her more than ample bust line.

She was ready after finding a pair of six inch heels Sill only hoped that Tristan was

taking her to someplace where she could show off her finery and show those who

didn't know that she hadn't only moved away and gotten finer but she had also

refined that which at nineteen or twenty had yet to be refined. She was ready and all

that remained was the night. In all reality Sill didn't expect much. Sure

Elizabethtown had grown but was it ready for her. Sylvia wondered.

Seeing Alex's limousine, it's nose sticking out into the road Sylvia cursed. Despite

all she had said to mommy she really hoped there would be no drama. All she really

wanted was some peace. She'd gone from Atlanta to New York and from New York

to North Carolina. Always seeking the same thing—peace of mind. But it didn't

matter where she went trouble seemed to follow and this time it was in the form of

one Alex DuMont.

Stepping out of the car packages overflowing, Thomas emerged from the limo and quickly made his way to Sylvia hugging her and relieving her of some of the many packages she was carrying.

"So good to see you Ms. Stanton," Thomas said a wide grin covering his face.

"And you Thomas. How's life been treating you in the Big Apple?"

"Still a rat race. Nothing's changed. Same ol' same ol'."

Sylvia sat down in the front seat of the limo and glanced the tabloid laying folded on he front seat as she bought time before confronting Alex once again while Thomas busied himself unloading the packages from her car. Sitting there she smiled thinking of Alex's favorite line. 'Persistence overcomes resistance'. She smiled again thinking that he had to be one persistent S.O.B if he thought he could overcome her once she'd made her mind up. And in his case her mind was firmly made up. The truth was she did not want him. Despite everything mommy had said on his behalf she wasn't falling into that rut again. There was nothing mommy or Alex could say to sway her otherwise. Her mind was firmly made up. Despite his wealth, charm and good looks and all the stuff about his making a good father for her baby she didn't want him. Yes, she had felt something for him at one time but that had been then and this was now. Whatever it had been was gone now. Sylvia contemplated her next move while leafing a day old tabloid sitting on the front seat. She recalled the days when she had adorned that very same tabloid with Alex. Leafing through she wondered who had taken her place.

Turning the pages it wasn't hard to see that Alex hadn't missed a beat in her absence. There he stood in all his glory surrounded by beautiful women while he stood front and center, locked arm-in-arm with everyone's latest heartthrob Nikki Minaj. Sylvia's blood boiled. She jumped up then caught herself. And then quite

125

miraculously she smiled. Why was she getting upset? Isn't this what she wanted?

A chance to rid herself of Alex DuMont. Now she had a reason. A reason to

support all her unfounded suspicions. What was she but just another notch on his

belt? 'Well, Mr. DuMont it was time to see just what you're really made of', Sylvia

thought to herself.

Gathering herself and making sure the smile was etched on her face she stepped

toward the front door.

"Oh, Alex you're back. What's up? How was business?"

Surprised by the warm welcome, Alex hugged Sylvia warily not sure of what to

expect next.

"I'm good and you?"

"Couldn't be better," she replied on her way through the house to shower and change

for her upcoming date. "Will you excuse me, I'm running late," she said rather

nonchalantly.

"You're leaving? I just got here."

"So, you did. I'm sorry. If I had only known," she said as she entered her bedroom

closing the door behind her.

Alex looked at the elderly woman gently bouncing the cooing baby on her shoulder

and simply shrugged.

"You know Sill about as well as I do. So don't look at me. I did the best I could but

she's headstrong as a mule. Got that from her father's side I guess."

Sylvia lay across her bed, a large smile across her face.

"Take that Mr. DuMont. Certainly gonna test your mettle tonight. See how much

persistence you really have 'cause Lord knows I have more resistance than any one man can stand.," she said chuckling to herself. "First round Sylvia Stanton in the blue corner," she said aloud before pumping both fists high in the air.

Deep in thought Sill heard a light tap at the door. Fearing it was Alex she jumped up from the bed.

"I'm getting dressed," she yelled.

Recognizing her mother's voice, the young woman relaxed.

"I'm running late mommy. Give me a few minutes and I'll be out."

Hearing her mother's footsteps walking back towards the kitchen, Sylvia made a mad dash for the bathroom turned on the shower full blast and stepped into the steaming hot water. Moments later she was fully dressed. Splashing a touch of Chanel on she modeled in front of the full-length mirror, smiled at her appearance before heading toward the kitchen.

"Damn, baby you look…"

Before he could finish or the elderly woman could reprimand him for the profanity there was another tap at the door, only this one was louder. Sylvia pulled out her compact, checked her make up before asking Alex to please get the door.

"Evening ma'am," Tristan said to the old woman. Nodding at Alex briefly his eyes were fixated on Sylvia.

"My goodness you have certainly come into your own Sylvia. The years have certainly agreed with you."

"Tristan and Sill are old high school friends," Mrs. Stanton said interceding in an attempt to pull Alex into the foray and ease the tension growing in the room. Sill on the other hand was eating it up. She loved the attention and was well aware that she both men's undivided attention.

"Oh, I'm so sorry Tristan. This is Mr. Alex DuMont. I believe this is the man you were attempting to deliver that rather large load of lumber too. Was that Monday?"

"Glad to meet you Mr. DuMont. And thank you for your business. Met Sylvia over their on the site inquiring about the nature of the construction. We grew up together. Old friends I guess you'd call us."

"Is that all you'd call us? Tristan was the star basketball player in high school. All the girls were crazy about him including me," Sylvia laughed.

"I had to wait in line like everybody else and when I finally got my chance to date the star basketball player I jumped at it only to be dumped by All-World a week later," she said. "I was just telling him that and after a good deal of begging and pleading he very graciously decided to give me a reprieve," Sylvia said grabbing Tristan's elbow.

Tristan blushed, not expecting this at all.

"It was good seeing you again Mrs. Stanton. And nice meeting you Mr. DuMont. C'mon Sylvia I have reservations at Alexander Devereaux's for eight and it's already eight-thirty."

Sylvia glanced back at the house and smiled and waved goodbye a big smile at a peeking Alex who stood their mouth open a surprised and angry look covering his face. Tristan held the car door open as she slid in and again remarked on how good she looked.

Dinner couldn't have been nicer. Tristan had reserved no only the table but he entire second floor of the plush restaurant some fifty miles from Elizabethtown. Looking ou over the beach Sylvia couldn't have dreamed of anything better. A lone bartender stood at the ready. And while the waiter brought Maine lobster after Maine lobster Sylvia was quietly surprised that Tristan had taken I upon himself to

128

place order as well as his prior to their arrival. A bottle of the best champagne was cracked and placed before her and each time it seemed she was half finished her glass more was poured. Tristan seemed content with the Coronas served to him with the same frequency as the champagne and each cracked lobster shells as if it were heir last meal.

"Nice touch. You certainly have a nice way of making a first impression," Sylvia commented apropos of nothing. "Do you do this for all the girls?" Sylvia asked feeling the effects of he bubbly.

"Hardly. But an old man once old me that a man is only apt to come across one great one in his lifetime and this only one thing worse than missed potential and that's a missed opportunity. And when you come across that one great one in your life you'd best seize the opportunity," Tristan said smiling and looking deeply into her eyes. She averted her eyes from his.

"And what's all that got to do with me?" She replied innocently enough.

"Well, the way I see it is that because I was young and dumb with a brain full of cum I missed out on my great one. I missed out on the opportunity. God somehow blessed me and gave me a second chance. I won't blow it this time. I swear I won't."

"Is that right?" Sill said sipping her champagne and waving no to the waiter who was intent on pouring her another glass.

"Not to dissuade you Tristan but I've come back to Elizabethtown to relax and get my life back in order a little. I've got a newborn and right now all I'm really concerned with is devoting some time to my baby and being a good mother. I don't really have time for anything else."

"So you say, but I'm a pretty good judge of people and from what I gather your Mr. DuMont seems to feel differently."

"You always were pretty perceptive Tristan. And you're right. Mr. DuMont is a firm believer in persistence overcoming resistance but and I guess it has something to do with the male ego and the idea that you can accrue anything with money. I'm afraid he's in for a rude awakening. You see I told him the same thing I told you. Made it as clear as I possibly could and if he chooses to spend his time and money here in Elizabethtown there's little I can say or do. Bottom line though is I'm not interested."

"Hope so," Tristan said. "Because when you finally decide that you want to settle down with your soul mate I sincerely hope you look this way first and I'm your first choice."

"You always have been and probably always will be," Sylvia leaned across the table and kissing him lightly on the cheek.

"Are you ready?"

"Yes, and thank you so much Tristan. I had a wonderful time."

"Hope this is just one of many to follow."

"Perhaps in time."

"That time can't come soon enough. Guess I've got enough to keep me busy with my business and all until that time comes," he said the disappointment showing in his voice.

Chapter 10

Sylvia arrived home at a lil' after one a.m. The house appeared quiet as Tristan walked her to the front steps. Always a gentleman he grabbed her, hugging her tightly before kissing her lightly on the cheek and telling her goodnight. Turning to go into the house she waved to Tristan letting him know she was in safely. She watched as he pulled out of the driveway before pulling the door closed and locking it.

"Where the hell have you been?" Alex shouted loudly.

Sylvia, still smiling, turned to the irate young man and just stared.

"Do you know what time it is? Where have you been?"

"My daddy's dead and mommy's trying to sleep. I'm thirty eight years old single, independent and don't see anywhere where I have to answer to you or anybody else."

"Oh, you're going to answer me. I didn't come all the way down here for you to be out half the night gallivanting around with some country assed nigger."

"Excuse me, but I don't believe I owe you an explanation concerning anything or anyone. Contrary to what you may believe, you are neither my man nor my husband. So don't get it twisted. I thought I made it perfectly clear to you that we are not in any way connected. If at one time there was even the faintest idea that we may have had something those days are long gone and forgotten by me. Maybe it's time you accepted that and moved on."

"That may be all well and true but as long as you're the mother of my son I'm going to hold you accountable for your actions and that doesn't mean you out all hours of the night with strange men."

"Whoa! Hold up! And what in God's name makes you think that that's your son. See that's what I'm talking about. Men and their egos… I make love to you once or

131

twice, better yet have sex with you and you swear you've fathered a child. You're not only egotistical, you're delusional to think that I'd ever let you father a child without knowing you first."

Alex was devastated by the fact that there was even the remote possibility that the baby wasn't his and had to swallow hard at the notion that she had been with someone else aside from him. Why had he even considered that he'd been the only man in her life up until this point? After all whatever had attracted him to this beautiful thirty-eight year old woman had to have had the same affect on other men. Why had he been so blind, so shallow to think that he only was the only one who could attest to her intelligence, her charm, and her attractiveness? But now was no time for an epiphany. Yet, before he could respond the older woman awakened by the sudden screaming and yelling walked into the kitchen.

"Lord Jesus what does a soul have to do to get some sleep around here?"

"I'm sorry to have awakened you Mrs. Stanton but let me ask you what kind of a woman with a newborn baby comes stepping into the house at two a.m. in the morning. She doesn't call and let us know that she's all right or anything. That's just common courtesy and consideration."

"Why do I need to call you for anything?" Sylvia replied. "I told you the only man I've ever answered to was my daddy and he's dead and gone. Furthermore, I asked mommy to watch Josh and she agreed, knew where I was going and was okay with that. That's the only person I have to report to whether you know it or not."

"As far as what kind of woman my Sylvia is Alexander, I must say that I resent your implications. She must have some special qualities about her that keep you coming back to see her when she's made it more than evident that she's not interested in seeing you. So instead of asking me what kind of woman she is you might acknowledge the woman you're so in love with in a more positive light. As a daughter and a mother I know that I couldn't have asked for more."

Alex hung his head in shame.

"I apologize Mrs. Stanton. It's just that I…"

"It's just that you let that little green headed monster raise his ugly head instead of checking it and going to Plan B and devising a new strategy for trying to woo the woman of your dreams. Let me tell you something I've learned over the past seventy something years Alex. You should never question the moral turpitude or speak badly of any woman you've chosen as yours. It not only puts the woman in a negative light but also makes a

Alex hung his head in shame.

"I apologize Mrs. Stanton."

"You owe me no apology, Alex other than waking me up. I believe the one you owe an apology to is the one standing in front of you," the elderly woman said before turning and making her way back to her bedroom muttering something about how children are always children and never really leave the nest.

Alex continued to stare at the floor as Sylvia delighted that her mother had come to bat for her simply gathered her things, checked on Joshua and made her way to her bedroom. She lay down fully dressed and thought of the evening, the cuisine, and the conversation. Tristan, despite his fan club had always been sweet. And despite all the accolades that a storied basketball career had bestowed upon him Tristan had somehow managed to remain both sweet and humble. His laid back demeanor was all the more attractive now that she'd had a chance to bathe in the hot lights of Atlanta and New York. Now that she'd come full circle and returned to her roots she needed nothing more than an unassuming man who she could relax on the front

133

porch with under the warm moonlight and share her inner most thoughts and dreams with. And from all accounts Tristan was that man. Sure Alex had money but then what man had she known that didn't. And there was no doubt that Alex treated her like a queen but there were just far too many skeletons in the closet for her. No, Tristan's life was a simple life. There were no allegations to underworld ties or killings. There were no rumors of drug trafficking. There was no need for bodyguards posing as butlers with criminal pasts. No, there was nothing criminal or complicated. Life was simple here. A lumberyard worth millions, a few contracts that kept him afloat and the will and determination that only spelled success in her eyes. The only thing missing was a strong woman to support him and keep him from the sharks that refused to see a Black man prosper even as of this late date in this little old redneck outpost known as Elizabethtown.

A knock brought her back from her daydreams, and even as tired as she was her excitement over the evening refused to let her sleep. She answered it reluctantly. The mood of the evening still upon her she answered reluctantly.

"It's me Sill. Can I just have a minute of your time?"

Cracking the door she answered.

"A minute and no more Alex. I really don't have time for drama in my life. All I'm looking for is a little peace. Elizabethtown affords me that. Please don't bring me the drama."

"No drama baby. I just want you to know that I love you. I didn't mean to get angry baby but I was worried. I don't know Tristan other than your mother recommended him to do some work for me. But I don't know him to trust him with you and if anything had happened to you I don't know what I would have done."

"That's one of the problems and why we aren't together any longer. It's just that reason. I'm afraid I don't know what you would have done either."

"Don't tell me you still believe I had something to do with those two young boys that got killed up in Harlem? I've told you I didn't have anything to do with that. I even went back and confronted Abdul and he gave me his word that he didn't know or have any involvement with that incident whatsoever. What more do you want me to say? What more can I possibly do? I've done everything you've asked and still you treat me like you don't know me."

"Listen Alex. I'm bushed. I had a long ride and perhaps a little too much to drink and I'm beat. Can't this wait until tomorrow."

"No, Sill it can't wait. In case you haven't noticed I'm crazy about you. I've searched high and low and taken the better part of a year just to find you. I haven't been able to eat, sleep or do damn near anything half way productive because my every thought was you and all I get is a cold shoulder and kicked to the curb when I finally find you. Do I really deserve this?"

"Alex, I'm truly sorry you feel the way you do. It's not in my makeup to hurt anyone and especially you. I was new to New York and you made me feel at home in a city that has a reputation for being cold. You took me under your wing and made me feel right at home. I appreciate it but in all truthfulness I have little or no faith in men. Believe me I've been hurt enough not to want to ever hurt you or anyone ever. I just want to find some peace of mind and although I enjoyed you and my stay in New York I just feel it's time for me to slow down, settle down and get back to my roots. Whether you believe it or not I enjoy the long quiet days and even longer quieter North Carolina nights. This life really suits me Alex."

"And as long as you're a part of my life it suits me as well, Sill. That's what I think you're missing."

"Alex, I think you're missing the point. I grew up here. I'm a 'lil country girl and no matter how far I stray that's what I will always be."

"I can adjust, Sill baby. In fact, I already have. Baby, I've been a New Yorker all my life. Been down with the hustle and bustle 'til I'm plumb worn out. And I've come to love it here with you and your mom. I really do. It's something I've never known, something I always believed was nothing more than something in a fairy tale but being here with you has made me believe that this dream could be a reality."

"I'm sorry you eel that way Alex. I didn't mean to hurt you if I did. I guess I have a bit o a confession to make but you see I came to New York because I was running from a past that was so full of hurt and pain that I swore never to fall in love or fall privy to another man in my life. And I must admit I was doing fairly well and rather enjoyed my lifestyle until you happened along. When you came along I fell like I so often do to not only you but to everything you represented. You were the bright lights and the big city. You were like a whole new world. You were all the things a girl dreams of. You were my knight in shining armor. You were handsome, rich and debonair. Then just like that I realized you were human. And all that glitters is not gold."

"All you have to do is change your perspective. And all those dreams of knights and fairy tales can be true. You know there's nothing in this world I wouldn't do for you Sill. But instead of taking me as I am and letting me shower you with my love you'd rather test the waters and fuck with my feelings."

Hearing Alex curse caught Sylvia off guard and she drew back up a bit. Gathering her wits she reclined. After a minute she spoke.

136

"Baby, you can have any woman in New York. Why do you want to settle for a lil' ol' country girl like me.

Hearing the words Alex looked deep into the dark recesses of Sill's eyes hoping to garner some clue to the sudden change of heart from the charming yet coy young woman he'd had the occasion to meet in New York less than a year before. Searching desperately, he was still clueless.

"But baby," he started before she rudely cut him off. Not sure if it was the Crys-Tal or the fact that she was tired of pacifying his feeble attempts at wooing her or just the fact that she was simply tired of men playing and trying to pacify her just so they could get into her pants. Alex was no different just trying to make the pussy permanent. And she wasn't having it.

"Alex, I don't know what to say other than to stop wasting your time. No matter what you do all your hopes and dreams are falling on deaf ears. I don't know how plain I can make it but on the real I'm not interested."

"You can't mean that, Sill," he said a tear rolling from the corner of his eye.

"I've said it with all the possible tact I can muster."

"But Sill…"

Again she cut him off. Tired and weary of the conversation, her patience gone she had no intentions of hurting him but if it was one thing she detested it was a groveling man.

"If you haven't noticed I'm in a relationship with Tristan," she lied hoping it would eliminate any further debate.

The look in Alex's eyes let her know her premonitions were correct. He stared at her and she was sure she had never seen such utter anger and contempt in his eyes or anyone else's eyes for that matter. He was livid; his eyes burned blood red and were piercing. Sylvia was shook. Panic ran through her and from the look on his face she thought of the two teens killed in Harlem on that fateful day and the thought that he'd been part of it came rushing back to her.

He glared at her once more before turning briskly and walking away.

Moments later a car pulled up outside and after addressing an envelope stuffed with something and placing it on the living room table he turned glared at Sylvia once more before exiting the tiny house slamming the door behind him.

Sill knew he was upset when he didn't say bye to Mama but just didn't know how angry. Men in his position seldom took losses whether it be in business or their personal lives. It didn't take a rocket scientist to know that and Sylvia was sure from the look in his eyes that there were sure to be repercussions. She didn't know how or in what form it would come but she was sure there would be hell to pay. And there was no doubt mommy would be upset but hey she had to do what she had to do and she was tired of him pushing up on him trying to get where she knew he'd never get to without some kind of minor miracle.

The next morning Sill woke to the shrill cries of Christopher. Glancing at her cell she noticed it was close to ten o'clock and the baby was soaking wet, his face flushed and red from crying. Scooping him up she placed him in his bassinet after warming a bottle on the stove and getting the tiny tot a fresh change of clothes. 'Where was mommy?' She thought aloud before seeing the note on the kitchen table stating that she had some errands to run. The baby's cries grabbed her attention and she had to admit that as much as she loved being a mother, her mother was certainly a godsend. She never awoke to her son's cries because mommy made it her job to get the baby up feed him, and bathe him before Sylvia had even gotten up. Before she could gather her thoughts, bathe, change and feed the baby her

138

thoughts digressed to the previous night and the look in Alex's eyes. The thought chilled her to the bone. Quickly she changed her thoughts since there was little she could do now. Besides he'd be a fool to do something stupid and risk his growing empire. Especially over a woman when he could have his pick of the litter.

The days and weeks passed quietly enough and though mommy was at first annoyed at her daughter for letting Alexis get away she seemed to forget over time and even the mention of his name

Became all but moot within a month. Sill, still remembered the look in his eyes but even that memory faded with time. And just as soon as it had all begun everything was back to normal. All thoughts of returning to New York had all but faded and the dreams of opening a tutorial program were all but gone as well. Tristan visited occasionally but was across the street everyday either unloading timber or clearing some parcel of daddy's land. And mommy still seeking a son-in-law in earnest made sure that if she couldn't have Alex then Tristan would most certainly do as an adequate replacement. The monstrosity that had Sill puzzled for so long was finally taking shape. And Sill was finally able to make sense out of it but Lord knows if it was a house it was the largest house she'd ever seen rivaling the Biltmore and the mansions in Southampton she had had the occasion of visiting when in Alex's company. It had no place in some backwoods southern hick town such as Elizabethtown. That was Alex and mommy and mommy certainly did deserve this and more but there was no way in the world mommy could have possibly afforded this. Not even a wing on this house. And despite her angering him and sending him packing he had continued to build. No, this was all Alex's doing. Well, mommy was in collusion, mysteriously receiving not only a new Blackberry already activated but whenever that phone rang the older Mrs. Stanton always seemed to need secrecy. At first, Sill thought that her mom was trying to cover for some mystery man. But when she would go directly to the construction site across the street after each phone call and speak to the foreman Sill knew the calls were from Alex.

So, he wasn't out of the picture but he wasn't certainly out of her life. Every now and then Sill, just out of curiosity, would stroll across the street and take a peek and see how progress was coming. Despite how she felt she had to admit the estate was simply gorgeous. Now in it's final stages, she counted thirteen bedrooms, seven baths and countless other amenities that were hardly necessary for a woman of mama's age. It was beautiful. Sill only hoped that Alex's building her mother a home would not serve as another reason for his sporadic visits but then he and mommy had culminated a relationship of sorts during there time together.

Sylvia crossed the street and spoke to Tristan briefly. She had become more fond of him and his unassuming ways as time passed and was surprised that he hadn't made it a point to push up on her after her comments on the ride back from dinner several weeks ago. The mere fact that he hadn't triggered her interest more than a little bit. Several times she caught herself staring at him from a cracked blind in her bedroom window. He still maintained his good looks even in a pair of Levi's and Timberland. And when her nature rose on several occasions and mommy had to run and errand or do some grocery shopping she'd pull up that ol' Queen Anne chair daddy loved so much, lock her bedroom door and grab the KY jelly and masturbate until she'd come two or three times. At other times, when he wasn't around she'd simply wander over and pick up a few tid bits on Tristan from one or more of his workers on what he did on his time off. But more often than not she'd return home knowing no more than when she started out. It was all always the same.

"Ma'm I wish I knew. Every now and then he goes bowling with us if we're short a man but for the most part this is his social life. All the man does is work. Guess he just hasn't found anything other than this to float his boat. A few years ago it was doing everything in the world to make sure his mother had everything in the world she could ever dream of. His mother couldn't have asked for a better son but since her passing he does little more than work."

Although pleased to hear this, Sill was convinced that there was some woman somewhere fulfilling his needs. After all, there wasn't a man in the world that could easily accept rejection from the likes of her and walk away. Leastways none she'd run into. Well, that was up until now so there just naturally had to be a reason. And the most likely reason was another woman even if his workers said he didn't. But then again men had a way of covering for each other and why would they tell her anyway. After all, if one of them had an opportunity to hit it then they could all share in the glory vicariously. That's just the men were. Unlike women who tended to be more like crabs in a barrel and would do anything to stand in the way of progress if it wasn't their own. Still, the more in the dark Sill stood the more she was curious as to what made Tristan tick. As the days and months went on and she bought things for mommy's old home, the home which had always had plenty of space for she and mommy and daddy her mother bought this and that with the intentions of surprising her daughter with Alex's gift to her and her own decorative taste in furniture and the like.

Sylvia had a full awareness of what she intended for the home she'd grown up in but made no haste to unleash her intentions afraid that it would offend her mother and thought not of hastening her to move out of a house she'd resided in her last fifty years. When she finally had the nerve to make mention of the move she was met with quite a surprise.

"Baby, Alex had that house built for you as a wedding gift for you. I'm quite happy right here in this old house. A couple of more years and I'll have it just where I want it," she chuckled softly. "I was hoping to have you in there by the end of the week."

"You're not serious mommy," was all Sylvia could muster so stunned was she.

"Tristan, has been basically supervising all the construction and says it's ready now except for a few minor details and he and I completed the walk through yesterday. Do you know it's the largest estate in Bladen County? I told Alex that you hardly needed something of that size and that we were a simple people but he insisted and when I didn't approve of the blueprint saying that it was much too large he made Tristan his acting foreman. I thought it a mistake but he and Tristan worked out some kind of agreement where he got the contract even though he's never actually taken on a project of this size before. Matter-of-fact, I believe this is the first home he's ever built from the ground up but somehow he reassured Alex that he was capable and I do believe there was some added stipulation. But I think it's just what Tristan needs to pursue his career as an architect and get him into A & T's School of Engineering. If you ask me Alex made Tristan give his word that he would resist pursuing you if he wanted the contract and his help in getting accepted into school. You know one of those gentleman's agreements."

So that was it. It all made sense now. And here she was thinking that Tristan was seeing another woman. And mommy was seldom wrong, especially about things that affected her family. Why that bastard. At first, Sylvia was angry at being the underlying motive in a business deal. What made matters worse was that Alex had

142

not only disregarded her wishes to be left alone but was now using his power and money to affect her social life. To make matters worse, sorry ass Tristan who had pretended to show so much interest had dumped her again; only this time it was worse. This time he'd dumped her not for love but for money and a chance at advancement. And if there was one thing she was sure of it was that she was worth so much more than a contract no matter how much it was worth and a few strings pulled here and there. Not to be outdone she was moved in and settled by the end of the week and between she and mommy had the estate partially furnished, well comfortable enough anyway for her to set up residency. From all appearances it seemed Alex had disregarded everything Sylvia had said and was sending the older Mrs. Stanton a check a week for furnishings. Sylvia was angry although she refused to let her mother see. How dare that man simply override her wishes? Who was he anyway to just disregard her wants, needs, and desires to fulfill his own shallow superficial needs? All she was to him was this week's toy, this week's plaything, only to be cast aside when he grew bored with her. The fact of the matter however was that Sylvia Stanton had never been and would never be his or anyone's plaything. She had been used and abused by men more than once in her life and she'd be damned if she'd ever let it happen again. Oh no! She had a plan where he'd feel her wrath and know that he wasn't just another beautiful body devoid of a brain. And as far as Tristan went she had a thing or two for him as well.

She loved her new home, which was estimated to be in the neighborhood of twenty-two or twenty-three million but could do nothing to sway her mother to join her in it. Instead she opted to stay in the old house her now deceased husband had built for her and their child so many years before. So, at mommy's request she kept the baby. Never being a morning person, Sill hardly argued with her mother's request. A month later she was nicely settled in. There were fewer and fewer workers milling around nowadays although Tristan made sure he made his daily rounds to fix all the minor repairs and Sill made it a point to look her sexiest often times sunbathing in her skimpiest bikinis by the side of the pool when he was due to arrive. The conversation slowly began picking up as the days passed.

"You know you're the first so called man that has actually shied away from me when I told him that I wasn't interested in pursuing a relationship. The rejection usually just spurs them to pursue even harder. But then you always were a different breed."

Tristan smiled cordially.

"Guess, I am. I usually take what people say at face value and if they tell me they don't want to be bothered then I don't bother them. I understand people needing their space. I'm one of those people," he said smiling again before walking off.

Seething now, Sylvia watched as Tristan checked the gutters and drainpipes before jumping in Ford truck and roared off down the highway.

'Well, if that don't top all,' she remarked to no one in particular now more adamant than ever that she'd have him begging by the end of the week. It was already Tuesday and she knew she didn't have that much time. But her mind was made up. She wasn't all that interested in Tristan but his sudden disdain had made him all that more appealing and the simple fact that a slight warning and a promise of a business promotion had caused him to spurn her made him all the more delectable in her eyes.

"Will just see if he collects any of the accolades from Alex. They'll both lose if I have my way and when is it that I haven't gotten my way?" Sill said to herself smiling.

Wednesday and Thursday she was more than a little friendly when Tristan stopped by to do his daily check and she had to wonder if these routine checks were a check on the house or had Alex put him up to checking on her. In any case, he always seemed to find something to do, whether it was the molding or some tiles in some of the bathrooms. He always found something to do.

"What are you doing for dinner on Friday night Tristan?"

"Didn't have any plans."

"So, why have dinner with me. Some say I'm a fairly good cook," she said giving him her best imitation of Mae West.

"Let me check my schedule and I'll get back to you Sill."

"That's fine," Sylvia said wondering what the hell could anyone have on their schedule in this little one horse town. You ain't in the NBA anymore asshole. Ain't nothing here but free time. Sylvia hated to admit it but she was totally dejected and frustrated by his being so nonchalant and assuming about the whole state of affairs. Any other single man would have jumped at the opportunity or even the possibility of being with her for an evening and this asshole had the nerve to check his schedule. His attitude nevertheless had a converse affect on her. Oh yes, she was not only determined to have him but she was gonna turn him out. Have him at her beck and call. His refusal this time would be his last. So, with painstaking patience she spent the better part of Thursday evening planning and plotting on just how to awaken Tristan's dulled senses so he'd wake up and smell the coffee. With a great deal of restraint Sill made sure that she wasn't visible when he went stopped by and went about his daily routine. The new house, however, gave her a closer and better view of Tristan's movement than she had from peeking from behind the blinds across the road. And his rejection of her only turned her on more. She let her skirt

145

drop to her feet and began touching herself lightly before forcing herself to stop. No, she wanted to be on her best behavior and ready when he approached her tomorrow night but then again knowing his slow ass he'd probably never get around to seducing her. Still, there was the remotest of possibilities and that was all it took to pull her skirt back up despite craving her daily orgasm. She made it a point not to see him, not to interact, and when he rang the doorbell she made it a point to ignore it. She wasn't giving him any room to back out.

Friday arrived with all the swiftness of hurricane waters and Sylvia making sure not to defer to mommy for any help lest she'd be have to worry about having mommy spending the day not only giving her advice on how to prepare the meal but also advice on how to get and keep a man. And being that those weren't her intentions and didn't want to nor could explain her intentions or motivations to her mother she'd just as soon leave her alone.

Around three o'clock a knock came at her back door. It was no other than Tristan smiling graciously.

"You never did give me a time for dinner."

"What time do you get finished?"

"Don't know that I ever get finished."

"You really love your work, don't you?"

"That I do. Gives me a reason for living. Don't know what I'd do if I didn't have it. I really don't know what I'd do without. I don't know how people feel constructive without…" he stopped suddenly knowing she wasn't employed and not wanting to step on Sill's toes already having felt her wrath on several occasions.

Sill smiled.

"I do understand. You don't have to cut your thought short. I felt like that for longer than you'll know. Guess I just burned out dealing with the bureaucracy but I still have all intentions of pursuing my dreams."

"Maybe we can talk about that over dinner tonight."

"Maybe but I don't think my dreams are the most interesting of subjects. I'm sure after twenty years we can think of a lot more interesting topics to discuss and do."

"We'll see. My last job should be finished around seven, seven-thirty. How's eight-thirty sound?"

"That's fine. I'll see you then," Sill said smiling and blushing deeply.

The day proceeded at breakneck speed. Sill all of a sudden had so much to do and so little time. She'd already gotten a French manicure and had her hair done. Only thing left was to pick her dress up from the cleaners bathe and put the food in the oven. Still she didn't feel at ease. For the first time in her life, she was going to combat those that plagued her that ailed her. She was going to feed her needs at the expense of someone who never ever had her best interest at heart but had given her up at the first chance for him to prosper. Now she was going to do this. She was adamant about it. She put the food in the oven at about eight knowing that he'd be there any minute. But she wanted time to talk, to flirt, to once again reacquaint themselves. A short time later, she adjusted the tight black mini skirt, threw on the black six-inch heels, touched up her lipstick, and reapplied her mascara before heading for the door. It was obvious she'd been through the routine several times before but this time was different. Usually some brother was coming for all intensive purposes to see how good his game was. To see how much game he had and how much he needed to seduce the very intelligent, very beautiful Sylvia Stanton. Now as she opened the front door the shoe was on the other foot.

"Tristan…"

"Hey Sill, just a little housewarming gift," he said handing her a bouquet of long stemmed red roses.

"I can think of some other ways of warming the house," she said smiling regretting the words as soon as they left her lips. She knew what she wanted and knew how badly she needed it but she had to be cool. Receptive yes but not too forthright and play it cool she told herself before kissing him lightly on the cheek.

He smiled before breaking into laughter.

"Did I miss something?" she asked unnerved by the sudden laughter and her own faus paux.

"No, I just thought about how I caught myself the other day when I said how I'd die without working and caught myself because I thought I may have somehow offended you. Now looking at all of this," he said still smiling and looking around the room, "I think you've worked enough for the both of us. Not trying to insinuate anything and don't know what field you were in or anything but you seem to have done quite well for yourself."

"I guess I did alright," she said wondering if there were a double entendre or he was being sincere. In any case, whether he meant it in a bad way or not didn't matter. Before the night was over she'd have him eating out of her hand.

Sylvia grabbed him by the hand, leading him over to the sofa and sat beside him.

"Thought we might chat for a few and clear up any questions and misconceptions you may have about where I've been and what I've been doing. Then you won't tend to assume things and insinuate things like you just did," Sylvia smiled this time not regretting a word from her mouth.

"And what does that mean?"

"Nothing Tristan. Nothing."

"If I said something to offend you I apologize. That wasn't my intention."

"I'm sure you didn't. I just wanted to set the record straight. And since we're being honest, I have to admit you look quite handsome tonight."

"You ain't doing too bad yourself," he said smiling glancing the long slit that veiled the long chocolate thigh.

Sylvia crossed her legs purposely hoping to have just this effect on the gentleman sitting so close to her. And then leaning over placing one hand on his thigh she used her free hand to grab the back of his head pulling him closer and kissed him passionately. Resistant at first, he soon fell quickly into her clutches returning the kiss and feeling a feeling he hadn't known since he was a child he responded in kind. Still, he was reluctant.

Sylvia feeling his eagerness was careful not to give him too much. After all, her only intent was to tease him, to tantalize, to arouse that which had laid dormant for far too long. Seemingly having done this she broke the kiss off suddenly and excused herself.

"Oh, Tristan, let me check the steaks. I almost forgot. Don't know where my mind is."

"I'm not sure either but I'd certainly wish you'd go back to wherever it was," he said smiling. Sylvia ignored the remark and headed for the kitchen. Moments later she returned; a glass of red wine in each hand.

"Sorry 'bout that. Now where were we?" She said smiling coyly.

Tristan stood taking both glasses of wine from her hands and placing on the living room table then pulling her towards him.

"Dinner will be ready in a minute."

"I'm all for skipping all the appetizers and heading straight for the main course."

"And what might that be?"

"Hopefully it's you," Tristan said smiling as he pulled her close to him. Sylvia not as receptive this time pushed him away.

"What makes you think your desires are mine?"

"Oh," he said suddenly taken back a bit.

"Didn't we just talk about assuming?"

"You're right. I stand corrected. So what is it that I can I do for you?"

Sylvia smiled pulling him close again. He drew close touching her lightly on her chin raising it slightly to kiss her but she turned her head.

"We're not dancing so there's no need for you to lead." She said before placing her hands on his shoulders and pushing him to his knees. Understanding now he knelt before her. She lifted her dress and pulled his head to her and spread the lips of her vagina with her free hand. Glancing up at her briefly she was more forceful this time pulling him to her.

"You said you were looking for an appetizer?"

He did not respond, could not respond as she forced his lips to meet hers. Almost as if on cue his tongue darted in and out of her now moist pussy.

"Ummm," she moaned in response to his quick thrusts. She wondered if he could tell just how wet and moist, and how much she missed the soft kisses. She absolutely loved the attention given to her now and knew that it wasn't the fact that it was Tristan. It was the idea of having a man fall to his knees while she lorded over him while he catered to her every freakish whim that turned her on so. They'd all do it at her request but then that had never been a problem. The problem was they thought she should reciprocate. And the ones that didn't think that thought they

150

should shower her with gifts and other goodies in appreciation. And perhaps they should have but that was no longer what she wanted from a man. She didn't need a man. She didn't need a man, nor his time or his money. Correct that. What she did need was a little bit of his time. She needed just enough of his time that he could work her stuff, leave her sore until she needed another dose and then be on his way. And that was Tristan's purpose tonight. Oh, there was little doubt that it felt good as he stuck his tongue in and out of her now soaked vagina but she refused to think of how good it felt for fear of coming and when she was on the verge, on the very brink of letting and shuddering and sputtering to a thunderous orgasm, she grabbed his head within her hands and held there. No, Tristan. It wasn't gonna be that easy. He'd have to work to get her to orgasm tonight. He seemed willing. And an hour and a half later he was still jabbing his tongue in her now dry vagina, salivating to keep it moist as he did so. On the edge of that same orgasm she pushed his head away again.

"Now I want you to lick and suck on my clit, Tistan."

Replacing his head she forced his head deep into her pussy while he sucked and gasped for breaths. Didn't matter if he could breathe as long as he steadily lapped at her ever-protruding clit. Humping his face now she could it rising and still she was not ready. Pushing him away once again she turned, her ass in his face now and bent over.

"I want you to lick and fuck my ass with your tongue while you massage my clit, lover."

Doing as he was told, she felt the impending orgasm mounting. She was ready now and as his fingers worked in unison stroking steadily in and out of her vagina so did his mouth accompanying and sucking on her clit, his tongue deep in her ass. Sill felt

151

herself coming now and as her back arched she turned grabbing his head and thrust her clit into his mouth.

"Suck it bitch." She screamed. "Is this what you wanted? Take this shit. Drown in my come bitch."

Tristan was shocked but did as he was told.

"Suck it motherfucker," she shouted as she came over and over again.

Sylvia looked down at Tristan who seemed content to continue to stick his tongue in an d out of her now throbbing pussy and she had to admit she was almost willing to let him bring her to another rousing orgasm but with a good deal of trepidation she refrained. No, she would much rather have just a taste and keep him at bay and come collecting when she was in need. She was convinced that she didn't need a man, a relationship, just a man that was equipped to quell her needs when she was tired of doing herself. They were all equipped but only a few she'd come across could actually move her. And despite her attitude Tristan could. Still, she could think of no other purpose for him other than doing what he was doing. Still, he was convenient and most of all he was safe. His business kept him more than a little occupied so she knew she wouldn't have to worry about him bugging her constantly. Pulling her dress down and wiping the beads of sweat from her top lip she looked down at Tristan who remained on his knees wondering if she was finished or if she had other demons she needed to have exorcised. Seeing that she appeared to be gathering herself he stood up.

Neither said a word when they heard a car start up in the driveway. Looking at each other Sill made her way to the front window. She prayed mommy hadn't been her nosy self as she hadn't purchased curtains for the front windows and everything that happened in the living room was easily observable from the driveway. She hated to

152

think what mommy had seen and wondered how in the hell she'd explain this one. Tristan who was still fully dressed was equally if not more embarrassed made his way to the front door.

"Think I can get a rain check on the main course?" Tristan said smiling. It was late and if he had any plans for his future with Sylvia he knew all roads ran through the elderly Mrs. Stanton and there was no way she'd approve of him coming from her daughter's home at ten or eleven o'clock at night. She was respectable, church going woman and he knew from his own mother God bless her soul that no respectable single women entertained any churchgoing man past nine o'clock at night. That's just the way it was and though he loved Elizabethtown and that old southern tradition there were time such as these when he thought it time the South caught up with the world instead of being mired in the past.

Stepping through the door, he was relieved to find that it wasn't Mrs. Stanton at all. And then his heart stopped as the long black limousine slowly backed out of the driveway. He could barely see the occupants but recognized Thomas chauffeur's cap and realized that it was no other than his current employer, Alexander DuMont. Sylvia must have realized who the occupants of the car were at the same time because both stood fixed in place as if they'd both just seen ghosts.

Tristan's concern was more practical. He thought about the agreement he had with Alex. He was supposed to watch Sylvia but only from a distance and report back to Alex on any unusual findings in exchange for Alex letting him put some of his architectural designs in place on one of the largest most expensive houses in that part of the state. He'd gladly accepted knowing what Alex really wanted and that was for him to steer clear of Sill and he'd accomplished that—well—for the most part except for tonight. Alex had held serve when it came to his part of the deal. Paying Tristan

153

more than his business was worth to design and oversee construction of the home all Tristan had to do was stay clear of Sylvia. Tristan knew there'd be a price to pay but had no idea what it was. He'd been paid in full. The monies already deposited but with a man like Alex DuMont there were so many ways he could make you pay for your indiscretions and Tristan knew that none of them were good.

Sylvia had similar thoughts as she watched he long black limo back out of the driveway and head down the highway. She'd broken all ties but still she was in his house and not only was she in his home, she'd been caught making love in plain view. And there was no doubt he'd seen her. If he hadn't there's no doubt he would have come in. Again Sylvia thought of the two teens that had been killed in New York. She'd never really believed that Alex didn't have something to do wit the murders and the thought loomed large in her mind as she thought of him now.

Chapter 11

There was no word from Alex and Sylvia began to seriously believe that the last episode probably did more than anything else Sylvia could have possibly done to dissuade Alex. Nevertheless she didn't take pride in the way he'd been dismissed. Still, she was glad it was over. Mommy made her feel even better when she admitted that she hadn't heard from him either. Tristan received his last payment from Alex on time so all seemed well. Sylvia met with Tristan on several occasions over the next couple of weeks but he not feeling all that comfortable at Sylvia's home not so much because of Alex but more so because he had no desire for Mrs. Stanton to find out and lose respect for him. After all, she was one of the elders and very well respected in the community. A negative word from her and it could go along way in hurting not only his business but also his reputation. So, at his insistence he agreed to meet Sylvia but only if she agreed to come to his house. And since he was catering to her every need that was the least she could do if she wanted her needs met. And from what Tristan could gather, Sylvia having an insatiable appetite when it came to sex could hardly refuse. Still, she'd done nothing to soothe either his needs or desires and hardly seemed interested in doing so. Truth of the matter was she didn't seem to be all that interested in anything he had to offer other than the fact that he was—well—rather proficient at satisfying her cravings. Her means of achieving an orgasm were rather different to say the least. Well at least they were to him. Not once did she seem interested in making love or any of the things he had grown accustomed to from the women he'd come to know. No, she was simply interested in her own gratification and her gratification seemed to only come when his mouth was attached to her vagina and he had a couple of his fingers

155

up her ass. Truth be told he didn't mind her freakiness or fetishes or the fact that she didn't seem interested in reciprocating. He was sure she would in time. He simply figured that she'd been so accustomed to catering to the needs of her male partners that she'd grown bitter and calloused and was now turning the tables. He was sure that he wasn't the one she had issues with and was cognizant of her past and the fact that she'd been raped during her college days and had spent time in an institution but he continued to remain patient. She was after all essentially the same shy, little schoolgirl he'd met as a junior in high school and to his way of thinking the only woman he'd ever truly loved. So, he would show patience. He could wait it out until she trusted him, until she figured out that he wasn't the same as all the rest of the men out there who were simply interested in seeing what and how far they could go with her. Then when they'd had their fill they'd drop her and keep on moving. Now she'd had a baby in her search for love. But Tristan believed himself to be different and so he continued to kneel down and submit to Sylvia's demands on those days when she needed to release her demons and exercise her passions before him. In his heart and soul though he believed that she would eventually see the light, see that he was somehow different from those that she'd known before and come to appreciate him as someone genuine with no hidden agendas or underhanded motives.

Sylvia, on the other hand, had grown less communicative and truly believed that Tristan had finally come to acknowledge his role in her life, had come to accept it and from all the fervor and enthusiasm he exhibited in bringing her to multiple orgasms accepted it. Each tryst ended with her downing what was left of the bottle of Merlot he'd begun buying for her weekly visits. This evening was somehow different and though he understood her plight, he was still somewhat perplexed as to why she didn't ever mention the two of them consummating their relationship. This was becoming an increasing concern with Tristan. And for some reason the Merlot would not let him mask his growing displeasure.

"Perhaps you don't recognize or maybe you just don't care Sill, but you've been coming to see me for the better part of a month now and has it ever once occurred to you that I haven't even gone as far as kissing me since our first night together?"

Sylvia had been expecting this conversation for some time now. Still, she wasn't ready when it came. She was glad she'd come at least four times though when he stopped.

No longer did she push him away always allowing him to continue until he was exhausted. But recently he'd begun stopping well short of where she wanted to go. Was he getting tired she wondered. Lord knows he should have been. She was working his ass to death and wasn't giving up shit. Yet, if he was fool enough to go along with the script who was she to make adjustments. But she knew it was only a matter of time before the question would arise as to when and why she hadn't reciprocated or even thought about his needs and wants.

"Tristan, I'm afraid if I answer honestly you'll both lose respect for me and end up hating me at the same time."

"They say the truth will set you free."

"Truth of the matter is I'm worn out Tristan. Men have worn me out. Physically and mentally... I haven't been in a lot of relationships; not that I think you have to be in more than one or two. It just depends on the depth and gravity of the relationship and I have always been one to give a hundred per cent."

"I believe that about you too, Sill. That's why it's so hard for me to believe that you haven't made a move to love me as much as I love you and I'm not just talking in a physical sense."

"I hear you."

"I'm not interested in you in a physical sense. No, wait. Let me rephrase that. Lord knows that didn't come out correctly. You don't know how much I use to fantasize about having you in a purely physical way when we were kids. Thank God I've grown up some since then. That's not to say I still don't fantasize about you at times but I think at this point in my life…"

"I would have thought at this point in your life that you would have had your fill being that you had the chance to travel the world over."

"Don't stroke me Sill. I've been in love with you ever since we were kids. I kind of figured that you'd been through the war. I've kept tabs on you, you know. I heard what happened to you at A&T and hurt and cried right along with you. I was there when you got married and followed you as far as Atlanta when I lost touch because momma was sick. And through it all I've had all I could do to not just track you down, wrap my arms around you and bring you back home. But your mother told me to have patience. She told me you'd be back when you'd had enough. And I guess she was right. Now I'm on my knees paying homage to you because in some small way I figure it's my responsibility to make right all the wrongs that have been cast your way. But to be honest Sill, I have no idea where your head is at."

"That makes two of us," Sill replied. "I guess I'm pretty much content to just continue the way things are. I guess I'm pretty much like everybody else. I have my needs but they're nothing out of the realm of possibilities. I'm comfortable—you know—financially. I don't really want to be involved in a relationship. That's just not where I am in my life."

"Where are you in your life, Sill."

"To be honest, Tristan, I just don't know. I guess like a lot of women in this society I was taught to be subservient to my man and support him in his efforts but I've done that and was good at it but it left me with a void. Made me feel like I was selling myself short by not realizing and fulfilling my own potential, and my own dreams. And no matter how much I gave, and believe me I'm not the least bit bitter, those men were better off for having known me. But I don't feel like my efforts were really appreciated and I ended up neglecting myself. So, now I'm kinda adamant about making up for lost time and realizing some of my own dreams. Do you feel me?"

"I do," Tristan said laughing. "It's funny you say that, Sill but that's one of the reasons I'm not married. Never met a woman solely interested in being independent. They never seem to want to do anything other than wanting to hang on my coattails. And you know as well as I do that we can both do bad by ourselves and we can reach the heavens with no help so I guess I understand you a little better than you may think I do. I don't have any problem with your thought process. Seems logical. I just don't understand why you feel confident to strip naked in front of me and yet you can't talk to me, confide in me."

"Like my daddy used to say, 'all things in time'," Sylvia replied grabbing her jacket and heading for the door.

"Will I hear from you," Tristan asked.

"First thing in the morning. And believe me Tristan I heard you. I'm not blowing you off. Just trying to get home. Mommy's had the baby all day and I know she's probably wondering where I am."

"I look forward to it baby. Got a couple of appointments in the a.m. Give me a call around lunch time or better yet why don't you meet for lunch."

"Sounds good. Why don't I meet you at Applebee's on McPherson Church at around noon?"

"Okay but my treat," Sill stated a little embarrassed surrounding Tristan's sudden revelation concerning her intentions.

"If you say so, m'love." Tristan said grinning broadly. "Maybe we can finish this conversation and I can finally get a handle on what it takes to get to the heart of Sylvia Stanton."

"My heart," Sylvia said laughing out loud now, "When you find out you let me know. Cause far as I know it's been turned off and shut down for as far as long as I can remember. Lord knows I wish I could revive it but I've tried and it looks like chances for that happening are somewhere between slim and none."

"You know a few weeks ago when you invited me to dinner I truly believed I could become the special person in your life."

Sylvia smiled.

"Trust me I'm not so cold that I didn't notice. I just can't let it affect me. I've been down this road so many times and no matter how much I want it to have the kind of storybook ending mommy used to read to me when I was a little girl it just never seems to work out that way."

"Doesn't mean you stop trying or give up hope. You're not the only one who's been through the war Sylvia. I think Sade had me in mind when she wrote Soldier of

160

Love. It's hard to believe she could have had anybody else in mind. I mean I have truly been through it. And countless times too. It's like I had an "x" marked on my back. Seems every woman I sought took my kindness for weakness and I actually came to despise women for a while. I really did."

Smiling again, Tristan looked at her suspiciously.

"You're smiling?"

"I'm not laughing at you by any means. It just seems like we led parallel lives."

"I'm serious. I had had my fill of the opposite sex. It got to be so bad that I eventually moved back to this booming metropolis," he laughed. "And you're still smiling."

"I'm smiling because those are the same reasons I came back. I came back to get away from all the drama."

"I can imagine. I spent about three months in New York and damn near lost my mind."

"It wasn't New York. It was people. I loved New York. It's one of the few places I could actually go that didn't have that small town mentality. I could actually lose myself but you know me. Always finding a way to get involved in something I shouldn't be involved in. I actually did my best to avoid all the bright lights and hoopla."

"That's funny because every time I looked up you were in the gossip pages," he laughed. "I told you I kept abreast of you and your whereabouts."

"I see."

"And you weren't in bad company either."

"That's debatable."

"Well, I have to admit that the only person whose company I saw you in was Mr. DuMont's and I must say that's pretty good company to keep."

"See, there you go assuming again. Mr. DuMont was merely a neighbor."

"I'm neither speculating nor assuming but when someone of his stature and reputation rides down here every other week to see you I would gather that he's more than just simply a neighbor."

"I can't venture to say what his motives are but to me and what I've tried to explain to Mr. DuMont is that we'll never be more than friends. Never."

"You may very well have explained that to Mr. DuMont and I'm not in any way dispelling that that was your intention. But if that was it I can certainly attest to the fact that he didn't get that message. This is or I should say was confidential since I'm about to tell you but Alex made it quite clear to me and in no uncertain terms that I could have the contract for this house if I did one thing and one thing only."

"And what was that?"

"To basically stay away from you."

"Is that right?"

"You know I wouldn't lie to you, Sill."

"And he paid me a tidy sum for me, a novice, to build a house of this magnitude and to better yet stay clear of you. Of course our deal is consummated now and he no longer can hold me to anything."

"Are you for real? And you took the deal?"

"Yes. I took the deal. First, of all, I saw the way in which you and he interacted and it was clear to me that you weren't interested and aside from that if you had to make a choice between his good looks, money and power and me and my country ass I figured you'd choose me so I let him do his thang and try to wine and dine and woo

162

you because I knew you weren't as shallow as he seemed to think you were and that it was only a matter of time before he'd either see the light or give up hope."

"You're a mess. Let me get out of here. Mommy's gonna kill me. She's had the baby all day and… But anyway I'm already late so go ahead. I like your take on things. It's different and refreshing. You know you're on point about a few things but go ahead I'd like to hear your whole take on it."

"There's really nothing else to say. That's about the size of it. My mother always said patience was a virtue and I've spent a large part of my adult life trying to learn it. But Alex's persistence really tested it. There were a few times when I wanted to tell him to take his money and stick it up his ass and get the hell away from the woman I loved but I refrained because I had faith in you and I knew that if you were the woman I believed you to be that you'd let him know in your own time and in your own way and we'd be that much more secure if I just let it play out. Was I right?"

"Possibly. And I must admit that you're pretty perceptive. Well, at least in my regard you are. Money isn't what makes my boat float. And that's not to say that I'm not infatuated by it. It's just the perception of money that he had distorted. He truly believes because he believes that money is the end all whereas I like the idea of acquiring money, not possessing it that lights my fire. I like the idea of making money, acquiring it from nothing. That's what really spurs me on, not the idea of having or hoarding it. He never understood that. Still doesn't. He actually did think he could wine and dine me but I don't think for a minute he was under the impression that he could buy me nor did he attempt to at any point in time. What his money did to him was tell him that he couldn't be denied. I did like that about him though."

"What's that?"

"The idea that persistence overcomes resistance. I like the fact that some people are resilient and believe that with hard work and with a firm constitution anything can be accomplished."

"He believes that?"

"And I as well, in most cases. Just don't believe that that's applicable when it comes to me. And frankly I felt it a little discerning that he thought that I could be had like any of his Wall Street commodities. That's the wrong approach to use with a woman—at least this woman."

"I hear you. So what's the right approach?"

Sylvia winked at Tristan.

"You're on the right track. Listen let's finish this conversation over some Appletini's tomorrow at lunch."

Sylvia returned home to find her mother balancing the baby on one hip and stirring a pot on the stove with the other hand. And though Sylvia was in a cheerful mood, as she thought about Tristan's take on the whole situation and finally being able to clear the air where he was concerned she noticed immediately that her mother was not quite as cheerful. She immediately grabbed the baby. Holding out her arms the baby immediately clutched harder at his grandmother's blouse and let out a scream that made both she and her mother cringe.

"Damn shame when a baby don't wanna go to its own mama," her mother commented reassuring young Christopher as she moved him from one hip to the other in an effort to console him. "Boy, hardly knows his own mama. It's a damn shame," she said in an attempt to comfort the small child.

"That's because you've spoiled him to death," Sylvia said realizing her mother wasn't happy with her early morning exploits.

"Maybe you're right. Spoiled you and look what's become of you. All you think about is yourself and your own happiness," she said grabbing a potholder and taking the chicken from the oven. Here it was a quarter to one in the afternoon and the older woman had already cleaned her house, fed and bathed the small child, and prepared her dinner and Sylvia had yet to begin her day.

"What are your plans for the day young lady?"

"Well, outside of working on the project I really don't have any mommy," she said knowing that mommy had something in mind.

"Might be a good day to start bonding with your son. You know I'm getting older and not going to be around much longer and when I'm dead and gone this little fella's gonna need his mama."

"Oh, mommy you'll probably outlive us all. 'Sides you're too mean and ornery to die. God don't want you coming up there raisin' no hell," Sill said laughing as she hugged her mother giving a big sloppy kiss on the cheek.

"You watch your mouth girl. God don't take kindly to nobody talkin' ill of his children." She said smiling. "Now go on and do whatever it is that you gotta do so you can watch this youngun'. I got a two o'clock meeting down at the church and ain't got no time to be draggin' no babies around."

"Alright mommy. Just let me get cleaned up."

Sylvia had reluctantly moved into the monstrosity of a house across the street but still kept a cache of clothes and other belongings here with mommy letting mommy know that this would always be her home. And it was. No matter how much she decorated the house and Lord knows it was a project in itself the fact remained that

165

when she thought of home her thoughts always reverted back to the little single story red brick house she'd grown up in. It was all she had ever known and all the love she'd ever known emanated from there. She had never experienced the love she found so warm and comforting as she had from her mother and father since she'd left and that had been more than twenty years ago. Yes, she'd found success and money but never the love. Making her way into her bedroom she heard Christopher's cries again and her mother's soothing voice quiet the baby. She smiled. She had to be one of the luckiest people alive. No matter what her mother's cantankerous ways might insinuate she knew that her mother's love was constant and unwavering when it came to her. Sylvia smiled again as she closed the door to her bedroom. She recollected on the move to Elizabethtown and now was glad she'd done it. People were just so much more down to earth. Sure there was the thing with small towns and gossip. After all, what else was there to do? But aside from small town there was just so much less drama. Sylvia turned and layed across the full sized bed. She felt a sudden twinge and smiled again. She was sore and as she let her hand slide between her legs she suddenly became moist, her thoughts suddenly switching to Tristan once more. Closing her eyes she could actually see Tristan kneeling before her. She'd made him disrobe completely today before she would let him touch her. He'd obey just as she knew he would and made him stand before her. She was surprised at how shy he was and reveled at the idea that she could not only make him strip naked at her request but that she commanded the kind of respect that she could make a man and not just any man but this man who she knew desired her strip naked and stand before her. The idea that she had this much power had aroused her and after commanding him to bring her some lubricant made him not only stand before her but also made him bend over and spread his cheeks as

166

she examined his goodies. She immediately became aroused and instead of letting him fall to his knees as was her usual custom Sylvia began massaging herself, slowly, methodically. Tristan upon seeing this grew hard and she was amazed not only at the length but the width of his member. He was certainly more well endowed than any man she'd ever known. When he could no longer stand the sight of her massaging herself, he whispered, 'Sylvia please', barely loud enough for her to hear. Cognizant of his pleas she nevertheless ignored him but found herself coming at the mere sight of his long hard, dick. She suddenly found herself gasping for breath and shuddering hard with each plea he made to let him have her. But if at any time she'd even remotely considered letting him sex her those days were long gone after seeing the enormity of his penis. She couldn't understand why she hadn't thought to realize just how much he was working with. After all, he was more than six five and upwards of three hundred pounds but heaven knows he wouldn't be coming anywhere near her with that thing. Now here she was lying across her bed wishing she'd let him at least try. Sure she'd come several times while commanding him to bend over and to stroke himself while she watched and yes, it had fulfilled quite a few of her long-standing fantasies. Then as she had Tristan assume his usual kneeling position she completely exhausted herself as she ground her pelvis into his mouth and tongue coming repeatedly the spasms gripping her whole body making her go rigid and gasping for breath on several occasions. But that had been then but she was home now and after experiencing a twinge of pain here and there from coming far too much and far too often from Tristan's constant sucking she not only found herself wanting but yearning to feel his member in her again throbbing pussy. As her hand slid parting the lips of her vagina, Sylvia knew that not another day would pass where she would go without knowing the pleasure of a man's penis inside her moist vagina. Locking the door to the bedroom she returned to her bed and with reckless abandon slid three fingers into her soaken pussy. When this wasn't enough she went to her dresser drawer, dug to the bottom and pulled out the huge black vibrator.

When it had first been given to her she thought it a mere novelty gift but now after seeing Tristan first hand she knew that women did use such things in pleasuring themselves. Placing it firmly on the floor she lubricated herself before straddling it and easing down on it. The beads of sweat burst forward on her forehead as she grimaced in pain but after two or three times her wet pussy absorbed every inch of the eleven-inch dick. Riding it she wanted to scream out from sheer pleasure. It was a feeling she'd never known before as the thick black dick filled her completely touching every side of her vaginal walls and at the same time penetrating so deeply that it she felt it push against her ovary with each thrust. She truly wanted to scream out agony but it felt so damn good she took the pain and took it deeper each time she came down on it. On the verge of coming she felt a scream rising from deep within her and then realizing mommy was still in the house she bit her lip drawing a sparkle of crimson. The sweat now broke out on the ridge of her nose as well as her forehead. And then just as suddenly as it had begun it was over. Sylvia lay back exhausted.

"Sill, you in there?"

"Yeah, mommy," she said putting the toy back in its proper place before opening the door.

"You alright baby? You looked flushed. Come here let me feel your head."

Sylvia walked over towards her mother who after placing one hand on her daughter's back and feeling her forehead was immediately alarmed.

168

"Girl you're hot as a firecracker and just as clammy. Lord, it's just like having two babies in the house. Here sit down. Let me get you a cold rag to put on your head. How do you feel baby?"

"I'm fine mommy. Really I am," Sylvia protested.

"You sure baby? Cause I can call Sistah Jasmine and tell her to go ahead. If you're sick you shouldn't be around that baby, you know. Baby's are susceptible to all kinds of germs we adults can fight off but that baby can catch something and liable to wind up in the hospital or worse dead. Their immune systems aren't ready to fight off things we take for granted. Shoot, that baby catches something as simple as the common cold and the next thing you know he's in the hospital with a case of pneumonia. I'm serious, Sill. You can't be too careful. Let me go call this woman now."

"Mommy I'm fine. I just broke out in a cold sweat. It happens from time to time but I'm okay. Really, I am."

"Well, you can't be too careful. Go over to the house and lie down. I'm gonna make you some homemade soup. Just go lie down and call me if you feel any worse or need anything."

Sylvia knew it didn't make any sense to argue with mommy and had to smile at the thought of mommy. She was truly blessed to have such a caring mother. Oh, she fussed a lot but it was mostly just idle chatter. The truth was the woman would do anything for her daughter.

Sylvia kissed Christopher bye as the baby pulled away from her preferring his grandmother and afraid that Sill was going to take him. It was starting to become a pattern with baby Christopher; this rejection of her and Sylvia was starting to become unnerved by the baby's response. Perhaps mommy was right. Maybe she

169

did need to spend more time with him. But it certainly wouldn't be today. Mommy didn't want her anywhere near the baby. Tomorrow, however, would be a different story. She'd take Christopher whether he liked it or not.

Sylvia chuckled lightly to herself as she crossed the road to her palatial estate. The thought that mommy was sending her home because she was sick from coming too much tickled her. The old woman may be knowledgeable about a host of things but when it came down to sex and achieving the ultimate orgasm Sylvia knew this was an area where her expertise was unsurpassed. And tomorrow sometime after lunch she'd show Tristan that although he'd traveled the world when it came to being with a real woman he was in uncharted waters. The brother would have all he could do to just stay afloat when it came down to loving her and though he was good she'd always deemed herself the shit when it came to lovemaking. She had never had a dissatisfied partner and was all too often told that she was the best they'd ever been with. Lord knows if there were a place on her resume for the talents she possessed there was no doubt in her eyes that she'd be on the Fortune 500 list of richest women in the world. Hell, Oprah would just have to suck it up and take a back seat to a woman possessing a true gift. And whereas Oprah drew millions of women to view her she knew if word got out concerning her prowess and these much coveted and treasured gifts, which she alone possessed she'd probably be referred to in the same vein as the goddess Aphrodite or Cleopatra. Sylvia smiled at the thought.

Once home she was quick to shower and climb into bed just as mommy had suggested. Her thoughts, however, soon returned to Tristan and their impending date. The image of him which loomed larger as the days passed was enormous now and although she was a little cross for letting the thought of him take up not only so much of her thoughts today but so much of her time as well. She wondered what

170

was truly wrong with her. How could she let men come into her inner sanctum and without fail take up so much of what she tried to guard herself against? No matter how hard she tried to fend them off they seemed ever present and always there to sidetrack and distract her from what she really wanted and needed to progress in a forward and positive direction.

For close to a year now she had fended off the likes of Tristan and Alexander with almost no effort whatsoever but alas and as was true to form the wall had inevitably come down and here she was again in the same situation she had tried so adamantly not to become prey to.

Lying in bed Sylvia contemplated her dilemma and was hard pressed to come to a viable solution. Inevitably, whether she was trying to or not she somehow always ended up in some man's bed. She had been through the same dilemma, the same impasse, the same stalemate and quandary so many times that it hardly bothered her now. She finally chalked it up to her sex and in some ways attributed to her rape, and let it go. There was after all, no need to fret over what was inevitably a flaw in her makeup. How did the young people say it nowadays? 'It is what it is.' And so with that she closed her eyes content to let it be what it was, thought of Tristan big, hard, firm, muscular body coming to her in her favorite brand of deep, rich, dark, chocolate and closed her eyes content with the world.

Chapter 12

The alarm clock buzzed in her air. She'd set it for four thirty hoping that she'd get up and relieve her mother of the baby but had obviously set it for the a.m. and accidentally slept through. A whole day wasted she thought and tried to rise from the bed but found herself to be sore and incapacitated. Perhaps mommy was right and she was coming down with something. When she went to throw her legs over the bed she felt the ache from her toes straight up through her neck. Whatever she had contracted had come with a vengeance. It then dawned on her that her workout yesterday coupled with her new found toy had been more strenuous than just her usual midday routine with Tristan and this brought her a smile. If yesterday was taxing, she could hardly wait to see what today had in store for her. Still, first things first. She'd promised herself she'd spend more time with Christopher who was becoming more and more like a stranger to her.

After her two mile morning run, she'd come back, take her normal shower and be just in time to grab Christopher who'd be waking up for his six o'clock feeding, bathe him, dress him and bring him to the house where she could spend some time with him and give mommy a break. By the time mommy ran her morning errands it would be sometime around noon and she'd be just in time for her date with Tristan whom she had to admit she'd gown rather fond of. He was rather laid back and assuming but at this point in her life she desired little more than that. No longer did she want a man trying to climb the corporate ladder or grasping to be king of the hill. No, for her purposes she was quite content to be shadowed by a man who had sown his oats and was satisfied to just kick back on the front porch after a long, arduous day at work and hold her, with few words and a gentle breeze blowing out to the ocean. And Tristan fit the bill. She hated to admit and would have died twenty years ago if anyone had told her that her fate lay in the deep recesses of North Carolina with some local boy. Yet, here she was doing exactly that and happy doing it. She couldn't even imagine marriage after what she'd been through in her life but God forbid if it were to happen she believed Tristan to be her choice. He was her father reincarnate. Simple with a subtle sense of humor, he was if nothing settled and comfortable in his own skin. And if there was something she wanted and needed Lord knows he had the tools to supply it.

Lacing her sneakers she smiled before hitting the pavement to put in her two miles. Glancing in the mirror before stepping out onto the old country road, Sylvia complemented herself on how quickly she'd lost the baby fat from her pregnancy and how fit and toned she'd become in so short a time. She'd make any man proud to call her his wife and she knew it.

Returning from her run she found mommy already up and Christopher dressed and sitting in his highchair. His eyes followed his mother around the room and when she went over to kiss him and pick him up she was pleasantly surprised that he reached for her.

"Boy, hates to be confined to that high chair. That's your son all right. You were the same way. You hated it too. Seems the only place he wants to be is in my arms. Guess I spoiled both of you," her mother chuckled.

"Thanks mommy. You couldn't just let me think that he wanted to come to his mother."

"Oh, Sill you know I'm teasin'. You know that baby loves you. He's just a lil' colic is all and he knows that I'll pamper him and try to ease his pain but you'll always be his mother."

173

The thought made Sill feel better about the relationship between she and her son.

"I'm gonna take him over to the house so you can get a break. Okay, mommy?"

"That's fine. I know the ladies down at the church auxiliary probably think I just abandoned. Haven't been to a meeting in close to three weeks and ya know Sistah Jasmine can't run it by herself."

"I'm sure," Sylvia commented nonchalantly.

"Don't get smart young lady."

Sylvia's head jerked up suddenly. She really hadn't meant anything by the comment.

"I wasn't mommy. I was just saying Miss Jasmine ain't never been no Michelle O'bama."

Her mother chuckled lightly.

"You right. Sistah Jasmine is sweet as she can be but Lord knows she'd need a GPS to get around in a one room house."

Both women laughed.

"Make sure you feed him again about eleven, eleven-thirty. I should be back around twelve or twelve-thirty at the latest. You have anything planned?"

"Well, I'm going to finish up on my proposal and try to tie any loose strings together on my project and that's about it. Oh, and I'm supposed to meet Tristan for lunch at twelve."

"You two are getting kind of serious ain't you?"

"No, and don't go reading nothing into it. We're just friends mommy."

"How they say it? Friends with benefits," she remarked laughing.

"Oh, mommy you need to stop being so ornery and devilish."

Her mother laughed.

"Ain't being ornery but it don't take no rocket scientist to tell when Tristan done tweeked your cookies. You come walking in here with that same look your daddy used to have after I'd rock his world."

"Oh, mommy! No, you didn't."

"Yes, I did. On the regular too... How you think you got here? Used to work that man so bad he couldn't even turn his head to look at another woman. I had him so trained and so strung out all he could do was focus on my cookies and me. Never left his eyesight...

I used to have him where he'd wanna take off from work and I'd tell him if he took a day off then he couldn't have any of my goodies and don't you know that man worked for seven years straight. And in all that time I think I let him taste my cookies twice."

Sylvia was horrified by the thought of her mother and father making love while her mother doubled over in laughter.

"Now go on and take your baby home. I'll be back in time for you to get yours tweeked if you let me get outta here," the old woman laughed.

Sylvia smiled, grabbed the baby and went over to the house and minutes later watched mommy pull out of the driveway. The old woman still had plenty of get up and go and Sylvia only wished she still had the same stamina when she was in her seventies. Then again Sylvia just hoped she had the stamina to keep up with Tristan today. She knew it had been sometime since he'd been with anyone. Well, at least that's what he'd told her. And somehow she believed him. Nevertheless his bout with abstinence could have a debilitating effect on her if he should lose control and she'd certainly made him wait long enough. She knew the choice was up to her but was it really? It was as though it was only a matter of time before her cravings, her needs had to be assuaged and she always but always fed her needs. Her habit had grown and so had her ideas for fulfillment. And with Tristan firmly in her sights she planned on fulfilling her every need.

With Christopher sleeping she called mommy to let her know that the baby was fine and sleeping peacefully. She then called Tristan to cancel lunch since she didn't want to rush mommy and agreed to meet at his house instead. When he agreed she quickly hung up and began getting her outfit ready. She was gonna rock his world today and wanted to see the passion driving, wanted to feel it deep inside her. And so without further adieu she searched her closet to find the cantaloupe sundress and grabbed a pair of six- inch heels to match. There was no need for a bra or panties and after ironing a few of the wrinkles out and showering she found the jar of Vaseline and lubricated herself.

Sill felt good. There was no premise, no façade. She was sure this time, sure of so many things. She was sure that she was not in love so love couldn't cloud her emotions, her thinking, or her better judgment. She wasn't a fool though and knew that the opportunity could still arise and after her conversation with Tristan yesterday she knew that even if she wasn't he was.

There still lay that possibility though and she refused to rule that out. But unlike past experiences she gave herself the opportunity to breathe. No longer could he or any man for that matter be able to make that decision for her. She was in control of her life now and it was she that would make the decision to love or not to love. Sill had to admit that she felt something for Tristan but she hardly felt the need to bring any more drama to her life and like it or not *all* relationships came with some sort of drama. And if it was one thing Sill didn't need in her life it was drama. She liked the relationship she had now just the way it was with her calling the shots and

Tristan doing as he was commanded. Sure, he loved her but that didn't necessarily mean the feelings were reciprocated on her part. Sill remembered daddy telling her when she was just a teenager that any man who really loves you will be there for you and you could always tell because most men wanted sex and if you refrained from letting them sex you and they stuck around then chances are they really interested in you as a person.

Sill heard her father's words as if it were yesterday, the words reverberating in her head. She had always heard him though she'd never taken him to task until now, until it was damn near too late. But she heard him loud and clear now and though she was no longer interested in love she was still gonna make damn sure that anyone interested was sincere and genuinely interested in her as a person. Those hadn't been her intentions—well not her sole intentions—where Tristan was concerned but daddy's scenario had played out nicely. Tristan had certainly put in his time and effort. Now here she was thinking about giving him a taste.

"Hey mommy. Just calling to check on you and see where you were."

"Oh, tired of playing mommy or does Tristan have your hormones all in an uproar?"

"Oh , mommy we're just friends. It's nothing like that at all. We're just having lunch is all," she lied.

"And I guess you need me to watch the Christopher?"

"Would you please? It'll only be for a couple of hours."

"You know restaurants have high chairs too."

"Mommy, I can't take Christopher."

"I certainly don't see why not. Think a fine dining experience would serve as an enlightening experience for my baby."

"Stop playing mommy."

"I'm not."

"Please mommy. I'll only be out for a couple of hours."

"Girl, you're about one worrisome child. Give me fifteen minutes. You just be ready when I get there."

"Okay, and thank you mommy for being a dear."

"Oh hush girl. I'm just hoping when you get this one you don't go and mess it up like you did the last one. Tristan's a pretty good catch if I do say so myself."

"Will you stop it mommy. Nobody's trying to catch or hold anybody and get married. I told you we're just friends."

"Okay! Okay! I'm pulling up now. Bring the baby over and you can be on your way to have lunch with your friend."

Sylvia peeked through the living room window, pulled up the back on her sling back heels, grabbed Christopher and his baby bag and headed over to mommies.

"He's been great mommy. Doesn't seem colic at all if you ask me. He's been smiling and cooing his little behind off all day."

"Probably so glad to see his long lost mother he didn't know what to do," she said smiling sarcastically.

The baby reached for his grandmother as Sylvia pecked Christopher on the cheek before turning around and heading for the navy blue SL5 Series Mercedes with beige interior she so adored.

"Won't be too long mommy," Sill said.

"Don't be. Anything past five o'clock and you'll find Christopher on your doorstep," her mother chuckled as she tossed the baby in the air and watched the wide grin break out across his face each time she did it.

Sylvia pulled in front of the Victorian styled Tudor home that was just short of a mansion with it's acreage of land that made it an estate and once again marveled at the well manicured grounds and smiled. Tristan had certainly come a long way since they were kids. Still he had no idea how much further she would take him on this day and she grinned at the thought. Checking her makeup and smoothing her short set once more Sylvia knew that she'd be hard to resist and tapped lightly at the door. Tristan along with two other men who appeared to be leaving led the way. All three men were slightly stunned to see the sexy bombshell at the door.

Awestruck, the shorter of the three men broke the silence with a fairly loud grunt followed by, "Damn!" and then just as quickly but perhaps a not nearly spontaneous he turned to Tristan and apologized. "Sorry boss. Didn't mean to disrespect your house but she caught me off guard and well it just slipped. Sorry ma'm. Didn't mean any disrespect."

"None taken," Sylvia replied knowing now that she'd achieved her goal.

The two men slid by eyes still focused on the attractive young lady.

"Hey Bill what were you a grade behind me weren't you. You should remember Sylvia Stanton."

"Nah, can't say that I do. Sure would like to though," he answered. didn't have but two. You must remember."

"I remember Sandra Petty and then there was that real skinny chick. I think she was a freshman then. Those are the only I can recall."

"This is that real skinny chick," Tristan laughed.

"Get outta here. You mean…"

Tristan laughed heartily still shaking his head.

"Naw," Bill repeated hardly able to believe his boss man. But not knowing Tristan he looked again.

"Why it damn sure is," he said looking deeply into Sylvia's eyes and then giving her the once over again.

"Damn sure ain't that skinny lil' skinny chick anymore. Excuse me ma'm. Like my friend here we're not quite as refined as boss man here. I guess we're still a lil' rough around the edges," he commented before spitting out a mouthful of that black tar southern men have a fetish for.

"Guess that's why I get the girl."

"U right," Bill replied never taking his eyes off of Sill.

"Well it's certainly quite nice meeting you," the shorter of the two men said, "and do excuse our rudeness. I'll call you later boss. Answer the phone."

"Can't much blame him if he don't," the other commented as they walked away.

"Sorry about that Sill."

"Not a problem, sweetie. Guess I have picked up a few pounds since high school."

"And all in the right places too," Tristan smiled.

"Thank you, thank you, thank you, you're far too kind."

"Just being truthful is all. Have a seat, Sill. Had to run up to Fayetteville this morning," Tristan said heading towards the kitchen, "Anyway I was thinking of you as I passed Bella Villa and picked you a little lunch on the way."

"*Know you didn't,*" she creamed.

Tristan smiled from ear-to-ear.

"Oh, but I did."

"What did you get me? No, don't tell me. You got me the veal."

"Is there anything else that you eat?" he said laughing. "Wasn't what you'd call a particularly hard guess."

"Am I that predictable?"

"Well, when it comes to food I gotta admit you aren't the hardest person in the world to figure. Are you ready to eat?"

"If I said I wanted to start with dessert would you be offended?"

"No, I wouldn't be offended but the truth of the matter is I never even thought to get dessert."

"It's alright sweetie. But if I'm so predictable at least tell me what I'm dreaming of when I'm thinking of dessert?"

"I haven't the faintest idea."

"Sit down sweetie and relax and let me help you focus."

"What's there to focus on Sill?"

"You m'love. You've been lovin' me for the last I don't know how long and in all that time I've been a selfish brat."

"I enjoyed every minute…"

"Hush, Tristan. You are a gentleman. But the truth is I have been nothing short of a self-serving spoiled brat only thinking of myself and my satisfaction, my needs, my immediate gratification and you catered to my every whim, my every need and craving. Let me return the favor m' love. All I want you to do is lean back, close your eyes and let Sill do the rest. All I want you to do is enjoy."

On this day, Sylvia was the one that dropped to her knees. Spreading Tristan's leg she moved in between them and immediately became aroused when she noticed him gazing down at her. Slowly, seductively she unzipped his zipper and slid both his trousers and his boxers down past his knees and then to his ankles. Reaching for his

throbbing member she was surprised to find herself within his clutches.

"Sorry Sill but no future wife of mine is going down on me. And especially not

you."

Sylvia was thrown for a loop and didn't know how to react.

"Baby as good as you've been to me..."

"Now you hush. Tristan's tone change and Sylvia noticed that he'd gone from his

usual cordial, friendly tone to a no-nonsense tone almost the same one he used with

his workers.

"Baby I want a wife. I don't want someone that feels she has to sex me 'cause I

made good love to her. This ain't no tit-for-tat shit. I can go right up to Hay St. and

get somebody to go down on me and toss 'em a few dollars. I don't want or need to

be sexed baby. I'm not looking for that. Now if you'd like to let me show you the

way that's done then you can gladly follow me," Tristan said standing now.

"No, perhaps I should go," Sylvia, said softly a bit perturbed and confused by the

rejection. "I didn't mean to offend you Tristan. Trust me my intentions were good."

"They may well have been but the way to hell is paved with good intentions," he

replied.

A bit taken back she had to admit she'd never seen him in this light, so forceful, so

adamant, so strong and although she wasn't sure whether to be offended or simply

angry over his rejection she felt herself suddenly very moist and very attracted to

him at this moment. Still, there was something that bothered her. Was he actually

comparing her to those tricks on the ho patrol. And before she was going anywhere

with this man whether it be upstairs or out the door to end this relationship forever she needed to know what his inference meant. She wasn't a ho because she was trying to please him.

"Now would my future wife care to accompany me to the bedroom?"

Sylvia was feeling Tristan and dropped her hand to feel the moistness between her legs. She had no objection with going almost anywhere but at what expense. She was not going to be insulted no matter how badly she wanted and desired him. No, he had some explaining to do first.

"Maybe I didn't understand your analogy sweetie so do me a favor and explain it to me before we proceed."

"Oh, come on Sill. What man wants to call a woman his wife when her first act of lovemaking is her on her knees with a dick in her mouth. You know what I call women like that. Well, let's just say they get no respect from me."

"And let's just say you gets none of this and no love from me. Here I am trying to reciprocate and you want to demean and call me a damn 'ho'. You know you have a lotta shit with you."

"Oh, come on Sill. You know I have the utmost respect for you. I'm doing my able bodied best to make you my wife. I just don't want a wife that sucks dick. I don't now how else to put it but you stop and think about it. What man wants a wife who drops to her knees? And if she's willing to do it for you how many more has she been willing to drop to her knees for. I mean that's just common sense. That shit is for common street trash not for a woman I intend on calling my wife. I'm serious I don't want a wife that sucks dick. I don't know how to put it any plainer. Do you feel me, Sill?"

"Yes, unfortunately I do. Would you please let me out Tristan?"

"Ahh, Sill I didn't mean anything. You know how I feel about you."

"Well, if I didn't. I do now. Let me explain something to you that you may not understand Tristan. Those women that you refer to are working, laboring or as you so crassly put it sucking dick for a dollar. Although the act may be the same, the reasons for doing it are completely different. It's still a labor but when I kneel before you it's a labor of love. I don't suck every man's dick that I come across or happen to date and the reason I happen to do it when I do it is because I'm giving my man that very special part of me because he is my man and I want him to know it and I want him to know that there are no bars up when it comes to pleasing my man. You need to understand that. You need to know that however slight it may be that there are nuances to even such things as oral sex. You need to know the difference between a woman that gives her all to please her man and someone that sells the same service for a dollar. Don't know if you're aware of it or not but there is a difference and when you find out give me a call."

"Once again I put my foot in my mouth and I am sorry if I offended you Sill but I have to stick to my guns on this one. Any woman that drops to her knees to pleasure a man by sucking his dick is a woman that I wouldn't choose to call my wife."

"And as if that's some great achievement."

"What's that?"

"To be called your wife…"

"Well, there are some who would deem that a noteworthy ambition."

"Must be some pretty shallow women out there."

"You'd be surprised."

"Well, what do I know? You may be right. But this one isn't even considering the option."

"Aww Sill…"

"Sorry and not that it was ever a thought but now since you bring it up I think I'll pass. And when you grow a little call me. You know it's funny how a man who has traveled the world over can actually be so small-minded. Be good Tristan."

"C'mon Sill, don't leave. C'mon babe. Let's talk about this. You know I've never been the smartest or most tactful person in the world. You know I say things that I really haven't thought a lot about. That's why I need a good woman to balance my act."

"I don't know about all that Tristan but I will afford you the time and space to work on those issues."

"Sill, trust me I didn't mean to offend you."

"Baby, it would take more than you to offend me. All you did was let me know how shallow you really are. And to think I had all thoughts of blessing you. I was seriously considering gracing you today with some of Sylvia's goodies. Thought about letting you get up off of your knees. Even considered accepting you as an equal and maybe even cracking the door to my heart to see if you knew how to act if I were to let you in. But you fucked that up nicely. But then I don't know why I expected any different. After all you're nothing more than typical male. Should have kept you on your knees groveling 'til I got bored with yo' old country ass. But no, I tried to be nice only to meet with the same old fucked up shit. See, that's why I don't have time for men or relationships. They're all the same. Full of the same drama and bullshit. I come over to do you, to reciprocate, to tell you I appreciate all the shit you've done for me since I've been here and tell you not to give up hope. And what do I get? You tell me that when I get on my knees the same way I've you have been doing me for the past—I don't know how many months—that I'm belittling myself—that I'm acting like one of the whores down on Hay St. Motherfucka you're crazy as hell."

"Okay, okay baby. You're right. I concede. You made your point clear. It's just that I got a chance to travel a bit and I gotta admit that my way of looking at things got kinda jaded by the types of people I ran into. Most of the women I met weren't the least bit interested in me or who I was. All they knew was what I did for a living and all the fringe benefits that went along with being in my company."

"Groupies?"

"Yeah, groupies if you wannna call 'em that. But all they saw was the fame and the money. And the first thing they'd wanna do is drop down and do me hoping that I'd get hooked and they'd get to share the spoils—you know some of the fringe benefits."

"And?"

"And I guess I was too stupid to see at first. Then when it came to me that they were using me and using me up when I'm thinking more like this could possibly be Mrs. Right. I saw them for what they really were."

"And that was?"

"They were little more than two bit ho's trying to ride for free. So when a woman drops to her knees that's just a natural correlation in my eyes."

"And what could you possibly think I'd want from you Tristan? I've been and independent woman for as long as I can remember. I don't need a man for every reason. If there's something I want I can get it myself and if I can't get it then it wasn't mind to have."

"I hear you, Sill."

"What I do is because I have feelings for you and no other reason. I do what I want because I want to. Do you understand?"

"I do now. Clearly. Is there any chance we can start over."

"I don't know Tristan. I just don't know."

Tristan got up moved towards the woman, grabbed her in his arms, pulled her towards him and kissed her gently his tongue finding the deepest recesses of her mouth. Rigid and unforgiving at first she soon came to relax in his warm caress and moments later readily gave herself to him. A tear ran down her cheek. Tristan felt the side of her face then tenderly wiped the tear from her cheek.

"What's wrong baby?"

"You hurt me Tristan. All I wanted to do was make you happy." She promised herself that no man would ever make her cry again but here she was crying again over some man.

"I'm so sorry Sill. Those were never and have never been my intentions where you're concerned. I promise you it'll never happen again."

And then he grabbed her hand and led her up the long winding staircase to the bedroom.

There were no tears on the ride home although the pain in her midsection was close to being unbearable. No matter which way she turned in the driver's seat her she hurt. But oh how it had been worth it. Reluctant at first, she had gobbled up Tristan's manhood with almost reckless abandon and when he looked hesitant and slow about giving her all of it she reversed roles and rode him like there was no tomorrow taking every inch of his eleven inches as if it was meant for her and only her. The pain, though excruciating at first was mixed with a pleasure she never known and though the tears flowed freely now there was no hurt and with each and

187

every penetration she could here herself screaming. She had never known anything quite so delightful and her reservations about loving and giving of herself as well as her qualms about relationships dissipated with each stroke. She was not alone in her ecstasy and heard Tristan begging her to stay with him.

And with each plea she seriously considered accepting his offer. They'd parted with him begging her to stop. Drenched in sweat he'd grabbed her hips after he'd come the last time and refused to let her move. Both were exhausted but Sill not having known anything quite like this in her life didn't care. If the world were to end tomorrow she knew she'd found happiness.

The ride home was wrought with mixed emotions but if there were boundaries she knew now that the line of demarcation was now gone, nonexistent. She would marry this man, raise her son in the same way in which she'd been raised, in this small southern town and maybe, just maybe, for the first time in her life know peace and contentment. The lovemaking had been good, more than she had ever expected but it wasn't the lovemaking that had torn down the walls. It was the closeness, the intimacy and well the lovemaking helped to a degree. But no longer did she have the strength to fight the fact that was so overwhelming and that was that there commonalities far outweighed their differences. And after all, no matter how far they traveled and in what circles they found themselves in the fact remained that they were both basically small town at heart with good ol' southern values.

She couldn't wait to tell mommy the news and even though Tristan hadn't proposed she knew with just a small twist of his arm he would. The thoughts eased the pain and as good as it had been she knew that their lovemaking would have to be contained.

Mommy was ecstatic when she heard the news and two weeks later they were married in a small ceremony down at city hall much to mommy's displeasure. Sylvia had always wanted a honeymoon and as was Tristan's way he let Sill decide where she wanted to go and Sill who had long dreamed of visiting Jamaica. He'd gotten everything he'd ever dreamed when Sill agreed to marry him. Everything else was second nature to him now and in the weeks following their marriage and in preparation for their honeymoon Sill found herself in the midst of not only raising Christopher and moving from the monstrosity she'd tried to make a home to becoming not just Tristan's business partner but the owner of a large lumber company of which she knew nothing. Tristan had all but resigned his duties and centered his every waking moment to making sure that Sill was happy. In any case, she learned the business pretty much in record time thanks to both Tristan' accountant and his lawyer. It was not long before she had a firm grip on what it took to make the business work and profitable. From what she gathered Tristan was no slouch when it came to business and had accrued quite a loyal patronage. And if she had respect for what he'd become in the last few years it grew five fold in the ensuing weeks when she went over his books and business dealings. It wasn't the money however, but the relationships and what he did in order for it to prosper the way it had. And unlike Alex business was no more way for him to pass time and make a livelihood. The moment he had Sill in the fold it became his pastime and no longer his motivator and although she was swamped with the idea of being not only a mother but one of the largest lumber suppliers in central North Carolina she never mentioned a word to Tristan who was simply ecstatic with the idea of keeping Sill happy. She was even more ecstatic that he had taken Christopher under his wing and made him his own. Now instead of Christopher only wanting to be with mommy, he now only wanted Tristan.

Mommy called and stopped by now more often than when Sill resided right across the road and all in all everything seemed to be as Sill had always dreamed about. It was as if all the stories and fairy tale endings were now coming true.

The next few months were everything Sylvia could have wished for—well all except that one night when Tristan had gone bowling with some of the guys and had a bit too much peppermint schnapps or whatever the hell he'd been drinking. He'd been jovial as usual and she acquiesced with no hesitation when he went about seducing her. But where he'd always been gentle with her he made love with all the gentleness of a pack of wolves. Sylvia remembered the first round. She'd come quickly and he was always cognizant of that but not that night. She came til' she was spent and still he was hard and seemed neither in no hurry to come or wanted to come. She didn't know which it was but she knew that alcohol slowed the reaction time but this was crazy. And it seemed he grew even more than she'd come to know. When he finally came and rolled over she tried getting up to go to the bathroom and revive herself after the onslaught and found she could barely walk without clutching on to something to keep her knees from buckling. Three days later she was still recovering though she took pride in the fact that she could accommodate her man's every wish even though it sometimes killed her to try.

Months passed and though they had their skirmishes the way all newlyweds do in coming to form new boundaries and getting to know each other the one thing that was unmistakable was their love for each other. And though they did their best to remain out of the limelight and remain low key they somehow were still the talk of the town. After all, it wasn't all that common for two local kids who had made good

190

to come home to little ol' Elizabethtown to set up shop with all the glamorous places in the world awaiting them. But here they were and though masked their success in humility the fact was that these Blacks had made it despite the odds.

Mommy was so proud of Sylvia's marrying and finally settling down that there wasn't a thing Sill requested that went undone. And when it looked like Sylvia was staring to get bored the old woman would always give Tristan the heads up and before Sylvia could protest they were flying to New Orleans or New York or somewhere just so Tristan could see his wife smile. Now it's been said that Black folks don't know nothin' about the days of wine and roses but if ever a couple did it was Sylvia and Tristan who spent their days basking in the summer sun and loving each other's company. All was good and Sylvia was sure that she'd found everything that she'd ever wished for.

"Sill, I been calling you for the last—I don't know how many hours—and you don't anser the phone. I don't know why you even bother to have a phone."

"Sorry, mommy," Sill said giving the old woman a hug. "I was out in the back pulling weeds and putting in some mums. Tristan pays Mr. Martinez to do it but I guess they don't have mums and azaleas in Mexico. He's cut down every flower I've planted so in between doing the books and looking after Christopher I'm trying to keep the yard presentable. Guess in my haste to get it done before Christopher woke up I must have left the phone in the house."

"Well, I guess that's why they have phone cases. There these simple little holders that you attach tour waist and it allows you to keep your phone near you in case you get a call."

"You and Tristan and your phones. You know there are days when I wish I didn't have a phone at all. I'm thinkin' 'bout having it turned off altogether."

191

"I hear you. If Sistah Jasmine calls me one more time I may just do that myself. Anyway, the reason I was trying to get in touch with you was because I know how interested you were in teaching and helping our less fortunate kids out. You always talkin' bout giving back and well I thought about you when they brought up the fact that they were thinking about opening a tutorial center and eventually a school."

"Who's they?" Sylvia asked as if she didn't know who mommy was referring to.

"The church. Who else?"

Sylvia smiled. She'd always gotten some delight in teasing the old woman and despite everything nothing had changed. It had been daddy and her pastime to drive the old woman up the woman with their antics.

"I know. I know mommy. But to tell you the truth between Christopher and trying to keep Tristan's business afloat I just don't have the time. You know he's all but given on the business if you ask me."

"That's just a temporary situation baby. He's just been distracted that's all. When the novelty of being married wears off he'll settle back into his responsibilities. He also knows something that you don't know Sill."

"And that is? I wish someone would please let me in on the secret."

"It's no secret baby. Tristan has put his every waking moment into the success of that business and he knows that you love him enough to know that and that you wouldn't let anything happen to it. He trusts you and he's letting you—no—he's giving you the opportunity to make it as much yours as it is his. It's a power move, a test, but he knows as well as I do that you won't miss a beat."

Sill smiled at the fact that her mother was so astute when it came to understanding men and their motivation.

"Got it all figured out? Huh, mommy?"

192

"It's my job to take an interest in my daughter's welfare," the old woman said smiling back at her daughter.

"Nice to have you in my corner…"

"Now answer the phone and I'll tell the ladies down at the church that you'll be glad to head up the program."

"Mommy don't do that. I can't handle it right now."

"Sill, let me tell you one thing. I know you're in love and want to do the best you can by Tristan but in marrying Tristan you don't want to ever lose what makes you. He wants you to be one in unison with him but a man like Tristan wants a woman that can stand alone, apart from him and that's why he chose you. Now you can aid him. That's what a wife does when it comes to her husband but Tristan is not the kind of man that wants a subservient woman and you are certainly not that. You let go the reigns and he'll take his business back. But it's you Sylvia Stanton, who he first fell in love with. In other words don't lose yourself or your dreams trying to aid him in his pursuits. How the young folks say it? *Do you!*"

"I got you mommy."

"Okay, so I'm gonna tell Reverend Dantzler that you'll accept the position as director of the program and Tristan will just have to understand. And I think he will with a smile."

"Thanks mommy. I probably needed that."

"That's what mother's are for. Our job is to clear the dust and the cobwebs. Oh, and by the way Sill I got another phone call today and I really debated telling you seeing how happy you are finally. You know some people live a lifetime and never know happiness. I guess we truly been blessed."

"I know that's right. There was a long time when I wondered if I was being punished. I really wondered how many crosses I was destined to bear. I mean I suffered."

"And I suffered right along with you baby. You don't know how hard it was for me to see my baby suffer so and I guess that's why I thought about not telling you about the phone call I received today."

"Well, I've come to realize you can't run from the truth. If it's a problem the best thing to do is man up and face it head on."

"Don't now if it's quite that easy, Sill."

"Who was it? A bill collector?"

"Wish it were that simple. No, I was stunned myself. It was Alex."

Sill stopped pulling weeds and stood mesmerized when she heard his name. She'd put him almost completely out of her mind. Her last recollection was the time he'd had Thomas drive him down here and caught she and Tristan standing butt naked in the living room. After that it seemed he'd all but vanished into thin air and although he was now a little more than a memory she hated the fact that was what it took for him to finally get the message. Still, he'd gotten the message and she was all too grateful that he was finally out of her life for good or was he?

Slowly recovering from her thoughts she turned and looked at the old woman.

"And what did he want?"

"Well, he was quite cordial at first. You know despite the picture you painted of him he's always been quite the gentleman where I was concerned. But today was somewhat different. I saw a side I'd never seen before."

"What happened?"

"Nothin' really. We started off talkin' about the flea market. You know how much he used to like that and then he went on to ask me if I'd picked up anything. And I said nothing worthy of putting on the Antique Road Show. You know it was like old times until I mentioned you."

"And why on earth would you do that mommy?"

"Come on now Sill, you know the only reason that man calls is to inquire about you. And for months I've been trying to let him down easily but Alex is relentless if nothing else. And when he called me today I really thought he was sincere when he asked about you. So, I told him how you'd gotten married and just how happy you were."

"And?"

"I don't know what happened but there was a long silence and then when he did speak again he asked me who you married and I told him Tristan and again there was a long silence before the phone went dead."

"Oh mommy you didn't."

"Yes, Sill I did and I'll tell you this. For the first time I believed what you told me about those two boys up in New York. I mean I'm a pretty good judge of people but I got an eerie feeling when I told him that."

"And you should mommy. I told you that he wasn't correct but you insisted that you know people and that he was all right. I never witnessed anything but there's something that's just not right about Alex. It was enough to scare me away and I'm worried that you may have put Tristan in danger now."

"Oh, Lord God I hope not. Baby you know that wasn't my attention. But you don't really think Alex would do anything do you. I mean seriously."

"That's the thing mommy. I mean I just don't know. I pray not but I just don't know. There's a side to Alex that's scary. That's what I was trying to tell you but you were so taken in by his charm and good looks that you couldn't see."

"You're right. He just seemed like such a good catch for you. I was just looking out for my daughter's well being. I just wanted to make sure you were secure and well taken care of. That's all. You know it won't be long before the good Lord calls me to join your father. I just wanted to make sure you were in good hands is all."

"I know mommy. You keep telling me that. I told you I'm a big girl now. I can take care of myself now. All you can do is lay the foundation. You did a hell of a job there. Your job is pretty much over now. I'm just building on the blueprint you layed out."

"I hear you baby but no matter how old you get I'll always be a mother, your mother. It's not something you just turn off because your child reaches a certain age."

Sylvia hugged her mother.

"I just hope that boy doesn't do anything foolish."

"You and me both mommy."

"We'll just have to be a little cognizant of his whereabouts and keep a watchful eye over him until this blows over. Then again I could be making far too much over the whole thing. I just had a funny feeling when I got off the phone. It's like a premonition."

"I had the same feeling after those two boys were killed in Harlem. But there's nothing we can do now mommy. Don't blame yourself though. The truth was bound to come out sooner or later."

"True. All we can do is hope that he has the common sense to concede. I don't think he'd risk his business for the sake of revenge though. He seems to be very intelligent and he didn't come to acquire either his fame or fortune overnight. It'd be awfully stupid for him to throw everything away over a woman."

"U right. But then I'm not just any woman," Sylvia laughed. "After a man has had a whiff of this he just can't have anything. It's hard to find a woman that'll do after any man's had a Stanton woman."

Both women laughed but the concern showed in Sylvia's face. She thought of calling Alex and talking to him hoping she could smooth any ruffled fathers but decided it would be inappropriate in Tristan's view and if she were to ask Tristan about it or mention it to him he'd come up with the typical male ego thing and his reply would be not to worry about it. So, really there was no reason to bring it up. Still, she had to watch out for him. It was her job to keep him out of harms way. They were scheduled to fly down to Freeport in the Bahamas on Friday night. Both loved to gamble and mommy was always coming up with these package deals on airfare and hotel fees that made it affordable. Anything to make and keep the happy couple happy but Sill thought it was primarily to get a chance to keep Christopher. Anyway, it was Wednesday which left them two days before their trip and then they would be gone for six days and during that time she hardly have to worry about Alex. If he was angry or thought about revenge in the time they were away he would have time enough to cool down and come to his senses.

Later that day Sylvia met with the pastor of momma's church and found herself consumed with the idea of starting an after school tutorial service. The good reverend, an elderly gentleman in his mid-sixties with an eye for beautiful women looked Sylvia up and down several times and when it was obvious that she had the credentials to run his program gave Sylvia all the liberty needed in making the program as success and after talking to the good reverend she actually saw the possibilities of all of her dreams coming to fruition. Excited by the endless possibilities she was further surprised that she ran the idea by Tristan he seemed more enthusiastic than she'd ever dreamed.

The days seem to drag on. They always do when you're waiting for something special to happen. It had been no different when she was a kid and Christmas was just around the corner. But that had been a long ago and Sylvia hadn't felt like this since—well since then. Now the hours, minutes and seconds seemed to take forever. Sylvia had plenty to keep her busy with the church program, the new rental property she'd just purchased over on Avalon St. and the baby. But the day still moved too slowly for her likes. Tomorrow was Thursday and her scheduled remained the same as it did today well that was she was to have lunch with mommy and do a little shopping for her trip. Thursday turned out to be a beautiful day. Tristan had to pick up a client at Raleigh International Airport at eight o'clock that morning and was promptly on his way at by six fifteen. Sill felt him kiss her lightly on her cheek but refused to her open her eyes, fix breakfast, and see him off. She knew mommy had done it every day for daddy but she just couldn't do. Between the baby, her exercise regimen and the long filled days that awaited her each day, it had become more and more of a struggle just to get up in the morning. This morning was no different and a half an hour later when she heard the door rise she dragged herself out of the bed and made her way to the bedroom window only to see Tristan ease out of the garage in the shiny black Mercedes which meant she'd have to make her rounds in his old beat up Ford pickup truck. 'Damn.' She'd asked him on several occasions why he was so adamant about keeping the old Ford pickup when he so enjoyed the

Mercedes and after all didn't it make a better impression on prospective clients. He'd agreed but that's as far as the conversation had gotten. He did admit that it wasn't the car so much as it was the satellite radio that he liked so much but she had all reason to believe that it was so much more than that since whenever he gave a bid on a job or had to meet a client he would take her car. Sill smiled as she watched the car ease down the highway and made it a point to stop by Mr. Glover's Mercedes dealership and order the identical C-120 for herself. Hers was already paid for so he shouldn't have anything at all to say when she pulled up in her brand new 2010. She smiled at the thought. If he had anything to say the trip tomorrow would certainly diffuse anything he had to say. She was also fixing his favorite meal tonight and along with the veal parmigiana she'd pop open a couple of bottles of Merlot and with mommy keeping Christopher so they'd have less to do to be on time their six o'clock flight she'd start their vacation right their in E'Town. And despite his initial protests she ran the damn thing behind closed doors. Sill grinned broadly when she thought of the first night she had made love to Tristan. There were no questions, no conversation this time. It was two o'clock in the morning. Tristan was still on his back and there was someone pounding loud and relentlessly. Tristan drenched in sweat and unable to move made a valiant to get up but Sill beat him to the punch. Who could it possibly be at this time of night? Her thoughts turned to her mother who had been complaining of chest pains all week and she hurried to the door only to find two of Elizabethtown's finest standing there.

"Ma'm we've received complaints from your neighbors that there was some loud noise and screaming coming from your residence. Is everything all right?"

"Everything's fine officer."

"Do you mind if we come in and take a look around. No I'm sorry. Come in by all means."

"Is there anyone else presently in the house," the first officer inquired while the other made his way around the house flashlight in hand.

"Seems like everything's in order here Jack," the one officer said to the other. "No sign of a struggle or anything."

"Mind if I speak to your husband ma'm. Just doing my job. Gotta make sure you're not holding him hostage or torturing the poor fellow."

"My husband's in bed but I can get him if you think that's necessary."

"Just doing my job ma'm."

"Tristan," Sill yelled.

Moments later Tristan appeared in her pink housecoat that came no further than his waist.

"My God baby, you didn't say we had company," he said embarrassed.

Both police did their best to hold back laughter.

"Hey Captain!" the older of the two officers said extending a hand to Tristan. He turned to his partner. "Played ball with this guy in high school. This was one of the best power forwards in the country. Tristan meet my partner Jack. Tristan went on to play at Notre Dame and the overseas and eventually with the Pacers. Hell of a ballplayer. Of course he used to wear gym shorts and a t-shirt. Now he's wearing pink robes. Guess time changes everyone somewhat."

Everyone laughed.

"Well everything seems to be in order. Sorry, for the intrusion captain. We get a lot of prank calls "

"No problem," Tristan said closing the door behind the two men.

Sill stood their smiling

"And no prank," Sylvia said after the officers were long gone. "I told you to put a pillow over your mouth."

It was memories like these that kept her going. Little had changed since their love affair in high school and what was really nice was that they truly enjoyed each others company. It was obvious that they were the best of friends. They complemented each other nicely. And though both went their separate ways and had their separate lives in the daytime, he to work and she to the church, they were like young lovers, texting constantly and calling on occasion. In the evenings, they met and all too often left one car somewhere and rode home together where they'd talk about their days apart and just about anything else that was on their minds. She feared that their closeness, their constantly being up under each other would be the thing that would eventually drive them apart but she'd deal with that when the time came. At home they'd share their evenings together talking about this and that and sleep would all too often come too soon and they'd be apart briefly. But right now her only thought and his too was how they could put a smile on the others face and make this last forever. She'd never known happiness like this in her life and she was ecstatic and she prayed that that day when something would change all this would never come. But if ever she had a dream, Tristan had fulfilled it and she gave thanks and praise now to the good Lord above with all sincerity. After all these were the days she'd dreamed of all her life. These were the days of wine and roses.

Now they were headed to the Bahamas for a brief respite and some more time to spend alone together and she only hoped that there would be cops knocking at her door again.

Surprisingly enough Thursday came and went with a rapidness she hardly expected and before she realized it was something after six and she was heading home. She'd texted and called Tristan all day long but hadn't been able to contact him. If he'd only listened to me and gotten a regular phone instead of that Cricket phone. He's so damn hardheaded. The damn thing loses reception when you cross the street. Go two blocks and it's out of range. Then again knowing Tristan, he probably hadn't charge it last night and it's dead. It was unlike Tristan to not call her or text her and she was starting to worry. But that wasn't her only worry and she didn't know how he was going to react to her latest news even though he hardly got upset over anything. Still, if her premonition was true she was sure there would be some reaction. She'd told mommy who'd stared at her for quite some time before saying anything, which was something for mommy who always had something to say about something. But when she told her that she thought was pregnant again her mother sat there motionless. Now she had to tell Tristan. She was pretty sure he'd welcome the news with great joy but the fact of the matter was that even though they'd talked about everything under the moon they'd never discussed the idea of them having children and she hated to just spring it on him so soon after they'd been married and had taken on the world in that span of time. Hell, with her schedule she didn't have time to spend with Christopher and if it weren't were for mommy and Tristan she never could have done it. And now there was another one on the way. Mommy certainly couldn't take on a newborn at her age. Hell, she had all she could do to take care of Christopher. She herself despite the anxiety was ecstatic. If nothing else it would bring them closer. And a baby was a gift, a blessing. But with the new rental problems they'd just bought, the tutorial program she'd just taken on, and the business she didn't see how she'd have either the time or the energy to take on a newborn. And then there were the financial responsibilities. They'd sat for the better part of the week and worked to figure out a budget so they'd both be able to retire in the next five years with what they deemed was a financial stability that would allow them to live the lifestyle the were living now. She'd already blown that with the purchase of the Mercedes she'd ordered today but had rationalized that away by putting a healthy down payment on that and by paying the car note out of her monthly allowance, which they'd agreed on, for such things as clothes and shoes and lunches with mommy—just miscellaneous stuff. There was little left after that. And now a baby? Sill was exhausted by the time she reached home. Yesterday seemed like eons ago. It had all been so easy then. The deliveryman was on his way with the car and it would soon be in the driveway and she'd have some explaining to do when Tristan got home but that was the least of her worries. The idea of her pregnancy was a whole 'nother story. So, Sill did what Sill did most of the time when things got a bit too much too handle. She threw on Soldier of Love. Sade's newest cd, grabbed a bottle of Merlot, found a book by J. California Cooper and sat down in her easy chair and sipped slowly. She enjoyed the bitter taste of the wine but even more than that she liked the relaxed mood it put her in. After a couple of glasses nothing much mattered. And so it was as she grabbed her cell and called mommy to tell her to give her a wake up call just in case she were to fall asleep. She still had to prepare Tristan's dinner. After a hard days work meeting with prospective clients and then the long ride from Raleigh to Elizabethtown chances are he'd be famished by the time he got home. She'd picked up two lobsters from Harris Teeter and a couple of T-Bones on the way home and with a baked potato and salad which required no more than fifteen minutes to prepare she'd have dinner ready when he got home. All she needed now was for him to call when he was on his way as he did whenever they arrived home separately.

Grabbing the book of short stories by J. California Cooper Sill poured herself another glass of Merlot, eased the chair back and began to read while Sade sang softly in the background. It was the second book she'd read by the author in a week and though the stories were primarily the same she enjoyed both the woman's writing style and the brevity of her stories. Heck, it was nothing to pick up one of her books, read a story, get a sense of completion and in her spare time if there was any, pick the book back up and read another story in it's entirety. It was easy reading, nothing taxing, and oh, how that woman could tell a story. Only thing was is that the women in her stories were so tragic, so depressing. Sill would read and thank the good Lord that she didn't have to endure what those women had to go through. And always but always there hardship was at the expense of men. Sill put the glass up to her lips, took a sip and put the book down and thought of the tragedies in her own life. She too had suffered similar indignities at the expense of men. Maybe that's why it made it so easy to relate. But those days were long gone. She smiled at the thought, put the glass down and leaned back, thankful that everything had finally come full circle and that life was good. Glancing her watch and realizing it was still early she put both book and wine down and closed her eyes for a minute.

What seemed like only moments later, Sill awoke to the sound of the phone ringing. "Girl, I was just getting the baby dressed and heading your way. You had me worried sick. You tell me to call you and then you don't answer the phone. I don't know what's wrong with you or why you even bother to have a phone. You never answer it."

Sill wiped the sleep from her eyes, poured herself another glass of Merlot and sat up.

"Shoot I've been calling for hours. I must have called twenty times. You told me to call you."

"I know mommy. I'm sorry. I must have dozed off but good. I'm exhausted. What time is it anyway?"

"Quarter after ten. Tristan home?"

"I don't know mommy. I just woke up. Damn."

"You watch your mouth young lady."

"Let me go mommy. Let me go see where Tristan is. Man work all-day and here I am sleeping. I didn't fix dinner or anything and I know he's starved and wondering what the hell has he gotten into. Man can't even get a decent meal. Let me go. And you know tonight of all nights I should have had my stuff together. Got this new car sittin' outside and ain't even discuss it with him. He's gonna be shocked when he sees that. And then there's the news of a new addition. Oh my God mommy let me get off the phone."

"Okay baby. I wish you luck. Call me back and let me know how everything goes. And Sill…"

"Yeah, mommy?"

"Don't worry so much. That man loves you to death and he's going to agree with almost anything you do. Don't worry and don't you sell yourself short. You hear me? Everything will work itself out."

"Thanks for the vote of confidence, mommy. I love you."

"Call me when it's over."

"I will mommy."

Sill called Tristan several times. Obviously not home, Sill checked the missed calls and text messages on her phone. Still no messages, Sill grew worried. This was totally out of character. He always called and when he wasn't calling he was texting. Sylvia would often wonder how he got any work done at all. But there was nothing—no text missed calls, no voicemail, no text—no something was definitely wrong. Maybe he'd stopped by the office. Sill called the job but only received his voicemail. She then tried calling but it went straight to voicemail. With no other recourse, she sat back in her easy chair poured herself another glass of Merlot which was now room temperature and waited. The wine had a soothing effect and accompanied with the subtle sounds of Sade she felt herself grow increasingly melancholy. A few more glasses and Sill began to dream wide-awake. Her thoughts were now scattered. Every conceivable possibility seem to come to mine but after considering Tristan being with another woman and the fact that he'd grown tired of her and just left she came to the realization that she was fishing aimlessly and the only thing she could do was just sit and wait. He'd obviously had car trouble and his phone was dead was more conceivable but the bottom line was that they were leaving at nine o'clock in the morning for the Bahamas and Tristan wasn't going to do anything to miss the flight. After a few more glasses of Merlot, Sill found herself fast asleep. The doorbell ringing startled her awakening her from a sound sleep. Glancing at her phone she noticed it was close to three a.m. Damn! It was about time. And where was his damn key. He better have a good damn reason for worrying her to death. Sylvia got up up and felt the pain in her back from sleeping in the chair. She stretched before taking her time to get to the door. He hadn't rushed to get home and she wasn't rushing now. Sill knew who it was and didn't bother to ask who. Opening the door, she was surprised to find the same two policemen she'd had the pleasure or the displeasure of meeting several weeks before.

"Evening ma'm."

Sylvia was shocked to see the officer and not Tristan's sorry ass. Where the hell could he be? Lord knows she hoped he wasn't going to turn out to be the typical man. He had done nothing to her to have her think that he was nothing but the best—well up until tonight that was.

"Mrs. Stanton I'm afraid I have some rather bad news."

Sylvia looked deep into the officer's eyes. Looking away it was no easy task to share whatever it was he had to say with the petite little woman in front of him. Tears welled up in his eyes and his voice broke into a thousand tiny pieces.

"Sylvia, as you know Tristan and I were close throughout high school and still remain friends to this day."

He turned away, pulled out a handkerchief and blew his nose and wiped away the tears flowing so freely now.

"What's wrong officer? What's happened to my Tristan," she yelled now grabbing the officer by his collar.

"Tell me. What's happened to him? Where is he?" She was panicking now.

"Don't know exactly ma'm. Raleigh police found his body sometime this morning on I-440, a single gunshot to the back of the head."

"Is he alive?"

"No ma'm he was found by state troopers this morning and was pronounced dead at nine nineteen this morning."

"Oh no officer! You must be mistaken. We're supposed to leave for the Bahamas this morning. He's terribly excited about our trip. He'll be home soon. Then you can talk to him personally."

One officer looked at the other both now realizing the woman was in shock.

"Ma'm is there a relative nearby that we can talk to or that can come and sit with you in your time of need?"

"Mommy. Where's mommy?" Sylvia screamed.

"You stay here. I'm going to go and pick go over and pick up her mom," the older officer said to the rookie cop before turning to Sylvia.

"Sylvia do you think you can find your mother's phone number or maybe phone her so I can get her to come over and stay with you for awhile?"

Sylvia stared at the officer, and noticed the tears dripping down his face. The grief obvious the officer who had once been Tristan's teammate and friend saw no solace, no way to relieve the pain and the hurt but to make his leave. Sylvia who had miraculously regained her composure called her mother. The older woman unaware of the happenings agreed to be ready when the officer arrived.

Mrs. Stanton bundled up the baby. Ready for the worst she got into the squad card.

"You're Beverly Jo's ain'tcha boy?" She said as she nestled the baby into the back of the squad in the car seat.

"Yes, ma'm," the officer whispered trying to hold it together. It was his job to keep it together, to be strong for those in need. But today's news hit him and he had all he could do not to break down in front of the older woman.

"Which one are you."

"I'm the oldest ma'm. I'm Jack," he answered still trying to hold back the tears.

"Your mama and me grew up together ya know. All through school she was one of my best friends," the old woman laughed. "They used to call us Bonnie and Clyde. Who would have ever thought she'd have a son that was a cop."

"Yes ma'm," was all the officer could muster.

"Ain't seen her in Lord knows how long. In a town as small as Elizabethtown you'd think we'd bump into each other every now and then. How's she doing anyway?"

"Mom moved to Fuqua Varina about fifteen years ago. She passed last month."

The old woman dropped her head.

"I'm sorry."

"Thank you ma'm. I'm sorry too."

"What do you have to be sorry about?"

"Your daughter's loss. Our loss ma'm."

"What are you sayin' son. Sill told me that Tristan had been in an accident."

"I'm afraid it's a little more than that ma'm. I'm sorry to say Tristan's been killed ma'm," the tears flowed freely now."

The old woman gathered her thoughts. It was all a bit much to take. And her first thoughts were of her daughter. Still, she felt for the man sitting next to her.

"You knew Tristan?" She asked still stunned but regaining her composure from the initial shock.

"Yes, mam. We use to be good friends. Played on the same basketball team in high school. He was like a brother to me. We kinda lost touch as we got older but I would always like to think of him as a friend."

"What happened?" Was all the old woman could manage.

"Not exactly sure, ma'm. All I know is that state troopers found him on I-440 this morning. Seems he was shot gangland style one shot to the back of the head. He was pronounced dead at nine nineteen this morning from our reports. I just got the news myself and was supposed to inform his next of kin so she could identify the body."

"Oh my God, poor Sill."

"Ms. Stanton your daughter's handling things pretty well—well as well as anybody could be.

The old woman sat silent for a long time before speaking. When she did her concern was only for her daughter.

"That poor girl's had such a tough life. You don't know what she's been through," she said aloud and to no one in particular. My poor baby..."

The squad car pulled up in the driveway and the old woman thanked the officer, grabbed the baby and made her way to the house as if each step were her last.

Opening the door she saw her daughter staring out the living room a glass of wine in her hand. She turned as her mother approached and welcomed the warm embrace as she felt her mother wilt before her. If at no other time, Sill knew that she needed to remain strong for the old woman who had stood strong for her so many times.

"Are you okay baby? Oh, Sylvia I am so sorry."

"I'm okay mommy. Really I am," she said as a tear rolled down her cheek.

"Oh, baby I am so sorry. It's such a crazy world we live in. Filled with so much senseless violence and Tristan was such a good man—wouldn't hurt a fly—oh baby, it's always the good ones. And so young... Oh, baby I'm so sorry."

Sylvia remained uncharacteristically calm in lieu of the events, which had just unfolded, and the old woman, always so perceptive had to take a step back for a minute. What was it? There was no doubt Tristan was no doubt Sylvia's soul mate. She had seen Sylvia with countless men friends or at least those that proposed to be so and though her daughter had always proved indifferent and distant Tristan had broken through that rough calloused exterior and brought out the best, the carefree little girl in her daughter once again. For the first time in a very long time her daughter had trusted, believed and felt free enough to give her love and her heart to someone. And that person had been this man, this man who North Carolina state troopers said was now dead the victim of a senseless gangland style killing. All preliminary reports said the killing was a case of mistaken identity. Yet, the fact remained that he was for all intensive purposes gone. Now all that remained was the memory and all the dreams and hopes of a life together. Hell, in a few hours they were to be boarding a plane for Freeport in the Bahamas. It was a trip they both worked so hard for, a trip that would see the culmination of all the hard work they'd put in in recent months and a chance to love each other. And now this. And Sylvia was acting like she'd lost no more than a part-time job at the local 7/11. The old woman and looked long and hard at her daughter's eyes but could detect any emotion—neither love nor caring—and wondered if once again Sill had shut down and withdrawn into her inner world. Was she lost in desperation? There was no clue as to what was going through the young woman's thoughts.

"That's why we called you over ma'm. Don't be alarmed. We come across this more often than not under extenuating circumstances. You see frequently when soldiers return from battle or the front lines. It's called posttraumatic stress, ma'm. Your daughter's simply in a state of shock. But she'll need you when she comes out of it. What I'd suggest is that you call a doctor in the morning. He maybe able to prescribe something that will help her deal with the magnitude of the situation. Sorta ease her grief and loss if ya know what I mean."

"Thank you officer," the old woman said never taking her eyes off her daughter.

"Not a problem, ma'm. Here's my card. Call me if you need any help."

"Thanks again officer," she said locking the door behind the two officers.

Turning to her daughter who still stood staring out the window as though she were expecting Tristan to pull up at any minute.

"Sill I'm gonna put Chris to bed and then I want you to change and get ready for bed too. It's been a rough night and I don't think your staring out the window's gonna help any. Lie down and get a good night's rest and we can talk in the morning. Okay sweetheart?"

Sylvia walked over to her mother, embraced her long and hard, whispered 'I love you mommy and headed upstairs and to her bedroom. The old woman was truly worried now and positioned herself in the hall outside her daughter's bedroom in full sight of Sylvia and waited to hear her daughter's breathing grow faint before she closed her own eyes.

Chapter 13

The old woman was up at the crack of dawn. The hard backed chair had taken it's toll on her back and she grimaced slightly as she stood. Sill was still asleep and she feared that worst when she awoke so she took the young officer's advice and called Dr. Ali and made her case. Agreeing to shoot by on the way o his office he'd leave some Tratazone to calm her and her sleep. As far as the old lady was concerned he couldn't get there soon enough. She'd witnessed Sill's behavior after a traumatic event that led her to psychiatric ward some years earlier and knew that her daughter could be a handful and knew that at her age she certainly wasn't a match for the strength and stubbornness of a woman grieving at a loss the magnitude of Sill's. She was only grateful that the two officers had been there to lend a hand last night. Still she was sure that once the grief hit her today she'd need them or somebody to control her daughter. Even as a little girl, Sill had been a handful when her temper got the best of her. And now this. There would be hell to pay but Dr. Ali promised upon his leaving that all the old lady had to do was call him and he'd send over a nurse's aid or two who were adept at handling unruly patients. Thanking him she showed him the door before checking on Christopher and then back upstairs to check to see if her daughter had awakened. The old woman was remorse but she had already come to the conclusion that although Tristan's death was a hideous and grievous crime that there was little time to grieve. Life came as a blessing. And death followed in whatever form and for whatever reason as a natural part of life. It was seldom a happy event but it was what it was. And for reasons we could do little about it would touch us all in some way, somehow, someday. What was more important was to protect the living and give them a reason to live full and fruitful lives until death reared it's ugly head and sought it's next victim. And Sylvia's life was certainly a life worth preserving even if at time she did not believe so. And it wouldn't be entirely out of the realm of possibility for her to consider it all. After all, she'd just lost the only man she'd ever really loved at a time in her life when everything was finally starting to become so clear and meaningful.

The old woman bustled around the house leaving Christopher downstairs in his playpen and came up to check on Sill. In the bathroom with the door closed and the shower running the old woman panicked. There were pills in the medicine cabinet and she was sure Tristan had a straight razor or two and Sill hadn't really said anything since she'd heard the news. Lord knows what was on her mind. Her mother panicked knocking on the door loud enough where Sill could hear despite the shower running.

"Baby, you alright?"

The door opened. Sill stepped out, a towel wrapped tightly around her.

"Where's the fire?" She asked her mother.

"No fire. I was just wondering if you were alright?"

"I'm fine. Don't worry. Just need to go down to the precinct and see if I can find out anymore, identify the body and then start to make funeral arrangements."

"Baby, are you sure you're alright. You're awfully cool for someone who just lost a husband."

"Have to be mommy. I'm hurt deeply but I have a son to raise and a mother that I'd like to grow old with. I can't let Tristan's death kill me and all those I love too. You will help me with the funeral arrangements won't you mommy?"

"Certainly baby," the old woman stared at her only daughter somewhat bewildered by her calm reserve.

"What's wrong mommy?"

214

"I guess I'm in a state of shock myself. I'm here on the verge of tears, ready to cry my heart out yet I know I have to be strong for you and you act as if nothing's happened at all."

"I told you mommy. I'm crying inside. I loved that man more than I've ever loved anyone and now he's gone but I just can't let go and just fall to pieces," Sill said wiping a tear from the corner of her eye. "All I need is for you to just be there for me."

"Aren't I always?"

"Yes, you are mommy," Sill said forcing a slight smile and hugging her mother tightly.

"Are you gonna be okay? Do you want me and the baby to come along?"

"No, mommy I'll be okay. Don't worry I'm not gonna do anything rash mommy. So relax those days are long gone. I just need some time to put things in order and give myself a little time to think but trust me mommy I'll be fine. Don't you worry 'bout a thing. I'm gonna check on what really happened, see if I can't get a handle on things. I should be back by dinner and like I said don't worry."

Sylvia pulled the Mercedes out of the driveway and headed towards the inner state and the state police headquarters in Raleigh. Once there she got no more than what the local police had told her. She then went to the morgue and made a positive i.d. of the body. She then headed back towards home but the morgue had been even a little more than even she could stomach and several times over the course of the ride home she had to stop and regroup. It was all a bit much and so unwarranted that all she could do was stop and cry. Over and over she looked for answers and heard herself again asking everyone and noone 'Why?' With no answers forthcoming she continued the long trek home. But by the time she'd gotten there and pieced what little info the police together she at least had a suspicion of who was behind her husband's murder. And the person she most suspected was no other than one Alexander DuMas. She remained calm though. She called his office and talked to Celeste. Celeste had been one of her sorors at A&T in North Carolina some years earlier. They'd always managed to somehow stay in touch and when Sill first arrived in New York she'd been one of the first people Sill had contacted. Later Sill had gotten Celeste a position with Alex's brokerage as his personal secretary. The woman was eternally grateful and remained indebted to Sill. Sill had never imposed on the woman but now she required her loyalty.

"Hey girl, I thought you'd fallen off the edge of the planet. Ain't nobody seen or heard from you in Lord knows how long. Where you been?"

"I'm back here in North Carolina. Just chillin'."

"Ain't much else to do in North Carolina but chill," Celeste laughed.

"U right."

"What happened? New York get too much for you?"

"No, actually I loved it but daddy passed and I just didn't want mommy to be alone."

"Oh, I'm sorry."

"Listen I need you to do me a favor C. I need you to get me Alex's itinerary and his whereabouts for these dates but I need you to do this on the down low," Sill said.

"Oh you want me to do some sheisty undercover, ruthless shit."

"Somethin' like that," Sill whispered.

"Oh, you know I'm loving that. You know sheisty is my middle name. And for what this motherfucker's paying me I'd be glad too. Ooops I forgot you're seeing him aren't you?"

"Girl where you been. That was over a year and a half ago. I've been married, widowed and had a son since then."

"Get out! Well congratulations and condolences. Damn I have been out of the loop haven't I?"

"Appears that way… Anyway can you do it?"

"Hell yeah! Anything I can do to hem this tight motherfucker up. He's the cheapest, tightest motherfucker I've ever worked for. I can't stand him. Is this your phone number?"

Yep."

"Okay! Give me a few minutes and let me see what I can find out and I'll give you a call back."

"Thanks Celeste. Not a problem. Anything for a soror."

"Okay , love call me as soon as you get the info."

"I will. He's not here today but his planner's on his desk so I'll check it right now and get back to you in a minute."

Sill hung the phone up, poured herself a glass of Chablis and waited for the call back before staging her next move.

A few minutes later the phone awakened her from her thoughts. Listening intently she smiled before hanging the phone up. Just as she'd suspected the date of Tristan's murder Alex had taken a personal day. This only confirmed her thoughts and put her plan in full effect now. Hell, she could have taken him to court or made allegations but all he would have done was have his cook or butler admit that he was home that day and if worse came to worse he could and he would wind up in court but he could afford the best lawyers in the world to get him off. Hell, and what were the chances of her even getting to court to testify. And without the star witness there would be no case. Besides Sylvia wanted to do this. She wanted despite her beliefs to be the mighty hand of justice of vengeance. Sylvia smiled at the thought. Vengeance is mine said the Lord but when it came to Alexander vengeance would be hers.

Sylvia not only her found out where Alex had been on the day Tristan had been killed but she also had Celeste give her his itinerary for the upcoming month. It was rather loosely filled leaving her lots of room to lure him in before making her move. She wondered if it was to soon to call him. The funeral was only a few days old. The anger and longing was still fresh in her heart. She wanted him to pay so dearly that she knew that if she acted now out of anger and grief that it would only end up being botched so she exercised something she had never been good at and that was patience. Besides it was far too soon to approach him considering her husband had just past. She would surely be considered lecherous and uncaring, a gold digger even and what would mommy think. She hadn't even bothered to tell mommy what she believed. But mommy was perceptive. She'd probably already come up with the same thing Sylvia had and just hadn't said anything. She prayed mommy hadn't considered the possibility of Alex being involved. It would certainly kill the old woman if she thought she was in any way responsible for Tristan's death.

Her family doctor had prescribed Vicodin and Darvocette and Sill never one to imbibe found herself taking them more and more. It was now the only way she could get through the long southern nights. Every idle minute was spent thinking about how she would make Alex pay for the grief and sadness he'd brought into her life. Mommy was concerned for her and it showed but she refused to talk about it. Any other time she had an opinion or at least some words of wisdom about anything and everything. But Sill believed that deep down inside she was taking the blame for

218

Tristan's demise. Neither woman dared speak of the murder each believing that with time all things pass and since there was nothing they could do now why belabor the issue. Mommy seemed so much more cognizant of the baby now and Sylvia knew the guilt was taking its toll on the old woman. Sylvia grappled with ways to assuage her mother's feelings but was so consumed with her own guilt that it was not long before she left the whole affair alone and simply concentrated on revenging her husband's death. The days were long and the nights even longer as she both schemed and plotted. And the months that passed were close to unbearable. She was by no means a criminal let alone a murderer. Her parents had raised her in the strictest sense to be a good Christian and she had never strayed far from the example that they'd set but now only God could save her and although she never once considered killing Alex when she'd finished tormenting him he'd probably wish he were dead. The weeks and months flew by and Sill eased up in the pursuit of her husband's killer. The police were no closer to finding a suspect than when they'd first found the body and by now the trail had grown ice cold. Sill had with the help of Celeste and some other good friends she'd cultivated while in New York had begun to put her plan into effect but without letting any of the parties involved knowing just what her ultimate goal was. And Celeste didn't need to know now. She was quite satisfied just dropping hints and letting Alex know that she'd talked to Sill and that she was doing fine and whatever lie she thought would enhance Sill's aura in his eyes. Reporting back to Sill with all the glee of a ten-year-old schoolgirl-playing matchmaker for her best friend in the schoolyard at lunchtime Celeste loved the mischief.

"Sill let me tell you how I shook ol' boy up today."

"I'm afraid to know."

"Girl, you know how I been tellin' him you got the school up and runnin' down there and you all successful and this and that. Well, I told him how your school has brought attention far and wide and how it's also increased your prospects."

"Oh, Lord Celeste. I don't know why I got you involved in this. I forgot you were the one that almost got our sorority sanctioned when you went and fed the previous line raw chitterlins' and that little girl from Cincinnati almost choked to death."

"Oh no, wait, hold up, Sill. That sawed off little trick got just what she deserved. She should've choked to death. I wanted to beat yo' ass for callin' EMS. That little ho was messin' with Akeem and she knew I was going with him or just about to be going with him. And you know I wasn't just gonna stand by and let some girl suck his stuff just 'cause she asks him to. And from what I hear that was that little bitch's specialty. Almost every AKA on campus had problems with her and their mens. Ol' girl had a reputation and a half. I mean we could all been slurping and burping but we were the ladies on campus so we wasn't runnin' around just suckin' niggers off. You had to put some work in to get that kind of treatment. So, when I heard all this shit about 'bout this little "b" I just wanted to see if she was truly as good as they said she was so I had her walk around with a raw, wrinkled, up piece of chitterlin' for a day since this carnivorous little bitch always had to have a piece of meat in her mouth. Wasn't my fault that she tried to deep throat the shit and wound up half chokin' to death," Celeste laughed.

"Shit came back to haunt you didn't it?"

"Yeah, but this is different Sill. I ain't sharing nothin' but tiny tid-bits of your life and I just watch him salivate over every word. Besides the shit I be tellin' him is true for the most part. Onliest thrill I get is watchin' Mr. Tightass wet his damn self whenever I mentioned your name. He up here actin' all high and mighty and the

220

minute I mention your name it's like he just stops like he a deer caught in a car's headlights."

"Well, you be careful Celeste. That man wields a lot of power and has a low threshold for pain. Trust me. I don't want anything bad to happen to you at my expense."

"I'm a big girl Sill. Trust. I ain't never gonna let no man hurt me. Guess that's why I'm still single at thirty-eight. The first sign of trouble and he either he gets his walking or baby girl gets ghost."

"You ain't never said nothin'. I know that's right."

"But on the real though Sill—all bullshit aside—I am so proud of you. I read the article about your school and how you've increased those poor kids reading scores in only a year. They said you have revolutionized the traditional school of learning. And they went on to say that Newark's Mayor Cory Booker came down to see you and your school and was seriously considering adopting your model for the Newark City school system. Girl, you gonna be paid."

Sill laughed.

"I don't think it's quite there yet. I believe Mayor Booker was just seeking some new innovations—you know—some creative teaching methods to implement in the schools being that we have basically the same population. That's all."

"That's all my ass. If Cory Booker came my way seeking anything—anything at all—I'm gonna find that little bitch from Cincinnati and get her to give me a remedial course into how to deep throat a damn dinosaur so I can be ready for that man. He's one fine ass specimen of a man ain't he?"

"Wasn't really payin' any attention," Sill laughed.

"If you ain't notice how fine Cory is then either your eyes done failed or your shit done dried up and died and even if that was the case I'd find someway to get that man to give me mouth-to-mouth and bring it back to life. Wit' his fine self… And you gonna tell me you ain't notice?"

"I will say he's terribly bright. That I will say about the brother."

"Oh shit. You either been down in the country too long or you just flat out lyin' Sill."

Sill laughed again.

"Oh shit! You fucked him didn't you Sill? That's what it is. You fucked him."

"I haven't slept with a man since my husband died and neither want to or have any desire to."

"You're serious aren't you?"

"Dead."

"You know what's funny, Sill?"

"No what's funny?"

"Funny thing is I believe you. Damn it's been over a year. That Tristan must have been one hell of a man."

"That he was."

"Okay sister girl, it's getting late and I got to get up and meet Mr. DuMas tomorrow so let me go but I will say this when I get finished telling Mr. DuMas about you and Cory Booker he'll be eating out of the palm of your hand."

"Night Celeste."

"Night Sill."

Chapter 14

The flight out of Raleigh International had been nothing less than peaceful and quick. Barely had Sylvia gotten a chance to close her eyes and drift off than she was awakened by the pilot's deep baritone.

"Ladies and gentlemen Flight 165 arriving at New York's Laguardia is about to begin it's descent. Our estimated time of arrival is one thirty and we seem to be right on time. At this time we are on schedule and should be arriving in about fifteen minutes. We ask now that you place your seats and trays in an upright position."

Sylvia sipped the last of her double of Jack Daniels and placed the tray in an upright position and clutched the plastic cup she held in her hand. She hated flying and no matter how much she flew she had never gotten comfortable with the idea. She didn't know if it was the anticipation of taking off or the rapid descent that she disliked most but she had come to the realization that she just didn't like flying. It would all be over within a matter of minutes and so Sill leaned back as far as she possibly could with her seat in an upright position, closed her eyes and thought of more pleasant thoughts. She thought of the many fall days and fewer winter nights she's spent with Tristan nestled up close to her in bed and smiled. Lost in her thoughts she felt the giant aircraft touch down on the runway and relaxed as she felt the 727 so coming to a halt.

Moving through the airport towards the luggage claim she felt a deep sigh of relief as she heard Celeste's voice scream her name.

"Hey girl! Sill! Sill! Hey girl!" Celeste shouted. The tiny woman's voice boomed out over the crowded airport and made Sill cringe. Out of all the well wishers greeting loved ones there was one voice that resounded and reverberated over all the others.

"My goodness C. There must have been close to a hundred and fifty passengers on that flight and you know the only voice I hear is yours. Damn girl, you're loud. I know you're glad to see me but damn. Good thing I wasn't trying to be discreet or on the download. Fuck being undercover!" Sill laughed hugging the woman tightly and grinning broadly.

"I'm so glad to see you. I swear you haven't changed a bit since back when we were in school. Matter-of-fact, I hate to say it but I think you've lost a few pounds since then. And you mean to tell me you were pregnant?"

"Was, but that doesn't mean I'm supposed to just throw in the towel and let myself go to the dogs. Does it?"

"No, but you know most women can't help but gain a few pounds during pregnancy and I'm just saying with middle age it's just…"

"See, there you go throwing me in the mix. You should by now that I have never been most women. I'm a diva baby and not just any diva I'm the diva president. I set the standard baby. I show 'em how it's done. You might wanna pick up a few pointers along the way." Sill said grinning and patting Celeste on the buttocks and grinning widely. "Might wanna begin with an exercise regimen. That's a start and maybe one day you can grow up to be just like me." Sill said chuckling loudly.

"Ooh somebody is really feeling themselves today." Celeste said laughing and grabbing Sill's arm playfully. "But to tell you the truth I'm really glad you're feeling yourself so much because what you're about to embark on is gonna take a world of confidence and Lord knows what else. I wish I could talk to someone.

224

You know just throw it out there and get some feelers because to tell you the truth what you're planning on is nothing short of suicidal."

Sylvia dropped her head. Celeste wasn't alone in her reservations. She had hers too but she'd come too far to turn tail and run now. She wasn't vindictive by nature but she refused to falter now.

"I've had my reservations too and on the serious tip I've thought about the task I'm undertaking and trust me Celeste you don't know how many times I've considered backing down but I owe myself. I owe Tristan and I owe my baby the right to know if my suspicions are true and then I owe at least myself to at least make it right/"

Celeste pulled Sylvia to the curb and flagged the closest cab. The women eased into the cab and waited while the cabbie loaded the luggage in the trunk.

"You know I love you Sill and would back you to the darkest, deepest, recesses of Hades and I'm here for you no matter what you decide. I'm just voicing my opinion is all."

"Thanks for being honest C."

"Never knew any other way to be…"

"Don't I know?" Sill laughed. "So what's on the agenda?"

"Just sit tight baby. What time do you have?"

"Two, two twenty-eight. Why? I hope you don't have anything planned C. Outside of handling my business all I'm really looking for is a little r & r. Seriously, I don't want to meet anybody, don't want to hit no new clubs, nothing. I'm serious C. I just want to chill, maybe do a little shopping. But outside of that I really don't want to do anything."

"I gotcha. Believe me you made that perfectly clear when I talked to you earlier in the week. If you want to be a poo putt that's on you. 'Sides Alex has piled up so

225

much work for me that I couldn't get away if I wanted to. I think he did it personally so I wouldn't get in the way," Celeste laughed.

"That's good because my whole purpose for being here is strictly business and right now he's my number one priority."

"Don't I know that. And you're not the only one thinking along those lines. Just this morning he had me clear his whole itinerary for the rest of the week. Made me reschedule every meeting and appointment he had. I'm telling you the boy's nose is wide open. It's like he's getting all his ducks in a row for the second coming and every now and then he glances up at me over his bi-focals to make sure I 'm following as if I didn't know he's preparing for your arrival when I'm the one that has him all gassed up over you with those wild tales I be tellin' him about you every time I get his ear."

"Just hope I can match up to the hype."

"Oh you're gonna blow his mind baby," Celeste said looking her girlfriend up-and-down. Rumors ran rampant back during their college days about Celeste's swinging both ways but she'd never approached Sill so she never gave it a second thought. Still, it was obvious that Celeste saw Sill as not only as a close friend but as a potential partner.

"You know I don't roll like that C."

"I know but I'll be the first in line should you ever change your mind."

Before Celeste could get the final word out her cell chimed in almost as if on cue. She didn't bother to answer but handed the phone Sill who stared quizzically.

"Answer it. Ain't nobody but your Mr. Wonderful. He asked me what time you were getting in and what was a good time to call. Did I plan this shit or did I plan this shit," she smiling sheepishly before grabbing he phone back.

226

"Let's wait. I'd like to see him sweat a little bit. He hears your voice on the first ring that fools liable to come all over himself," she said slapping Sill on the knee and doubling over in laughter.

The cabbie glanced in the his rear view mirror to see what all the laughter was about then shook his head and entered the Holland Tunnel into Manhattan.

A minute later the phone rang again. This time Celeste answered it and after a few short words handed the phone to Sill and stared out the window at the New York skyline.

"Glad to have you back in town Mrs. Stanton."

"Thanks Alex and how are you?"

"I'm good, even better now that I hear your voice. It's been quite some time."

"You're right. I guess you heard the news about Tristan."

"I did Sill and I am truly sorry. I asked your mother to share my condolences. I tried to get in touch with you so I could share them personally but was unable to. Believe me I know how it is to lose a loved one."

Sylvia wondered if he was purposely being sarcastic and immediately felt her pressure rise. No she had to remain calm and couldn't lose her temper or she'd blow the whole plan. But she had the distinct impression he was referring to losing her and she was in no means any comparison to the loss or death of a loved one. God knows he couldn't be implying that. Why that arrogant son of a bitch but Sill played it cool and did her best to shrug off the remark.

"So, how's Thomas doing?"

"Thomas is Thomas," Alex laughed. "He's my constant. Never sways he keeps me centered. He asks about you frequently. When Celeste told me you were coming I promised him I'd get you to stop by. He'd really love to see you."

"And you?" Sill asked feeling him out slightly.

"Would I?" he laughed. "I never wanted to see you go in the first place. Of course I'd love to see you. You know with all that's happened and come between us I'd still go to the ends of the earth for you, Sill. I waited when you had questions concerning my character. I waited through a marriage and I'm still hopeful. I'm still waiting. I'm a victim of your timeframe sweetheart. Whenever you decide you want me or have time for me one thing's for sure. I'll be there."

The words made Sill cringe but she was a trooper and hung in there. She was sure of one thing and it was this one thing that would enable her to pull off her plan. She had to appear sincere, make him believe that after all this time she'd finally come to her senses.

"I don't know about you waiting but you do sound sincere. Maybe we can get together you always wee a great host."

"Is that all I was a great host?" Alex asked the dejection noticeable in his voice.

"No." she laughed feeling his pain. "But listen why don't you get back to me. I know you're a busy man. Why don't you give me a call when you're free. You take care now." Sylvia said before flipping the phone shut.

"Didn't give him time t answer did you? That's what I'm talkin' bout. That's how *we* roll. And they say men run the world. Barack may be the president but you and I know Michelle's the one really runnin' the shit on the down low." Celeste said raising her hand and giving Sill a high five.

The phone rang as soon as the women commenced their charade as both looked at each other and burst out in laughter again.

"You did the right thing girl. Let him sweat. Shit, he's used to playing hardball. Let's just see how good he is at his own game."

"I intend on doing exactly that. Believe me."

The rest of the day proved uneventful and the two women contented themselves with sitting around Celeste's spacious condo on the East Side reminiscing about their college days and the various men they had the opportunity to come across in their lives. Sill's stories always paled in comparison since Celeste's included both men and women.

"Had this one chick who swore she was in love, little young gal. You know I touched her up right and the next thing I knew she was stalking me, you know, following me everywhere telling anyone I came in contact with that if they so much as breathed my way she was going to take them out. It got so bad that I'd peek out of my office window and there she was waiting for me outside of my job every day. And this wasn't your typical run of the millmistress. I mean this was all woman. I'm talking one hundred per cent USDA grade A prime rib. I mean this girl could punk Halle Berry. She was beautiful but she had that fatal attraction. You know the kind that drove Michael Douglas damn near crazy. Yeah, well she had some similar shit going on. Now you know I'm a sex addict but this girl was scary."

"So what did you do?"

"Wasn't anything I could do but ride it out. I curtailed the stalking but when she said she was ready I just assumed the position," Celeste laughed. "I know you were waiting for me to tell you how I whooped her ass but that's not always the case. You're gonna find out sooner or later that as good as you are in your own right there's always somebody better. I heard Muhammad Ali say that when he was on top of the world and it's always stuck with me. Told you that story for a reason Sill. Sometimes you're a winner when you concede. I don't think that's something you've ever learned. Losing isn't the greatest folly. Sometimes you win when you lose. Do you feel me?"

"I hear you," Sill said as she sipped at the glass of Gray Goose in front of her.

"Enjoy New York. Shop til' you drop then go back to the good livin' and hug that pretty baby boy for me. Leave Soddom and Gommorah for us heathens. You're better than this."

"I hear you," Sill repeated taking a long sip this time.

"And you still won't change your mind?"

"I said I heard you. Just give me some time to think about it."

"That's all I can ask."

No sooner had Celeste made the comment than the tiny cell to the right of her went off again.

"Believe it's for you," she said handing Sylvia the phone.

Sylvia palmed the phone and whispered gently into it.

"Sylvia here."

"Sylvia. Alex. I believe we were cut off the last time we spoke. Didn't want you to get the impression that I'd hung up on you. And I believe we were in the midst of setting up a dinner date or something along those lines when we were disconnected."

"Sorry, I must have missed that part of the conversation. What did you have in mind?" She asked now grinning playfully at Celeste.

"Damn you," Celeste said. "After everything I said you're still going through with it aren't you?"

"'Scuse me Alex, Celeste is trying to tell me something. Yes, what is it dear?"

"I said you're still going through with it aren't you?"

"Why no dear just planning on having dinner with an old friend is all," Sylvia lied.

"Okay, I'm going to leave it alone but you're going to get yourself killed. You're not playing at the shallow end anymore. You're playing in deep waters now," Celeste said before grabbing both glasses and topping them off with a fresh pour.

"What was that all about," Alex inquired.

"Nothing dear. That was just Celeste inquiring about whether I was going out to dinner or did she need to fix something?"

"And?"

"And I told her that since no one had asked me out I guess ordering a pizza or some Chinese would be fine."

"I just asked you out and you didn't respond. Stop playing with me Sylvia. Would you like to have dinner with me or not?"

"Oh, did you? I must have missed it. Why I'd certainly love to have dinner with you Alex but I wouldn't want to leave Celeste in a lurch. You don't mind if she comes do you?"

"Certainly not. Bring her as well. In fact, I'll invite a couple of more people and will make an evening of it. How's eight sound?"

"Sounds good to me. Let me check with Celeste," but before Celeste could open her mouth to reply Sylvia did.

"She said eight would be fine."

"Okay, I'll send Thomas by at around eight."

"We'll be ready," Sylvia said grinning broadly at the expression on Celeste's face.

"I see that motherfucker Monday to Friday from eight o'clock in the morning 'l five o'clock everyday fuckin' day. What the hell makes you think I want t see his ass on m day off?"

"Oh, be nice. Turn around and look at how you're living girl. I can guarantee you that a whole lotta sistas would love to be livin' this lifestyle and despite my feelings ya gotta be cognizant of who's paying the bills dear."

"I am cognizant but it's not as if he's giving me anything. I work hard. Believe me if that man parts with a dollar you'd best believe you're earning ever last dime of it. Trust me. It's a nice arrangement but it doesn't mean that I want to spend my free time in his dry ass company."

"I hear you babe but wasn't it you that told me less than fifteen minutes ago that you'd go through the deepest, darkest depths of hell if I needed you to?"

"Yeah, I said that and..."

"And I need you more than ever tonight baby. I want to get a good look at the layout and talk to the cook among other things while I'm there."

"And believe me you can do that without me."

"I probably could but you know what they say about two heads being better than one."

"Yeah, I also know the one about too many cooks spoiling the broth."

"Oh, Celeste I'm trying to do the damn thing. Can I get some empathy from your ass, some damn cooperation? You told me you'd help me and here you are bucking me at every turn. Damn!"

"Oh for the life of me why did I think you had changed? You're just as bossy as you were in college. Shit! Give me fifteen minutes."

Sylvia never understood why Celeste always put her through the winger when the outcome was always the same. She smiled knowing ta I wasn't so much a con game that affected Celeste. No she was one of the best at that. It was simply the love and respect she commanded. She'd never understood why or how she commanded either the love or respect but was more than glad she did.

The phone rang loud and long.

"Thomas is here." Celeste shouted. She hadn't bothered to answer but knew the number by heart. Only this time she wasn't summoning Alex but Sill.

"Damn you asked me to get ready and here you are taking your sweet ass time. I'll be in the car. By the way what is it that you needed me to do?"

"Just need to check out the house. I wanna talk to the help is all. You know get some insight into how things run—shit like that."

"C'mon Sill that building has the tightest security of almost any building in the city. You should know. You used to live there. Besides what if you did make off with a fewof Alex's priceless possessions. So what! If you asked he'd give you damn near anything in there anyway. You wouldn't be doing anything and it damn sure wouldn't make up for your loss."

"What is it they used to say about being all in the Kool-Aid and don't know the flavor? I always did like that one. I guess I really liked it because it fit you so well."

Sill laughed. "No one's trying to rob Alex and stop being so damn inquisitive. The less you know he better off you'll be in the long run. Now would you please tell Thomas that I'm on my way?"

"I swear I don't know why I like you," Celeste said as she lifted her long flowing black evening dress from the floor and closed the door behind her.

If Celeste looks good, Sylvia looked sensational. The extra time she'd requested had done her a world of good and even Celeste looked on appreciatively. Dressed in a navy blue evening dress laced in gold that hit her right above the knee her well toned thighs glistened firmly and though it was somewhat revealing it showed no more

233

bust line than was necessary to keep every male head in the house turning appreciatively. Alex was more than ecstatic to see her and even commented that his longtime friend and confidante was his guest of honor on this particular evening. His eyes shone with pride as even those he held in the highest esteem seemed to marvel at this enchanting creature who had taken this evening off to grace them all with her presence. Sylvia always the consummate lovely who always seemed to be in awe of the attention she drew and never looked uncomfortable in the midst of all the attention felt somehow out of sorts tonight. Although she had always been comfortable being the center of attention she was uneasy on this night. On this night when she had asked Celeste to run interference she realized that this small get together which was the result inviting of her Celeste had turned into a large gathering and left her no breathing room whatever. And where was the respect? If she were a friend of Alex's it just didn't seem right that all these rich preppy bastards in their Brooks Brothers suits and Jos A Banks money clips bulging with fifties and hundreds should be flexin' and pushin' up on her. But here they were not allowing her space to breathe let alone the time to get a sense of where Alex kept his stocks bonds and other monies. If she was right and Alex was street, he wasn't trusting a bank or any other financial institution to keep his money. Besides he worked in to closely with those institutions and I it's one thing he was aware of was the presence of thieves in the temple. And she knew like he knew that that was the last place he'd house his fortune. No the money was right here under their very noses—right there—possibly in plain sight. She just had to figure where but how could she with all these vultures looming. After about an hour or so, Sylvia knew about as much as she had when she arrived and resigned herself to the fact that there were just too many people to exact the knowledge she needed to carry out her plan in

234

any detail. No her initial plan was for the small trio to share a nice quiet dinner and Alex did as Alex always did and blew it all out of proportion. Now there were people everywhere and not only were they everywhere but Alex's little announcement about her being the guest honor made the curious ones inquire about what special qualities this woman must have to have her elevated in Alex Dumas' eyes. The remainder were simply paying their respects out of homage to Alex for being invited to Alex's home. Whatever the reason Sylvia was ready to explode under the despite it all.

"How's it going girl?" Celeste said handing her a drink. "Patron baby. I'll give it to him. Mr. Man knows how to throw a party. He doesn't seem to hedge on the good stuff."

Sylvia smiled.

"How's it coming? I don't know how you could possibly gain any information. Seems like anybody and everybody has been pushing up on you. I never knew you were quite the star."

"I didn't either but look Celeste what I need for you to do is look out for Alex while I snoop around the study. Better yet you can come with me so it looks like we're simply checking out his library and having an old fashioned heart-to-heart girl talk so he doesn't get suspicious."

"I gotcha. Let me run to the bathroom and I'll be right in."

Sylvia made her way to the big heavy oak doors and let herself in. No sooner than she

had, she felt a tug at her waist. *Damn. Who the hell could it be now?*

"Sylvia you don't know how long I've waited to finally get you alone," Alex whispered in her ear.

Sylvia startled, turned abruptly and managed a coy smile.

"I hardly think we're alone Alex."

"That's true and I do apologize. What started out as a quiet dinner party just sort of blossomed. I do so apologize. I wanted nothing more than to spend some quality time with you but…"

"There you are. Girl I've been looking all over for you," Celeste said ignoring Alex's presence altogether. "I saw you earlier but you were surrounded by a host of gentlemen," she said making sure to get this little dig in. "Didn't want to disturb you. Didn't know if any one of them was a prospective suitor or not but they all seemed to have the same intentions. At least it looked that way."

Sylvia dropped her head and smiled. She had never understood why Celeste was the way she was. She had always had an evil tint to her. She was just malicious in nature. Sylvia was just glad that she was on her side.

"She did have quite a few of good looking men around her didn't she? I was trying to get a word in edgewise myself but the crowd was just a little too thick. "

Sylvia blushed deeply and this time the gesture was sincere.

"You know when Sylvia was living in New York a couple of years ago the response was always the same. The men just thronged to her. I called myself dating her at the time and I'm gonna tell you any guy dating this woman better have a pretty thick ego. She's a male magnet."

"Oh Alex stop it. You know that's not true. The only reason people were around was to meet the woman on Alex's arm."

Alex smiled.

"I don't know about that but one thing I do know is that when we were in school you were attracting men like fleas on a dog. I do know that."

"And ain't nothin' changed," Alex replied giving Celeste a high five and grinning all the while.

"Hope you ladies will excuse me but I have guests to see to although I don't think I'll find any better company than you two. Sill knows where everything is so if you need anything just ask and I'm sure she'll be glad to get it for you. "

And with that said Alex turned and walked out of the library and down the long hall to the living room.

"Damn C. why did you have to rile him up?"

"Rile shit up? The niggas been riled up since you left two years ago. You know as well as I do that he's obsessed with your ass. All I did was feed him, you know give him a little taste, whet his appetite," she laughed.

"His appetite gets any wetter he'll be slobberin' all over the place. I think the trap you set is well laid now all we have to do is draw him in, gain his trust again and work him like only we can do. Now do me a favor and watch the door for me. I don't want the whole evening to be a total loss."

"I gotcha. Go ahead but be quick about it. You know he's going to swing back through here since he knows you're in here."

Sylvia opened each drawer of the mahogany desk and rummaged through the multitude of papers careful not to disturb the order of things and making sure everything was in its' rightful place when she'd finished. After finding nothing of either interest or importance she moved to the two metal file cabinets in the corner of the room where she rapidly rifled through its' contents. And then as if a deer caught in a car's headlights she stopped. Grabbing a file from the cabinet she threw the paperwork in her clutch and turned to Celeste smiling but Celeste was hardly smiling.

"Close the drawer he's coming Sill."

Sylvia closed the drawer softly as not to make any noise and eased over to the bookcase and grabbed a hand full of rather thin paperbacks by J. California Cooper just as Alex entered the room.

"Well, I'm glad to see there's something that I have that peaks your curiosity."

"I'm not sure that's all that peaks her curiosity," Celeste said grinning broadly.

"Hush Celeste. I was just lookin' at your collection of J.California Cooper. I'm surprised to find a man reading her. She's usually talking about female issues."

"I need all the help I can get when it comes to the opposite sex," Alex laughed.

"I know that's right. If you're referring to Sylvia you probably need a manual. Talk about high maintenance," Celeste said teasing her girlfriend good naturedly.

"Go somewhere Celeste," Sill said playfully.

"I intend to do just that. You two haven't had any alone time since you got here. Just give me a holler when you get ready to go Sill. Some of us do have to get up and go to work in the morning you know."

"I'm ready when you are."

"Ladies, ladies, I haven't even gotten a chance to spend any time with you."

"You spend eight hours a day with me every day so I take it that that comment was directed to Sylvia even though you said ladies," she chuckled.

"Chow good people."

"Your girl is really something," Alex commented.

"She's crazy as hell," Sylvia replied.

"But efficient as heck if you can get past the rough exterior. I've never had a better assistant. She keeps the whole office running and keeps me on my toes."

"I just hope you're compensating her adequately for all her efficiency."

"Why don't you ask her? I honestly think she's more than adequately compensated but I think that's more because of the people she knows rather than her office skills if you get my meaning."

"I do and I thank you."

"Enough about Celeste though. And I really must apologize about not getting to spend more time with you tonight. I just didn't expect…"

"Don't apologize Alex. I enjoyed the night and the food was excellent as usual. So you really don't have anything to apologize for. Besides there'll be other times."

"My sentiments exactly," Alex replied biting on Sills subtle overture. "Let's say tomorrow morning—say about ten. We'll go out on the island, around Montauk Point and do a lil' deep sea fishing. Whadda ya say? Let's make a day out of it?"

"That actually sounds like a lot of fun, Alex. And believe it or not that's always something I've wanted to do along with taking a cruise and going skiing in the Alps."

"Maybe that can be arranged. But for now can I send Thomas around for you at ten?"

"That sounds fine, Alex. Let me go round up this crazy woman and get her home or I'll have to hear about how I dragged her and kept her out 'til the wee hours of the morning."

"But it's barely nine o'clock."

"I know but you should know how Celeste has a tendency to overdramatize everything."

"She does have a tendency to do that," Alex laughed. "Then ten a.m. it is."

"Sounds good to me."

Alex leaned over and kissed her gently on the cheek.

The ride home had been quiet. Thomas being one of the reasons why and though he was certainly glad to see Sill she knew he was loyal and would say anything or proceed to give Sill any pertinent information about his employer without becoming suspicious and she wasn't sure if he could be trusted and since she wasn't sure she said little to say other than what was in order. Celeste being astute and following Sill's lead also said little buut kept it cordial enough not to arouse the older man's suspicions.

When both women were inside the apartment Celeste looked at Sill both sheepishly and inquisitively.

"Go ahead and ask but I'm only answering one question and one question only."

"What? I wasn't going to ask you anything. If anything I was going to comment on Alex's place. It is gorgeous. I always wondered how the other half lived and now I guess I know. But since you bring it up let me ask what made you kick him to the curb in the first place? When you first got here you seemed to simply adore the ground he walked on despite the fact that you claimed you weren't interested in men. So what happened?"

"Well, in all honesty C. I saw some things that didn't sit right with me and who I am as a person and when I questioned him I couldn't get a straight answer no matter how hard I tried. It was always some out of the way garbage to throw me off course and I just had to many unanswered questions about some really serious concerns. And when I questioned him it was sort of like Michael Corleone when he says to his wife Kay in the Godfather. He was like, 'don't ever question me about the family business Kay'. Do you remember that scene? Well, that's what it was like with Alex. I was with him when he got shot up in Harlem. I panicked and was scared shitless. But he was calm telling me not to worry and asking me if I believed in

240

Karma. I was dumbfounded at how easy and in-stride he took the shooting and then less than two days later they found two teenage boys shot dead on the same corner. And the description of the killer fit his bodyguard to a tee. When I brought it up he squashed it like it was a daily occurrence. It was at that time that I decided to distance myself from him but he followed me down to North Carolina and had some business dealings with Tristan and awarded him a contract with the clause that he stay away from me which Tristan did until he completed the contract. Later on Tristan winds up dead."

"I see why you had your reservations. But don't you think you're in over your head? If your allegations are true then there is a good possibility that you could end up the same way."

"That's true. All I have in my corner is that Alex is egotistical to a fault and as you know he can acquire what he wants but his ultimate challenge is making me his wife and he knows that all of his money and power are not enough to sway me. Still, it's crushing to his over inflated ego that the man that raises his hand on Wall Street and can lay waste to four or five men in Jersey can't have this 'lil 'ol country girl from North Carolina. I think that's what really bothers him. To tell the truth I don't think he really cares or loves me that much I think what really is eating at him is the fact that a woman has rejected him."

"Í believe you're right. And as long as you keep yourself at bay and just out of reach you'll having eating out of the palm of your hand."

Sylvia smiled.

"That's the plan."

"So where do we go from here?"

"Well, he's back on his high horse. He really thinks that he has a chance. He's supposed to be taking me deep sea fishing tomorrow but I don't have a bit more interest in deep sea fishing than a man in the moon and I'm already feeling like I'm coming down with a little something."

"Is that right?"

Sylvia and Celeste smiled at each other.

"You know fifteen or twenty minutes after we get on the road. I'm sure he'll want to turn around and take me home where he can pamper me and that's where you come in. While he's trying to pamper me I'm going to send him downtown to the seaport to get some porgies and crab legs. And of course you're going to blow his phone up with items that need his attention with the quickness. And while he's downtown taking care of business and catering to my needs I'll be searching for every investment he's made in the last five years. You'll be doing the same thing on your end."

"Okay you've peaked my curiosity. What's up? I'm a little lost."

"Well, I really considered killing his lecherous ass. I'm serious. When Tristan was first murdered, that was my only thought. For weeks it consumed me but then I looked at my mother and my son and I had to calm down and think—you know—rationalize shit and come to the realization that I couldn't lower myself to his level. Besides I remembered something my father once told me."

"What's that?"

"Daddy once told me that the worst thing you could do to a thief is steal from them and being that Alex's whole essence surrounds and is involved with money then the worst hurt and pain I could possibly inflict on him is to take everything of value from him. That would be a fate worse than death for Alex."

"That it would be but then again and although I don't condone killing anyone or anything if you rob Alex blind you best believe there will be retribution far worse than death if he doesn't kill you."

"Thought about that and I've already begun planning for the aftermath. I learned a long time ago that a contingency plan is always a necessity in any activity," Sill said laughing as she poured herself another healthy shot of Grey Goose.

"Going a little heavy on the Goose, don'tcha think?"

"Not hardly, not under the circumstances. Can you believe he has the unmitigated gall to act just like nothing happened? I can't believe this son-of-a-bitch can just knock off somebody, just kill somebody and act like it's all in the course of a day," she said tossing her head back.

"Well, if he can do that once or twice in the time that you've known him you can best believe that it ain't just start there and he's okay with it. Now go ahead and step it up to the big leagues and see what happens to your ass."

"Don't worry I can play the game. What you fail to realize is that I'm no novice at this game."

"I know you're good girl. I've watched you work. I give you your props it's just that…"

"Then you should know that men ain't nothin' but little boys that grew older. They can be worked and manipulated just like any five year old. And trust me I've been playing this game since I was knee high to a grasshopper. If I ain't perfected it by now, then shame on me."

"I hear you but again I think you're playing a dangerous game."

"Listen Celeste I love you like a sister and you know that. The last thing I want to do is put you in harm's way and if you feel that I'm doing that then I won't be

243

offended or hurt if you ain't down with this. Trust me. I know it's a dangerous game and like I said the last thing I want to do is put you at risk. So, instead of warning me just say Sill I'd rather not take part."

"You know I can't say that. You've been too good to me and besides you know I ain't never run from trouble or disaster. You know that anytime I have a chance at fuckin' up somebody's life or my own you know I'm always first in line," Celeste said grinning.

The following day came compliments with a dark, dull, gray overcast day and though Sylvia was anything but excited over her upcoming little venture she was up and at 'em by before5: 30, dressed in her Carolina blue jogging suit. She'd already finished her two-mile run, had stopped by the local meat store, grabbed a half a pound of that bacon she loved so well with the rind on it and was scrambling some eggs with a little Sade in the background when she heard Celeste stirring.

"Dag girl, you still getting up when the rooster crows," she said wiping the sleep from her eyes and pulling her robe around her.

"I've always been an early riser and you know what hey say… The early bird gets the worm. 'Sides I've got a lot to do and not a lot of time to do it. I'm only here for a week you know."

"I hear you."

"Fixed you a little breakfast," Sylvia said placing the plate of bacon, eggs, grits, and slice of holly in front of her. "Orange juice or coffee?"

"Coffee's fine. Black baby, no sugar, no cream. Just like I like my women," she said winking at Sill.

"Ain't nobody paying attention to your simple ass. If I rolled like that and let you'd have a taste, I'd end up turning you out and pimping your ass," Sill laughed.

"If anyone else had told me that I'd probably have gotten offended but your pretty ass could probably do just that so I'm going to leave that alone," she said leaving the topic alone. Inside Celeste smiled. In the entire time the two had been friends— what was it—thirty years now Sill had never avoided or condemned Celeste for her choices or her preference for women. They'd spoken about it openly, accepted the terms of their friendship and gotten along splendidly and much better than Sylvia's so-called straight friends.

"So, you're doing the deep sea fishing thing today?"

"Really don't think so. Things I need to do are right here on the East Side."

"So, you're going to take ol' boy home and work his corporate ass," Celeste said gulping down the coffee and grinning like a Cheshire cat. "I don't know what it is with me but as long as I can remember I've always loved to watch people being turned out. And I get especially excited when they're those little, straight-laced, tight assed corporate types from downtown on Wall Street. You know the kind—the ones with the one point five children and the two-car garage and home on Long Island that schedule sex around the kid's weekly sleepover at the neighbor's house. You know the one's who plan on having children around their doctor's recommendation on when they're ovulating. I give them one night with my freaky ass and I guarantee they've turned in their tighty whiteys for some boxers and turned in their little Caucasian wife, you know Miss Polly Fuckin' Purebread for some of this dark chocolate mousse. Ain't no different than the master in his big house creepin' and lyin' to the mistress about Sally Hemings. Fuck the missionary style. I'm talking riding him like he ain't never been ridden before, the turning him over

245

strapping my shit on and fuckin' his ass 'til he screams it's yours baby, and make him masturbate all at the same time. Shit, I got some shit that will make him think I'm a cross between Cleopatra and Michelle O'fuckin' Bama. And when he's gasping for what he feels is his last breath I'll sit him on the edge of the sofa, spread his legs wide open, kneel in front of him, grease him up and suck his shit like his dick is the last dick on earth before sliding two fingers up his ass and watch him come like he's never come before," Celeste said a grin spreading widely across her face.

"I always knew you had issues, girl."

"Oh shit, Sill I know I ain't tellin' you nothin' new. If I was Alex wouldn't be as strung out as he is. Just wish I could be a fly on the wall."

"I know your freaky ass does."

"Kick his ass, and whatever you do please keep his ass away from the office."

"I'll do that. Just make sure you go through all his files and make copies of everything so I can get a fix on what he's doing and where his most profitable interests are."

"I'll do that," she said before gulping down her last swallow of coffee. "Well, let me get ready for work. I'm supposed to be preparing for an internal audit and I know half of those fools ain't ready."

"Do you baby!"

"Always do. Keep me posted on ol' boys whereabouts. Don't want him sneakin' up on me while I'm doing my dirt. Feel me?"

"I gotcha. And oh yeah, breakfast was delicious."

"Thanks C. And be careful. You don't know who's watching."

"I know that's right. And you better be too. That Rakman gives me the willies."

246

Celeste made her leave and Sylvia packed her overnight bag. Chances were good that she wouldn't be seeing Celeste anymore that week if Alex had his way. And she was certainly going to appease his every wish on her way to drawing him into her confidence once again. The phone rang awakening her from her daydreaming and she was surprised to hear Alex's voice on the other end.

"Morning love. Wanted to make sure you were up and ready to go before I sent Thomas around with the car. Are you ready?"

"I was born ready," Sill replied.

"Okay, Sill, he should be there in no less than twenty to twenty-five minutes," he said before hanging up the phone.

Sill threw a dash of Elizabeth Taylor's new parfum on, grabbed her overnight bag, her cigarettes, refreshed her coffee and made her way to the balcony to contemplate her next move so as to make sure it went off without a hitch. Checking out her outfit, which she deemed nice enough but decided to change it after thinking about Celeste's take on the whole charade. What Celeste had said had made more than a little sense and though she played it off Celeste would never know how much of a freak she really was and after a good year of forced celibacy she was not only going to take him financially she was going to dispose of his mind, body and soul though not necessarily in that order. Looking at her outfit once again Sylvia felt this too casual even for the day, or at least what she had in mind. Deciding on a low cut, flowing, floral sundress, Sylvia grinned. No sooner had she poured herself into the tight fitting dress and pulled her sling

back heels onto her feet she heard Celeste's voice.

"Thomas is here. But hold on so I can catch a ride downtown."

"Okay, we'll be downstairs."

Moments later they pulled up in front of Alex's building. Sylvia exited, kissing Celeste on the cheek and thanking Thomas again.

Calling Alex, she was buzzed in almost instantaneously and was surprised to find no Rakman to open the door for her and the little blond chef on her way out.

Speaking briefly Alex grabbed her by the hand and led her into the dining room and seated at the table which was full of every kind of delicacy one could ever imagine from Belgian waffles to sliced cantaloupe. Sylvia hated to tell him she'd already eaten and took tiny portions of everything she'd ever had an inkling for. Her plate was a smorgasbord of morning delicacies. There was mixed fruit. Honeydew melon, along with French toast, bacon, sausage, poached eggs, canvassed her plate. And as Alex tried to catch her up on the ever fluctuating market and New York's nightlife Sylvia ate 'til she could eat no more.

"The boat leaves at eleven and it's a good two hour drive out to the point Sill so when you're ready let me know."

"Alex would you be upset if we went at another time?"

Alex stopped in mid-sentence almost speechless.

"I thought you wanted to go out?"

"And I would. I would like nothing better but just not today Alex. I'm feeling a little under the weather. Nothing to concern yourself about it's just a woman thing."

If her not wanting to go was a kicker then the 'it's a woman thang' really seemed to crush him. He had obviously planned a day where after all was said and done he'd surely make her his. He'd even gone so far as to give the chef and the butler off so he wouldn't be disturbed upon his return. Still, glad for her company he contemplated the alternatives. After all, it had been her choice and in the end this may even work out better. At least, this way he'd be able to enjoy her alone and in private.

"So, what is it that you'd like to do instead?"

"I'm game for anything but in all actuality I'd like nothing more than to sit back and just chill. You know me. I'm content with a good book, some good conversation, a good movie although from what I've seen I'm not sure they make those anymore."

"What's that?"

"A good movie. Haven't seen one of those in eons. The Casablancas and African Queen days are long gone."

"Sadly enough I think you may be right. But back to our itinerary for the day…"

"That's just it Alex. We have no itinerary and I'm fine with that. Why can't we be just two old friends with some time on our hands content to enjoy each others company without others around to interfere?"

"Sounds like a plan to me. I just know as active as you are I didn't want you be bored."

"And could you please tell me how I could possibly be bored in such good company?"

"You know I asked myself the same questions, over and over again when you left New York the first time."

"And what did you come up with?"

"That's the funny thing I never did come up with a good concrete answer but now that I have you here in the flesh why don't you tell me what happened. Nothing like getting it straight from the source."

Sill smiled.

"You still won't accept my original explanation will you? I told you before I left New York that there were too many unanswered questions that bothered me and when I left it was too ease my mind. I came to New York for some peace and to ease my troubled mind. I guess you could say I was running and when I met you I realized that I was opening myself up to more problems, to more issues that I was neither ready to deal with nor become involved in so I took myself to a place I knew. I took myself to a simpler life, a life I knew and understood, one that wasn't so complex. I just wanted a simple existence where I could achieve some peace."

"And you found the peace you were looking for?"

"I did until Tristan was killed."

"And?"

"And I found it—well that was up until then."

"And now?"

"I'm not sure. But this I do know. With his death I've become a lot stronger in my own right. And my faith in the Lord has given me the strength to endure more than I thought I ever could."

"Is that the reason you've come back to New York?"

"No, in actuality I just came to get away from Elizabethtown. There's peace there but every now and then a change of pace is good. So, I'd come and visit some old friends, maybe do a little shopping, take in a play, time permitting and see what else transpires. But no itinerary."

"And no mention of me…"

"I do believe I mentioned visiting old friends."

"Thought I was more than that."

"Don't know. Jury's still out on that one."

"Perhaps you need me to refresh your memory."

"Perhaps I do," Sill said smiling coyly. "That is if you think you can."

Alex rose from the table and made his way to the other end and took both her hands in his and helped her stand before placing his arms around her and kissing her deeply.

"Remember now?"

"It's starting to come back," Sill said smiling.

"Let me see if can't bring it all the way back." Alex said smiling before bring his hands up to her shoulders and untying both shoulder straps letting the dress fall to the floor. Bending over slightly he found her neck and planted several soft gentle kisses on it before nibbling her earlobes and running his tongue in small circles behind her ear. Ohh, how she loved this and he knew it. Moaning softly she was falling quickly now into the deep recesses of her feeble psyche.

She remembered now. She remembered Alex as being one of the most patient, most passionate lovers she'd ever had. And Lord knows he was proving it now. Her legs turned to jell as he ran his warm mouth over her shoulders and the let it brush against her dark, hard, protruding nipples. Taking one then the other into his warm mouth he suckled each gently as she felt the tiny droplets of perspiration bead up In her inner thighs. At least she hoped that was all it was. She wondered if it was merely perspiration or had she actually had an orgasm without her even knowing. She dropped her hand between her legs and knew that it was far too wet to be perspiration and cursed herself. But before she could gather her thoughts she felt his hand gently pushing her breast upwards and mashing them gently together. Leaning over once more he took both breasts into his mouth at once. Sill wasn't sure if it was the feeling of having both nipples sucked at the same time or it was just the

251

freakiness of having them suckled at the same time. Whatever it was it felt

wonderful and the harder he sucked the wetter she felt. Only this time she was sure

it was not perspiration as she came again and again. He was having his way with her

now. She'd lost control and could only think of how good it felt but it was he who

was possessing her and she knew that it was far too easy to let a man take her, have

her, control her and that had not been her intent. She dug down deeply , gathered

her resolve and before he could take her again found his belt buckle and tugged hard

until the buckle gave way and she had his hardened member within her grasp. She

hadn't remembered him being so large but then after Tristan there was hardly a

comparison. Using her free hand, she pushed him back and dropped to her knees,

pulling his pants to his ankles and took all eight inches into her mouth and sucked

hard. Gasping he le felt his hands grow limp and rest on her shoulders. Sylvia

sucked hard and fast, taking all of it now to the back of her throat. Several times she

could feel herself choking but refused to allow herself to release him or give in.

Alex moaned louder with each pull on his now rock hard member and Sylvia sensing

his growing tautness sucked even harder. Sensing his impending orgasm she relaxed

the muscles in her jaws and reached over to the tiny jar in her handbag. Sticking two

fingers in the jar with one hand and then doing the same with the other she wrapped

her one hand around Alex's dick and stoked him until she heard him scream begging

her to stop teasing him and to take it. Feeling him go taut she lessened the grip she

had on him and feeling him relax a little she smiled inside before increasing the

pressure.

"Oh, Sylvia baby. Please baby! You don't know how much I've missed you. I

could have died when you married Tristan but now you're back. Oh baby how I've

missed you. You don't know how much I've wished for this day."

I bet you have. Sylvia thought to herself. And then she smiled. Be careful of what you wish for she thought driving two fingers up his ass as she stroked him and watched as his sperm shot across the room in great arches.

"Goodness!" she commented as each stroke brought another wave.

When it was over all Sylvia could do was sit back and listen as Alex told her his innermost thoughts on everything from love and marriage to hedge funds. Sylvia listened intently picking up everything she could on what made him tick and where his real interests lay asking a question every now and then when she came across something that would make her plight just that much more profitable. She was surprised at how much he confided in her and wondered if it had been her mere absence or the blessing she had just bestowed on him. Whatever the motivation he had fallen pray and she was certainly glad he had. It would make her endeavors that much easier. And when he'd finished and leaned back across the bed to relax, she promptly took her panties down, stepped out of them, lubricated herself liberally and straddled him her ass in his face grabbed his ankles and rode him to another three or four orgasms allowing him to rest a few minutes between each. She knew he was spent because she was and with all the 'please baby, no more and what do you want baby, I'll give you anything', she knew she had him just where she wanted him. Not that she had any doubt but Celeste was right about one thing. Those tight ass Wall Street brokers were so caught up in doing the right thing, and portraying the right image that they could never let their hair down. Alex was no different. In fact, from what Sylvia could surmise he had the double indemnity of not only being correct as a broker with his Brooks Brothers, charcoal gray suits, black Cole Haan penny loafers and London Fog trench coats but he had the added burden of having to be Black man on a an all-White playing field. And it had been so long since he had

253

corresponded with Harlem and his Blackness that he had forgotten not only how be Black but how to love a Black woman in the way in which she needed to be loved. Now here he was reacquainted with a sista who he could have had but who was now intent only on having him as her mark. And so far gone, so far removed from this thing called love he really and truly believed that this was where she was and with a few dollars and a few good lines he could sell her the same way he sold those knuckleheads who came to see him hoping that his good fortune would one day be theirs.

He was right about one thing though. Sylvia hoped that one day his fortune would one day be hers as well but for entirely different reasons. Her motivation was not to acquire a fortune in and of itself. Her motivation was to acquire his fortune and only if and because she knew that this would hurt him more than anything else she could possibly think of.

There was little else Alex could when Sylvia finished with him than roll over and close his eyes but Sylvia was having none of this. She was going to sex him good, leave him sore and ravished but wake up wanting, no craving more. And so just when he was drifting off she brought out the tiny jar of Vaseline, once again lubricating her hand well and grabbing his now limp member and stroking softly, easily until it once again expanded in its thickness and grew 'til it could no more. He was moaning and thrashing now. She had a hard time concentrating with him moving so she relaxed her grip and decided to wait. Taking a quick shower and fixing herself a ham and cheese Sylvia returned a half hour or so later to find Alex in a deep sleep. Tip toeing cautiously to her overnight bag she grabbed two pair of knee highs and opening them not as to make a sound, she promptly tied his hands and feet to the bedposts as securely as she could before reaching once again for the jar of

254

Vaseline. Once again she began stroking him softly, almost lovingly until he stirred moaning.

"Oh baby, please let me rest," Alex said before realizing that he was bound and could not push her hand away. She was working vigorously now, squeezing harder and stroking him quickly and each time she hit the tip of his penis she would squeeze harder and whisper in his ear.

"Come baby. Come for mommy now! You told me how much you missed me. Show me baby!"

Alex's back rose from the bed arching upward as if he could catch the motion of her hand. On the verge of coming she let go.

"Oh my God! Baby! Oh Sill why did you stop? Please baby don't stop!"

There was a wet spot surrounding Alex, almost like the police chalk lines they use to outline a corpse but Alex wasn't dead yet and Sill wasn't finished torturing him. Once he was breathing normally Sill grabbed the now limp dick. Pre come dripped from the head and Sill only guessed at how many more times she'd see that before she'd eventually let him come to a full orgasm. She smiled to herself again as she thought to herself. 'Be careful of what you wish for.' Five or six more times Alex cried out for Sylvia to release from the threshold of pleasure which had now turned to pain.

"Baby, anything you want—anything—you just name it baby—anything! Please baby I'll do anything."

Sylvia knew his words were in earnest but then he would have done anything two years ago. It wasn't enough for me then and he certainly can't do anything for me now. If I need something I'll do it for myself. I've never needed help from any man and I certainly don't need any now.

Alex was sweating profusely now and Sylvia grew a little concerned. Besides she needed him gone for a couple of hours so she could check out his files.

"Tell me baby. Do you love me?"

"Has there ever been any question?"

"Didn't ask you that," Sylvia said stroking him deeply and then quickly massaging the tip.

"Oh Sill you know I love you," Alex said hoping, praying to have her relax her grasp.

"And what you do to express your undying love and devotion to me?"

"Damn near anything, baby you know that."

"And you're going to show me how much you do love me and show me the lengths you'd go to express it this week as well?"

"I will baby," he said moaning, still trying to free his hands.

"Do you want me to untie you or would you like to come for me?"

"I'd like for you to release me. I don't think I have anything left baby. I think you've taken everything I have to give."

Sylvia laughed at the remark.

"This is only the beginning sweetheart. Trust me."

"Anything baby. I told you anything."

"Then give me some come, baby."

And with that said Sylvia started stroking the tip of his penis again softly this time until she felt him grow in response to her touch. He was feeling her now and began to beg in earnest this time.

"Oh baby take it! Please let me come this time! Please baby! Please take it!"

"I'm gonna do exactly that Alex. I'm gonna take it all. Now tell mommy how bad you want it."

"Oh please mommy!" Alex screamed.

"Want me to fuck you, Alex?"

When there was no response Sylvia repeated the question this time grabbing his testicles and squeezing tightly. Alex screamed in pain but Sylvia acted as if she didn't hear.

"I said do you want me to fuck you?"

Alex was quick to answer this time.

"Yes, mommy I want you to fuck me," he responded.

"Beg me to fuck you," Sill responded wrapping her free hand around his balls once again.

"Oh mommy please fuck me," Alex replied.

"Lift your ass up off the bed," Sill demanded.

Alexis arched his back and made a bridge between the bed and his ass at which time Sylvia jabbed three fingers in his ass. Alex let out a scream that could be heard in the lobby twenty floors below. Sylvia didn't care. She was working him, cursing him.

"Give it to me baby. Give me the shit. Dammit! Give me some cum!"

Alex had never seen this side of Sill and it excited him though her fingers in his ass hurt like hell he was at her mercy and soon heard himself begging for me.

"Oh baby fuck me," at which time Sylvia rammed her fingers all the way up in him, squeezing the head of his penis and sucking it with a ferociousness he'd never known before causing him to cum in large bursts. But this only drove her into a deeper frenzy as she sought to make him come again and again. After the third time

257

when there was nothing left and he'd collapsed on the bed in a pool of his own sweat she untied him kissed him on the forehead and let him sleep for about an hour before waking him up.

"Alex darling would you do me a favor?"

Attempting a smile but obviously in pain he answered.

"Anything for you love."

"I was a little on the hungry side and I thought if it wouldn't be too much trouble you'd run down to the new Fulton Street Fish Market and grab a couple of lobsters for dinner."

"Okay baby. Let me take a quick shower and get myself together. I need to stop by the office too. I don't know if Celeste told you or not but we're supposed to be having an internal audit today."

"No she didn't mention it but don't be forever. I'll be waiting for you."

"I won't. Shouldn't be anymore than a couple of hours at the most. Anything else you might like?"

"No, nothing that I can think of off the top, maybe a couple of bottles of Merlot to take us through the evening."

"As you wish my queen. Do me a favor and call Thomas and tell him to bring the car around."

"Already done. He's downstairs waiting."

"You're really something you know that?"

"I do my best."

Alex showered quickly. He smiled as he dressed and wondered how he'd ever let anything come between he and this woman. But she had had her druthers and quite reasonably so. He had his misgivings about Abdul Rakman in her absence as well. Sure, they had been boyhood friends. And truth be told when the going got tough there was hardly a better man to have by his side but no longer were these the gang war days of their youth. Now it was a finesse game where brute strength and power hardly played a role outside of the few occurrences where they'd venture far outside the familiar confines of Manhattan. And now he'd become even more of a burden and it wasn't just Sylvia. More and more people were suspicious of him and what required such a fine and moral gentlemen such as himself to require a man of such limited gen-se-qua to be in his company and employ. One thing was for sure. Rakman was no butler. And for two years he had been without the woman he so loved and adored because she had questions about Mr. Rakman. He had never found the courage to ask Rakman about his role in the two boy's murder but then he knew what Rakman's answer might be and if it was one thing he didn't need to be involved in was murder and much as he loved Sylvia it wasn't worth him knowing. Besides knowing Rakman as he did he knew the man would never tell him anyway. What was it that he always said? 'What you don't know won't hurt you." And he knew and had to attribute Rakman in large part to his being where he was today. What was it that they'd both said when they were young men on the rise. Money over bitches. And so who was he to discredit or question Rak.man's action now that he'd made it. The sad reality was that one of the things he valued most in business and his personal life was loyalty and noone had ever been more loyal than Abdul Rakman.

Alex was a in a quandary. Turning around to grab a towel there stood Sylvia with a towel which she dabbed gently at his face and then as if she knew that his happy was dependent on her presence she drew the towel back and stood there letting her

sundress gently cascade to the floor.

Chapter 15

No sooner had Alex left than Sylvia called Celeste.

"Hey girl. It's me Sill. I just called to tell you that he's on his way downtown. I had him stop by the fish market so he should be there in the next forty to forty-five minutes. So, how did everything thing go with the audit."

"Well, you know when you're auditing yourself chances are that you're not going to find anything out of the ordinary. You know what I'm saying? I mean Alex is not going to embezzle from himself and most of these jokers make so much straight up that there's no reason for them to steal either and your boy gives such attractive incentives and bonuses that their all just too pleased to be in his employ to do anything stupid."

"That's true."

"On your end though there's some room for question but I'd rather wait 'til I see you to talk about that. I know this is a cell and they're safer than a land mine but I don't even feel comfortable talking on here if you know what I mean."

"I've taught you well," Sill said chuckling.

"Who taught who?"

"Listen I gotta go. I've got some scavenger hunting of my own to do."

"I hear ya girl. Be careful."

"Always."

Sylvia went downstairs and checked the front lobby. After a brief reunion with Sam the doorman she went outside to check and make sure that Alex was gone. 'I don't trust him as far as I can throw him she whispered. Wouldn't surprise me one bit if he doubled back to check on my ass.' Sylvia thought to herself.

But that was the farthest thought from Alex's mind at this point as he got in the limo and greeted Thomas warmly.

"Thomas my good man. How are you this morning?"

"Fine sir. Blessed, I tell you. Every day I'm able to get out of bed and see your smiling face is a good day."

"Well, that's great sir. Lot of people don't count that as a blessing. It's a wise man that knows."

"Listen Thomas," he said leaning over in the back seat. His ass was still a little sore from where Sylvia had loved him but now it was more a reminder of what he had to do than it was pain. "Have you been putting away a little something for your retirement as I suggested over the years?"

"Yes sir. You know I have my 401K and the investments you made for me. Why do you ask?"

"Well, I'm thinking about retiring and I just want to make sure you're alright before I get out. I'm by no means suggesting that you have to retire because I do I just want to make sure that you're financially set should you decide that you've had enough."

Thomas glanced in the rear view mirror and smiled.

"You're planning on marrying Ms. Sylvia aren't you sir?"

Alex smiled.

"Never like to count my chickens before their hatched but yes those are my intentions."

"Well, I wish you all the happiness you so richly deserve, Mr. Dumas."

"Thank you Thomas. I just hope Ms. Stanton is ready."

"I'm sure she'll agree."

"You were sure two years ago, Thomas and you saw what happened then."

"That was then, Mr. Dumas. A lot has happened since then."

"I just hope you're right. How do you think Abdul will take the news."

"Oooh, that's a rough one. Hard to call that one. You know he's a man of few words and he lives for you. I really think he'll be lost without you. You are his reason for being here."

"I hear you. But things change. I just hope he's put something away for a rainy day."

"Where are we going sir?"

"Fulton Fish Market."

"You got it. Sure wish I could be a fly on the wall when you break the news to him." Thomas laughed. "Mr. Rakman may be a man of few words but I think he'll have quite a lot to say when you break this bit of news to him."

Alex sat back. Rakman had been loyal. They'd been friends since childhood but he 'd done everything he could to point Rakman in the right direction and paid him handsomely. He should be financially set but Rakman's business was his and his alone. Still the only thing on his mind right now was Sylvia and if she had any qualms about Rakman then he had to go. Besides he had no need for a butler nor a bodyguard in North Carolina. And that's where it seemed like everything was heading. Pulling his cell out of the breast pocket of his jacket he dialed Abdul.

"Need to talk to you when you get a chance man."

"What's wrong boss? Everything okay?"

"Everything copasetic. Just need to have a face-to-face is all."

"Not a problem. How about six or six thirty?"

"I'll see you then, Rock."

263

There was no question. His mind was made up and he'd hardly wait this time. He'd wanted this woman since he'd first laid eyes on her. Sure he'd lost her but that was then and he was adamant about not letting her getting away this time. No, by the end of the week she'd be his. He'd go get her ring now since he was passing right through the garment district and propose to her tonight. How could she say anything but yes after this morning. She'd let all her secrets be known and why would she have done what she'd done this morning if she hadn't finally decided that he was the one for her. No, she was definitely letting him know, she was giving her all to him. And this time he wouldn't let her slip through his fingertips.

Meanwhile, Sylvia called Alex just to keep tabs on his whereabouts. He had just arrived at the Fulton Street Fish Market, which gave her more than enough time to find the information she needed. But after more than forty minutes of searching she'd found nothing of significance. Oh, there were a few minor stocks he'd recently invested him but there was nothing more than a few minor stocks that he seemed to be toying with but there was nothing of substantial value that would either make him or break him. She could only hope that Celeste had faired better in her queries. She was somewhat fearful of calling Celeste on the landmine and decided to wait until Celeste was off and call her on her ell at home but before she could do that the phone rang interrupting her thoughts.

"I sure hoped you faired better than I did down here. The man believes in the tightest of securities. If he has some net worth you'd never know it from here. How did you do?"

"Same here. Not a trace of anything here. He must have a safe deposit box where he keeps all of his important documents."

"I mean his entire client' files are here but nothing personal belonging to him. I'm afraid this is not going to be quite as easy as you thought it was going to be."

"I hate to admit it but I think you're right."

"You may have to take your game to a new level altogether, sweetie."

"Well, if that's what's needed then I guess I'll just have to."

"Gonna need to bring to bring your 'A" game baby."

"If that's what it takes then I guess I may have to do just that but the bottom line is he can't beat me. I don't know what game we're playing or whose ballpark we're playing in."

"I hear you, Sill. What can I say? I have always had faith in you Sill. All you've ever had to do was grab the bull by the horns and do the damn thing. When have you ever been unsuccessful? Listen Sill, I think that's Alex pulling up outside. I'll talk to you when I get off. Meet me for drinks up on 96th St. Under The Stairs at six. We'll talk some more."

"Okay C. I'll see you then."

Sill showered and put on a flowered housedress purposely making sure to leave both bra and panties off just in case Mr. Dumas had anything left and wanted to pursue her. Despite her anger and need for revenge she had yet to quell her thirst. But then there would be time for all that. Her aim was different this time. She was going to use everything she had, all her wily means to summon and hold Alex until she had caused him the pain which he had caused her. And this was only the beginning. It was five thirty and he'd just called asking if there was anything she needed.

"No, baby I just don't like being here alone. All I really want and need is you. Hope you're not tired. I have such an evening planned for the two of us."

"I have a little something planned for you as well."

"Can't wait." She answered playfully.

Not more than twenty minutes later, Sill there on her black patent leather pumps that had fuck written all over them and headed for the elevator doors which opened into the hallway and greeted Alexis whose hands were full of shopping bags and other items an wrapping both arms around his neck and one leg around his calf pushed him backwards onto the ottoman that adorned the front foyer. Planting a deep hungry kiss on his lips before parting his lips with her tongue and stuck her tongue deep inside her mouth. Trying to gather his thoughts, speak and put the bags down all to no avail he succumbed to her passion and felt her zip his zipper down and pull his pants down to his knees before quickly straddling him and guiding his rock hard member between her already lubricated lips. Moving slowly at first she felt harden more with each stroke until she was sure he was going to penetrate her ovaries and then just when she could feel it touching her kidneys she slammed down on it time and time again. There was nothing more she liked than the sheer pleasure with just a little pain and with each thrust she too became more rigid, more taut until that orgasm that she thought would never come and now thought would never sent wave upon wave shivering from the tip of her asshole to the tips of her nipples. And then there were the aftershocks that rippled through her that only made her want to come again and after lifting her head from his deep sighing chests she sat straight and began again. By the time she was finished this time, finding it so much harder to relieve herself this go round, she eased off make him both shiver and tingle, she gave him a quick peck on the cheek before saying 'I missed you', and heading for the bathroom where she took a quick shower.

Alex stayed seated on the ottoman, his world spinning, smiling gratefully with a look of satisfaction he had long awaited. Finally, and after hearing the water in the shower running for some time he got up to meet Sylvia coming out of the shower a long towel draped around her glistening body.

"That's some way to be greeted at the door. I could certainly get used to that after a long day at the office," Alex grinned as he watched Sylvia let the towel fall gently to the ground and put on her panties and bra. Damn she was fine. He thought to himself and wondered if she was really what his eyes perceived or was it the image of the woman that he'd long ago conceived in his mind. Whatever the case she was certainly the one for him and he immediately began to look for the ring he'd purchased earlier in the day. Finding it he'd already come to the conclusion that there was no reason to wait for pomp and circumstance and after that performance why chance letting her slip away again.

"Sylvia there's something I want to ask you?"

"Oh Alex, can't it wait til I get back. I was supposed to meet Celeste at Under the Stairs up on 96th Street at six. And it's damn near six now. I don't know why but I'm always running late. Anyway, baby can you just hold that thought 'til I get back. It's bad enough I planned on spending the week with Celeste and here I am with you so let me go. I'll be back pretty early. We're just going to have a couple of drinks and reminisce a bit."

How many times had he almost been there, right there on the edge of victory and for some reason or other he was always deterred. No, he refused to be put off. Grabbing her by the wrists he pulled her to him.

"I've thought about this for some time Sylvia and I don't know if it was me or the times or the fact that you just weren't ready but whatever the reason I've carried this with me since we first met and I know how close you and Celeste are but baby after today I'm sorry but this just can't wait."

267

"Okay sweetie, but make it quick. Do you think Thomas can run me uptown?"

"I'm sure he can if you catch him. Call his cell."

"Okay, but what is it that you need to ask me Alex?"

"Well, it's not like the mood and the atmosphere is conducive to me asking?"

"Oh, just ask Alex."

Dropping his head he sighed before looking her straight in the eye and grabbing both her hands in his.

"Will you marry me Sill?"

Stunned it had happened so quickly Sill smiled, grabbed her cell, before turning and smiling and replying 'yes' and heading out the door.

Alex fell back to the ottoman he had not so long ago gotten up from. He was ecstatic and for the first time in he didn't know how long the only thing he felt at this moment was loneliness. He realized now that he had no one to share his happiness with. And still, and even with no one to share his joy no sooner than the door closed Alex leaped for joy. Finally all that he'd worked for had finally come to fruition. Sylvia Stanton was finally to become the first and only Mrs. Alex Dumas.

Twenty minutes later the door opened and Celeste greeted her old friend with a hug and a kiss on the cheek.

"I know you're fit to be tied," Celeste inferred. But Sill seemed unshaken.

"Guess you didn't come up with anything on your end either aside from a tired pussy trying to manipulate that stingy assed motherfucker. I'm thinking that he's gonna be one tough nut to crack when it comes to him loosing some of his cash."

"Oh, I don't know. Whatcha got to drink Celeste?" Sill said a sly grin on her face.

"Just some Chivas. It's in the cabinet over the sink."

"Oooh, you're really stepping it up girl. I remembered the back in the day when you were drinking Wild Irish Rose like water and then gout out on the prowl to see which night."

"You a damn liar." Celeste laughed. I'll have you know that if I visited a men's dorm it had already been prearranged and if I got some it was usually because somebody wasn't putting it down correctly. I just picked up where they left off and showed 'em what a real woman could do."

"You let half the campus know." Sill laughed. "That's why I spent half my college life bailin' you out of some shit. But the worst was when Wilomena came after you with that .45. Talk about one scared chick. I remember you coming to my apartment. You remember. That's when I stayed off campus on Martin Luther King and you were there for about two weeks. You were scared to come out of the bedroom. That's when everything came to light and the sistas was ready to kick your ass. You know we were the elite, the pretty girls on campus. Everyone knew it and we walked around like our shit didn't stink and then before you knew everyone was calling us dykes and lesbians 'cause you couldn't be satisfied with fuckin' everyman that didn't have his shit under double chain and lock but then you got bored and started fuckin' their girlfriends too. That was the straw that broke the camels back. It took me a week just to talk Wilomena out of shooting your ass. I think she put out an APB on your ass and was asking everyone on campus who knew your ass if they'd seen you. Shit even scared me and you know I don't scare easy but she came to the apartment strapped and there you were hiding in the bedroom. I never laughed so hard in my life 'til I went in and there you were trying to slide your fat ass under my bed and your ass was hanging half out and the tears were just running down your face. That was some funny shit. I remember telling

269

you that she was gone and you wouldn't believe me. It took me the better part of an hour to get your fat ass from under the bed and then when you did decide it was safe enough to come out we couldn't get you out. Remember I had to call Donut and Gary G. to come and lift the bed off of you just to get you out? Damn that was some hilarious shit."

"Yeah, yeah, yeah!"

Sylvia took a long swig of the Chivas and leaned back smiling.

"I see you got jokes tonight. What the hell has you in such a good mood anyway. You told me you didn't find anything at Alex's place. And you know I didn't come up with squat so what the fuck? Guess your little attempts at revenge just sort of went down the drain."

"So you say."

"So you did find something since I talked to you?"

"No. But there's more than one way to skin a cat. What do you think Alex wants more than anything in the world at this point in his life?"

"That's a tough one." Celeste said sitting down, spreading her legs and taking a drink from he glass of Chivas and taking a deep pull on her cigarette. "That's tough to say when you're talking about a motherfucker like Alex. It can't be money since he's got all the money in the world. I guess when you have everything in the world the only thing left is having someone to share it with. So, if I were to place a guess I would say that what Alex truly desires is you. You are probably the one thing he most desires and the fact that you didn't choose him with all his money and ran off with someone else had to damn near kill him. So, I guess if I had to venture a guess at what he most desires most in life I would have to say it's you. How'd I do?"

Sill smiled.

"Well what's the answer? Are you going to keep me in suspense or are you going to tell me where this is coming from or not. I mean the game plan was to get into his pockets, and rob him blind. Steal the thing that's closest to him. And that's his assets."

"You're right. But neither you nor I seem to be able to get to either he nor his dollars."

"And?"

"And I told you there is more than one way to skin a cat."

"So, you've changed the plan."

"What other course do we have?"

"Not many that I can think of. Well, then again I have ways that have worked for me over the years."

"Such as?"

"Do you ever listen to me when I'm talking to you?"

"Always. It's just that you tell me so much shit that it's hard for me to pull a parable out that's applicable in this particular situation. Is this the one where Moses leads the chosen people out of Egypt and parts the Red Sea or is this the one about the father bull telling his young not to run down the hill and fuck the one bull but to walk down and fuck them all?"

Oh, go to hell Sill. I'm only trying to give you some insight so that you may be able to better manipulate the current situation to your advantage."

"Sorry! Damn I didn't know you were so sensitive."

"Well as you know O'Bama's running the country."

"I'm sort of aware of that."

"But in essence it's Michelle who's really calling the shots. Republicans and Democrats can lobby all they want. But it's Cookie who's running the country. And who's Cookie?"

"Cookie's the one who runs shit. She's the only one that keeps O'bama on his toes and keeps him eating out of Michelle's hand. Did I ever tell you about the guy that I had that used to pay my rent, my car note, the whole sha-bang for me when I first came back to New York? I broke him off a little bit when I first met him and he worked for three years to just get a whiff of it," Celeste laughed. "But the bottom line was that he didn't do anything for me so I wasn't going to indulge him. He never did get back there though and even though he didn't I have to give him props for trying," she laughed. "You feel me?"

"I do. Believe it or not I do," Sill said smiling smugly.

"Okay the jigs up. From what I gather you came up here with revenge in mind. And you were so adamant about it and now that you dropped the ball you make it seem like it's all good and I'm sorry but that's just not you. You're one that refuses to be denied."

"You're so right but just because we lost a battle doesn't mean we lost the war. Any good general always goes in with a contingent plan. You know if this doesn't work out what do I have to fall back on?"

"And your contingent plan is?"

"The same as yours and Michelle's. Although I'm not so easy as to put it out there as such."

"So you're gonna put yourself out there and having him begging out of your hand?"

"Something like that."

"Oh, come on Sill. What gives?"

"Well, if you must know. He asked me to marry him tonight."

"Oh my God!!!! No he didn't. Oh my God girl. You must have really tricked his ass good."

Sill could only laugh at Celeste's disbelief.

"Oh my God Sill. You must have taken him back to the ol' school. Did you work him girl? Oh, no! Not Mr. High and Mighty. Not God's gift falling for that country-assed pussy. Damn Sill, I don't know if I'm glad for you or glad that you pussy-whipped him. How bad is he?"

"Hell, Celeste I don't know how you measure that. I mean I sent him out for a bottle of wine and he came back with a proposal of marriage. Let me ask you since that's more your forte than mine. How bad is he?"

"Well, I didn't think he could have been any worse than when you married Tristan. I thought he was ready to throw the towel in then. I was ready to give him some of my Zoloft and Xanex but he slowly came back around and started acting half way normal again. I say half way 'cause ya know he ain't never acted completely normal. Then when you got in touch with him and had me feeding him all that shit 'bout who you were dating and what you were up to him I could've bet my last five that you must have been

Fed-EXing him the good good. I swear I didn't think he could get any higher. Damn girl. You must have been blessed with that bionic shit, the kind that'll make a nigger jump off a bridge. I swear I've known my share of men and I ain't never seen one so head over heels over some ho."

"See that's your problem. You simply don't know any nice girls. You've just not been exposed to a true woman—a woman with style, etiquette and class. That's why you're so utterly enamored by the way a game is played and what can be had if

273

played correctly. This is not a game for tricks and tramps but for true women for real. I'll give you a few pointers one day when I have time although truth be told I think it may take a lot more time than I care to concede trick," Sill laughed. She then raised her glass as if to toast someone and said to no one in particular. 'True playa for real'.

"Oh, my goodness Sill. But tell me honestly you haven't really fallen for him and gonna try to make this shit work. Tell me you're not seriously tryna make a go of this charade."

"Don't know yet?" Sill said looking more serious than she ever had.

"Oh my goodness. Don't tell me that you lost focus and he's got you eating out of his hand like the rest of New York?"

Seeing how disconcerted Celeste had become she ceased her teasing momentarily.

"Now who's choking on their own saliva? You should know me better than that C. As far as I know that man killed the only man I've ever loved. How could I ever love him or go through with a marriage within sincerity. But I'll tell you what, I'll do what I have to do, even if it means marrying him to do what I feel I have to do to make him feel what I felt the day those men came to me and told me my Tristan was murdered. Trust me Alex will know what it feels like to have someone he really loves snatched away from him."

"Damn girl I knew you were serious but I never knew you had it in for him like this."

"Well, you're off the hook C. There's no need for you to be involved anymore than you already are."

"You will let me know the outcome though won't you?"

"Sweetheart, believe me you'll be the first to know."

274

"I'm trusting you to use good judgment in any event."

"Don't I always."

"Only time will tell."

Chapter 16

If anyone knew Sylvia it was mommy and mommy knew that her daughter's heart wasn't in it even though she did her best to alleviate her mother's suspicions. "Baby you've been home a week and no matter how much you pretend you're happy you forget that I know you better than anyone and knowing my daughter I can tell when she's faking the funk. I've seen you when you've been in love and been happy. When you married Tristan—even before you married him I knew that man had everything you needed to scratch your itch. I mean you used to walk around him beaming. I mean you had a glow that I hadn't seen since you were five years old and would be out back making mud pies with lil' Todd Murphy. Boy did you love that boy. You cried your eyes out when he and his family moved away. The next time I really saw that look was when you met Tristan the second time around. So I know when my baby's happy. And though you may think you're doing the right thing by giving your son a father it's more important that you are happy. This is a commitment that you'll be forced to face everyday for the rest of your life."

"You're right mommy and I've thought about everything you've just said. I really have but this is something I really want to do.

"Okay, honey. I just want you to be absolutely sure you know what you're doing. There was a time when you were quite skeptical of Alex and his goings on. What changed your mind?"

"Well, Alex investigated his bodyguard and let him go when I agreed to marry him dispelling a lot of my fears and questions."

"Okay baby. I just want you to be sure and happy. I'm glad he dispelled some of your apprehensions. But I'll tell you something I was afraid to tell you a while back and I'm not saying this to hurt you by any means. You know I wouldn't do that. I love you too much. But you know I hadn't heard anything for months from Alex and then two days before Tristan died he calls and inquires about you and Tristan and me being the ol' fool that I am told him more than I should have and then a couple of days later Tristan is murdered going to meet an out of town business associate. I've never said anything to you because you're already overly suspicious and I didn't want you to get yourself in trouble but I thought about what you said about him being involved with those teenagers up in Harlem and well uh…"

"You know mommy that thought crossed my mind as well but I didn't want you to blame yourself for Tristan's death and I knew you were thinking that perhaps you gave Alex too much information and you were the cause of Tristan's death. So I never brought it up because I didn't want you to blame yourself for something you had nothing to do with."

"How did you know?"

"Cause I know my mother… But to be honest with you I never really got over the idea that Alex had those two boys killed in Harlem and so while I was in New York I had to ask. I had to lay it all in the line. And he reassured me by questioning Rakman in front of me about the whole affair and then gave him his walking papers. Made me feel kind of special—you know the fact that he would address the situation and then cut ties with his long time friend. That really meant a lot to me."

"But how do you account for him calling a day or two prior to Tristan being killed after not hearing from him for a month of Sundays. And you know when he did call I was the one that told him you had just gotten married—old naive fool that I was and then Tristan winds up dead. More than just a coincidence if you ask me."

"It would appear so at first glance mommy but ask yourself this mommy. Why would a man that has a choice of some of the most beautiful women in New York City and an empire to boot concern himself about a little ol' country girl like me?"

"Don't sell yourself short, Sill. For the same reason he made his way down here after you spent months hiding from him and found you and built that with all his business connections he had opted only to invite his parents monstrosity of a house over there. Don't play me Sylvia. It just don't seem right that as vehement as you were a few months ago you are now so accepting. And if I know my daughter like I think I do then I'd say you have something up your sleeve."

Sill smiled and gave her mother a hug and a peck on the cheek.

"Whether you know it or not I have the capacity to forgive and forget and move on mommy. I have accepted the fact that vengeance is the Lord's."

"But to marry the man that may have killed your first husband and the love of your life. That's a bit too much to wrap my little mind around and I've been a good Christian all my life. You're better than I am."

Sill smiled again. Mommy stared suspiciously but didn't venture a comment.

"Everything will work out fine mommy. You'll see."

It was to be a small wedding. The fewer people the better, Sill told Alex and he so glad to be getting the woman he had so long desired agreed without hesitation.

The following Saturday they were married. It was small but nice, only a few intimate friends and Sylvia was surprised that with all the people that Alex knew in New York and all of his business enterprises and connections he hadn't invited anyone other than Thomas his driver. Two days later they left out of Raleigh/Durham for parts unknown. Alex had insisted they keep it a secret so as not to be disturbed. But when Sylvia saw the white sandy beaches of Montego Bay she was ecstatic. Of course, she'd dropped more than a few hints about her favorite resort in the last couple of weeks with the hopes of his noticing and he had. Now here they were and where he insisted on renting the top room out at some swanky she told him to stay at a friends' time share a not far from the beach. The villa was beautiful and convenient enough. Everything was close by. There were tiny huts that doubled as restaurants where large Black women poured over large black kettles of peas and rice, frying pans full of red snapper and the sweet, sweet cassava which accompanied it. Coolers full of Red Stripe beer lined the walls. Sure there were the fancier restaurants only a stones throw away with their pink table cloths and fine China but those were for the tourists with their high brow tastes and deep pockets. Alex and Sylvia were more content doing and living as the natives lived—sparsely and frugally—tasting, savoring the best the tiny island had to offer.

At night they made love and Alex truly believed he'd died and gone to chocolate heaven. Never before had he ever had a woman make him feel the way Sylvia did and she did it with no effort whatsoever. It was almost as if she were they were high schoolers reliving their youth and the first big dance of the year. Well, at least Alex was.

Still, what amazed Alex more than anything about this woman he had so long craved to be his wife was the fact that she hadn't a desire in the world. Sure she had become somewhat wealthy in her own right but never, not once was there ever a discussion of money. Seeing things around the island she wanted him to have she would purchase it and tell him it looked good on him and that was that. And so in the second week of their month long honeymoon Alex took Sylvia to the largest bank on the island and basically gave her power of attorney over his assets. As

279

much as she fought the whole idea he felt it imperative and once he had things went right back to the way they had been. He read in the daytime, took dips in the pool and at night after dinner they either explored the island and enjoyed the clubs and casinos or had cocktails in the Jacuzzi before making hot, steamy love and drifting off to sleep in each others arms.

The following week repeated virtually the same scenario and Alex was more than tickled with the way things were panning out and couldn't wait to return home to their own home to let the scenario continue. Only on Thursday, their last week in Jamaica—they were due to leave on Saturday he had awakened early and gathered himself together, called the driver he had gotten since he arrived on the tiny island and had him drive all over the island picking up all the things she had chosen during their three week hiatus but had refused to allow him to buy. Once he had amassed all of the little trinkets, which included clothes and jewelry that he had seen her eyeing he headed back to their villa with intentions of wrapping it all and sending on ahead as a surprise. He called it taking a lil' bit of Jamaica home with you. And this way there was no taking it back because it was too extravagant or too expensive or too much.

Alex arrived back at the villa at a little after one that afternoon only to find it vacant. There was no Sylvia. At first he assumed that she like he had just picked up and decided to see some of the country on her own. He knew just how independent she was so nothing she did really surprised him but on further inspection he found her luggage missing too. Worried he called mommy but there was no answer there and so like any good husband Alex went to the authorities who knew little and seemed not only oblivious but uncaring as well. The only thing they could say was that he'd have to wait twenty-four hours before filing a missing persons bulletin and she –'d only been gone since this morning. Convincing himself that it was really nothing to be overly concerned with and just the idiosyncrasies of being newly married Alex sat by the pool a fifth of Glenfiddich by his side and a cooler full of ice. Sipping steadily he was soon asleep, and woke up to find it four o'clock in the morning and Sylvia still not at home. He was now despite the detective's advice worried and called the police officer he'd spoken to earlier with hopes of coming up with anything at all. But the desk sergeant on duty had not heard anything of an American Black woman. There had been a shooting in nearby Negril but from all reports it looked like a quiet night.

Alex tossed and turned for the remainder of the night—restless and unable to sleep—until sometime near mid-afternoon when he was awakened by the gimbly old lady who stopped by to straighten up the house each day. He could elicit nothing from her and had a hard time understanding she and her broken English when she did bother to give an answer.

A day later, when he still hadn't received an explanation suitable to his tastes he did the only thing left for him to do and that was to gather his belongings and head for home. After exhausting all avenues of possibilities he came to the conclusion that no matter what she believed or how much she loved him he should have never let Rakman go. Their was a good chance that in a country as poor and destitute as Jamaica was she could easily have been kidnapped and was probably now being held for ransom by some sheisty drug lord.

He's stop by their home in North Carolina and then amass a small army to come down and look into the whole affair but first he had to know if it wasn't he had said or done to cause her to get up and walk out on him.

The flight into Raleigh/Durham was short and after a few drinks he'd even manages to nap a bit despite the gnawing worry over what could have happened to her. Leaving the airport after claiming his bags he cursed aloud as he tried to flag a cab and then almost as if to add insult to injury when he finally was able to flag down a cab and let the cab driver know where he was going the cab driver had the nerve to ask for a deposit. Promising to return quickly Alex loaded his suitcases into the trunk of the car and dashed inside to the ATM only to find his account depleted and reading insufficient funds. But how could that be? Looking through his wallet he tried card after card but they all read the same. Still, he remembered his mother's old saying about keeping enough on you should something happen to make a phone call. Digging through the worn, brown, leather wallet Alex found the hundred dollar bill he'd folded so neatly some years ago and rushed out to the cab only to find it gone with Gucci set of luggage he'd paid close to a grand for.

"Damn!"

What else could possibly go wrong? He thought to himself. Minutes later another cab pulled up and drove him to Elizabethtown. Feeling a sigh of relief he knocked first at the old woman's house and when there was no answer crossed the street and went to his own home. Knocking and hoping, no praying, he waited for an answer but there was none. Listening, he heard a small commotion coming from the backyard. The sound of small children was obvious. Walking to the back he caught the eye of a young boy maybe twelve or thirteen who immediately ran to get his mother.

"Well, hello. You must be Mr. Dumas. Thank you so much for selling us the house and it was so reasonable. May I ask why you sold the house so cheaply? My husband wanted to put it right back on the market. He swears he can get four times what we bought it for. Well, who am I to look a gift horse in the mouth. You wait right there. I have a letter Ms. Stanton left for you a couple of days ago."

Stunned Alex waited as the woman left and came back handing him the envelope. It read. Alex don't bother looking. Besides, with your very limited assets I don't think you'll be able to do much looking if you chose to do so. I've liquidated most of your assets. Guess you'll have to get a job like the rest of us hard working folks. In any case, good luck with whatever it is you decide to pursue. Mommy always said vengeance is mine saith the Lord but I thought I'd help him carry the load just a wee bit. He has such a burden to carry you know. In any case, mommy, Tristan and I send our regards. Ciao.

CPSIA information can be obtained at www.ICGtesting.com
Printed in the USA
LVOW021914211212

312799LV00006B/177/P